JUSTICE OF BRENDA
THE WOLVERINE

JUSTICE OF BRENDA
THE WOLVERINE

Alex Markman

ASTEROID
PUBLISHING

Asteroid Publishing, Inc.

Library and Archives Canada Cataloguing in Publication

Markman, Alex
  Justice of Brenda, the Wolverine / by Alex Markman.

Issued also in electronic format.
ISBN 978-1-926720-54-8

Other novels by Alex Markman

Payback for Revenge

Messenger of Death

Contra-ODESSA

The Dark Days of Love

The Drama and Mockery of Fate

Table of Contents

Chapter 1

The peaceful, melancholic beauty of the rural scenery outside the car window was not in accord with the mood of Melissa Bonar. The thirty-two-year-old woman with nicely manicured nails, a simple but elegant haircut, and a calm, all-understanding expression in her blue eyes could easily be taken for a corporate executive. Which she was not. She was a homicide detective, heading for a trailer park to find a woman named Brenda. It was a place populated mostly by trash—criminals, alcoholics, drug addicts, and other people of low esteem who had lost hope for a better life and had no skills for a meaningful employment. Melissa never knew what to expect from the trailer people. Many were psychotic, with nervous systems damaged by years in prison, alcohol and drug abuse, with behaviour that had nothing to do with common sense or consideration for consequences.

"Enjoy the view?" asked the driver, gesturing with his right hand at the tranquil undulation of a golf course. The younger cop's left hand lay casually on the steering wheel. Larry was blond, very handsome, and armed to his teeth. He was just in his late twenties, but competent, hardened by many violent assignments. He smiled most of time, distracting the attention of young women.

Melissa nodded yes, although the beauty of the world was the least of her concern. She knew too well the other side of the coin: the ills of humanity, the horror and cruelty of its deeds happening every hour, everywhere, regardless of weather conditions and scenery.

After a brief, absent-minded observation of nature, she returned her thoughts to the task at hand. So far Melissa had not found any evidence that linked Brenda Rorke, the suspect, to the case that had landed on Melissa's desk two weeks earlier. A young man, Edward

Green, had been sodomized in his own apartment. The rape was rather weird: no trace of struggle or resistance, but rape it was, not consensual sex, for sure. His girlfriend had found him in the evening. The door was unlocked. She found Edward sitting in a chair, in jeans, naked from the waist up. The last drops of blood were still oozing from the cuts to his veins. She called the police. She might have saved him, if she had taped the cuts, but she was not up to the situation. She was hysterical, frightened, confused.

By the time the ambulance arrived, Edward was dead. It was the post mortem that had revealed that he had been raped not long before his veins were cut. Except for that, the death definitely looked like suicide. The sharp pocketknife used to make the cuts bore his fingerprints. His shirt was on the sofa, neatly folded, as if prepared for the night out. Everything in the apartment was in good order. No signs of struggle, or use of force. In sharp contrast to this neatness was the pool of blood, which was almost dry when the photographs of the crime scene—if it was a crime—had been taken.

"Did he say anything before he died?" the policeman had asked Edward's girlfriend.

"I've made out only one word," she said, sobbing and shaking. "Wolverine. He was out of his mind, though. He was almost dead. He didn't recognize me. It didn't make sense."

She said that Edward was a very nice guy, always in a good mood, had no enemies, had lots of friends, was a moderate drinker, and was admired by girls. After graduating university, he found a good job as an electronic engineer and was pretty good at his profession. She repeated that Edward had many friends, male and female, frequented parties, but intended to marry her, as he was, by her account, madly in love with her.

Wolverine. Assuming that was someone's nickname, Melissa ran through police records, and got nothing. But investigation of prison records found it in the files of the high-security prison for female offenders: Brenda Rorke, incarcerated for five years, and paroled six months ago. At the time of her release, Brenda had not been considered a high-risk offender anymore, so it took some time to find out her whereabouts; she had settled not far from Toronto with a man belonging to an outlaw biker gang.

Before setting off to meet Brenda, Melissa had carefully studied the prison file. Brenda's face in photographs, pretty though it was, did not arouse sympathy; however, it was not as menacing as some of her actions would suggest. She was a mix of contradictions. She had spent her early incarceration in the maximum-security pod, where the most dangerous cons, presenting security risks for inmates, were held as punishment for violence toward others. But later she had been praised as a nice, well-behaved, model prisoner, likable, and polite most of the time with correction officers. During her years in prison, and during probation, her behaviour had been impeccable. She had studied accounting and completed education programs, via correspondence courses while in prison, and then, while on probation, with evening courses. Her IQ and educational level were considered very high.

"Here's our pet Wolverine," Larry said, pulling in close to the driveway of a mobile home. A huge, Jimmy Carter–like smile on his face assured Melissa that she was being taken care of by competent hands.

"You sure we have the right place?" Melissa asked, stepping out of the unmarked car. Like a sponge, she was absorbing every detail of the neighbourhood.

Two cars stood in the narrow driveway, one after another. The closest to the road was a Nissan. It looked almost new, with sparkling chrome and a shiny black body, and should have been beyond the means of someone living in that neighbourhood. The other was a

Ford, a few years old, but in good condition. Neither car was in harmony with the cheap trailer.

"I've been here a few times," Larry said, stepping out. "Once I even had to clean my gun. I hate that job."

"You mean cleaning?" Melissa asked. She spotted a small number sign under the roof. Indeed, this was the house.

"Exactly." He sneered.

"Have your badge ready," she said with a frown.

"No need. If they ask about me, tell them I'm your lover."

"Shut up. Who would believe that such a Quasimodo is my lover?" Melissa pushed the car door shut and started toward the small porch. Sometimes Larry was too frivolous at work, but he was a good cop and meant no offence.

She looked back. Larry, in civilian clothes, was already smoking a cigarette, which entertained him in boring times. He raised his hand in a sign of encouragement.

Melissa knocked, prepared to wait. Unexpectedly, the door opened rather quickly. A woman stood behind the threshold, dressed in a light-green bathrobe. Her mane of brown hair was tightened into a long ponytail, and a touch of makeup indicated her good sense of balance when it came to her countenance. She was pretty, but not sweet in a feminine way: her face was hostile, and conveyed a strong, baleful will. Her robe opened wide at the top, showing firm, heavy breasts. Though they might not be an asset for one of the best and well-respected detectives in Canada, Melissa would have loved to have such bosom; there was no doubt that her husband, a dean of philosophy, would appreciate it no less than her intellectual capacity.

Melissa showed her badge and introduced herself in a calm but firm voice. "Are you Brenda Rorke?"

Not saying a word, the woman closed the door shut. Melissa stood for half a minute in silence, waiting, deciding what to do next. She looked left and right. No one was outside, although it was almost ten in the morning. That was good. Melissa didn't want any attention.

She was about to knock on the door again when it suddenly opened, and the woman came outside, closing the door behind her. She wore the same robe, but had put on sandals.

"What do you want?" she asked, rather unfriendly, but not with acidity, as Melissa had expected.

"Are you Brenda Rorke?" she asked again.

"Yes."

"Mind if we talk? This won't take long."

"Okay." Brenda nodded in the direction of a table set at the edge of the front lawn. It was of solid construction, with two heavy benches, the type used in public parks. Most likely stolen. "Let's sit there."

"Why not inside?" Melissa asked, following.

"My boyfriend is sleeping. He's not well these days."

They settled on the benches, facing each other. Brenda observed Melissa with the jealous scrutiny of a woman and the irritation of a former con.

"Do you know Edward Green?" Melissa asked, putting a photograph of a handsome man on the table. Brenda cast a casual, indifferent glance at the photograph and raised her eyes. Melissa watched her with acute attention, in search for that peculiar, hardly detectable twitch of lashes, or tiny muscle contraction, or unexplainable, unidentifiable, momentary change of expression, that signals a lie. She found nothing.

"No," came the curt answer. Melissa let a short pause sink in.

"Sure?"

"Sure. What about him? Why do you ask?" Her stare was heavy and depressing, like an ominous thunderstorm cloud.

"This man was raped, and killed…"

Melissa didn't have a chance to finish. Brenda interrupted her with an angry guffaw. "And you think I raped him? Mind telling me how I could do that?"

"Wait, wait," Melissa said. "You're not a suspect. I…"

At that moment, a tall and heavily built man in his mid thirties came out of the mobile home and stopped on the porch. The dense beard, bandana, and tattoos on his thick arms gave him the look of an outlaw biker.

"What's this twat want?" he asked, looking at Melissa as a pit bull eyes an intruder. Melissa felt goose bumps gathering on her neck. Was he the type who acted out on impulses of hatred and destruction? When drugged, those guys were loose cannons.

"Get back," Brenda commanded, not turning her head. The man hesitated a few seconds, then retreated.

"So you don't suspect me in raping this guy, whatever his name is?" Brenda chuckled. She put her elbows on the table, tangled the fingers of her hands together, and rested her chin on the back of her hands.

"You're making fun of the situation, Brenda. But you know…"

"I know you think that you're the smartest ass in the world," Brenda said, cutting her off. "All of you…"

This time Melissa interrupted her. "You're right. The idea of a woman as a rapist is usually something of a stretch. But the more I talk to you, the more I get the feeling that you had something to do with this."

Brenda's chin was still rested on her hands. Not a single muscle twitched on her face. Her stare said, "Die, bitch."

The brief stretch of silence put Melissa on edge, but she had enough self-control to wait for Brenda's response.

6

"Very good, woman. You write a report about your feelings, and bring it to the court as evidence," scoffed Brenda. "See if the judge cares how you feel. Though since you're a cop, I won't be surprised if your word would be sufficient."

"Let's change the subject," Melissa suggested. "Your nickname is Wolverine, right?"

A wry smile distorted Brenda's face. "It was. Long time ago. Now I'm just Brenda. So what?"

"So before Edward Green died, he said the name Wolverine. That's why I'm here. I just thought that you might be able to shed some light on the case."

"I can't."

"Just for curiosity, why that nickname? Any reason?"

Brenda shrugged. "Already looked into Webster, did you?"

Smart. Too smart, Melissa thought. "Yes, I looked into Webster. Among other things, it says, that the wolverine is a 'cunning, fearless predator that will attack almost any animal, including sheep, deer, and small bears.' Now, I can see you doing that, but not because you cannot control yourself. Your records say you can."

"You think I'm a predator?" Brenda asked with a trace of a smile.

"Yes. Do you mind taking a polygraph test?" Melissa asked.

Brenda narrowed her eyes. "What for?" she asked. She looked as though she was seconds away from darting forward and locking her jaws on Melissa's throat. Ready to pounce.

"Why else? To make sure you tell the truth." Something's coming. Melissa felt it.

"You wanna know if I tell the truth, eh?"

Melissa nodded. Brenda leaned forward.

"I don't give a shit if you trust me or not," she said. "There's no need for your fucking polygraph."

7

"I'd advise you to watch your language. My patience is not endless," said Melissa. "So far as the polygraph is concerned, it's for your benefit."

"Really? Okay, let's make a deal. I'll go to your fucking polygraph—oh, shit…pardon my language—if before you wire me up you give me a written note stating that if I successfully pass your fucking test, you'll never talk to me again regarding this case, that I will never be a suspect in that case, whatever that case might be…"

"Look, I can't give you—" It was one of the rare instances when Melissa felt like a fool.

Brenda laughed. "Shove your fucking polygraph machine up your ass, detective," she said, with cold, fearless hatred. "My life was ruined long before you came here. I don't care about it anymore. Now you'd better beat it outta here. It's not safe in the neighbourhood, you know."

Melissa swallowed the insult. Part of the job, she thought, although it usually made her sick. The conversation was going nowhere. Perhaps a tack that was more conciliatory—chitchat-friendly blabber, with neutral topics? All Melissa wanted was some tiny, miniscule detail, a feeble hint that might eventually help her with the case. Brenda might not have been a partner to the crime, but still she might know something about it, or about the people who did it. She obviously was a hard nut, able to withstand any direct pressure. Melissa already was sure about that.

"You have a nice car. Nissan is yours, is it?"

"Yes." Brenda frowned, studying Melissa's face. "How'd yah find me? You have a mole in the gang?"

There was a mole in her boyfriend's gang, but Melissa let the question pass. "It was easy to find you. You registered your own business, which you advertise on the Internet. You bought the Nissan. Beautiful car, by the way. Your website is really well done, too. You hired someone good for that."

8

For the first time during the conversation, Brenda's face softened into a faint smile. "I did it. Myself." She said it casually, but pride leaked through the effort to restrain her feelings.

"Where did you learn?" Melissa asked with genuine surprise.

"All by myself. In prison, and while on parole, I spent as much time at the computer as I could. Actually, there's lots of software that makes building a website easy. It's just a matter of time and patience."

"You deserve respect for that," Melissa said, with all sincerity.

Brenda shrugged and looked away, toward where Larry leaned against the car, smoking.

"My mother was a cleaning woman. She did her best to raise me, but it wasn't much."

"You have lots of clients, don't you?"

Melissa knew already that Brenda offered her services as an accountant: she did personal tax returns for individuals and bookkeeping and taxes for small businesses. She did quite well, as far as Melissa could tell. Her bathrobe was cozy, of good quality, and obviously not cheap.

"Yes. At times I'm busy into late evening." After a moment of hesitation, she added, "Anything I do, I try to do better than anyone else."

"You deserve a better life," Melissa said, with emphasis.

"Thank you." Brenda sounded almost friendly. "Actually, my life isn't bad. It could be even better, unless…"

Melissa's heart skipped a bit. "Unless what?" she asked.

Brenda uttered a short laugh. "Life plays stupid tricks on us."

9

"How'd you manage all of that?" Melissa asked. "Education, practice...it must've taken lots of time and effort."

"It does," Brenda agreed, more relaxed. "I didn't have a chance, like some, to go to a private school or a daytime university. But you know what? Learning isn't all hardship. It's fun. If you really want to learn, and have some brains, you don't need the best teachers in the world." She paused, and observed Melissa's face with acute but benevolent scrutiny. "Did you go to a private school?"

It was as an unexpected blow in the stomach. But Melissa did not want to lie.

"Yes, I did," she said, as calmly as she could.

Brenda nodded, as if saying, "I understand." And then, with the same smile, she said, "You came here because you wanna take me back to prison?"

Melissa gasped. "Look—" she started, but Brenda's laugh interrupted her.

"Good luck with that." Brenda rose to her feet, not listening anymore. She threw a glance at the car on the road, showed Larry her middle finger, and walked to the porch.

Chapter 2

The judge sentenced her to five years in high-security prison. For a girl only nineteen years old, it was a hard pill to swallow, but Brenda had prepared herself for the worst. For some reason, there were unexpected turns for the worst at every step she'd taken. Her intuition and gut feelings told her that humility, admitting her guilt, promising good behaviour, and begging for mercy would do the trick, and help turn back the tide of mishaps. However, doing that was so much against her nature and understanding of justice that she preferred to accept the worst-case scenario rather than trample her own soul and pride.

Of course, she hadn't know how bad worst-case could be, but that didn't break her resolve. She didn't fear the future; she was looking forward to it. On her way to prison, she expected all kinds of hardships, abuse, and violence, and was in a mood to fight back no matter what. Much later, she understood the reason for her bellicose mood. She saw the same thing in other inmates. The whole penitentiary system was humiliating, soul trumping. The more humans are humiliated, the stronger their reaction to any disrespect, and even more so for bullying or abuse. Repeated confrontations blind the mind, making it momentarily incapable of considering consequences. Brenda felt it stronger than any of the others. It wasn't just the prison misery that beat her down; she had also been humiliated in court beyond the limit of her understanding.

The federal prison camp was a relief after the jail, where she had to put up with small cells, foul smells, and lack of freedom. What a joy it was to walk around, breath fresh air, and look at the sky and know if it was dark or bright. The people did not seem especially hostile, at least at first, as she had expected. Some of the women even smiled and joked with her and the other new arrivals. Inside the barracks, called "cottages" there, inmates kept their limited spaces and meagre possessions tidy, and even tried to put up decorations, such as artificial flowers, to create an illusion of a sweet home ambience. But the long years of separation from the free world and normal life left an ugly imprint on their faces.

Brenda quickly learned that the seemingly peaceful atmosphere in the cottages was also an illusion. After all, the inmates had suffered many times through indignities and trials that humans are not designed to bear. Most of them were tense, with the fuse of patience burning down fast with the slightest irritation.

"Do the women fight here?" Brenda had asked the woman whose bed was next to hers.

"Sometimes," her cellmate said. "Usually people try to avoid it. It affects your chance for parole, halfway house, early release…you know. We all want to leave this zoo as soon as possible. None of us want to live with people like ourselves. We're trash, you know? We spread misery. It's our nature."

Brenda did not like it. However, she'd only been at the prison one week when the first fight broke out in her barrack. It was a Sunday, so most of the inmates were entertaining themselves outside, and only three other women were in. One of them, a large and stocky bully with a bad reputation, was serving time for murder. With a menacing, frozen stare, unblinking eyes, and protruding cheekbones, the woman sent chills along Brenda's spine at the first sight. Bluish bags under her eyes were the sign of bad health, likely kidney problems or indulgence in drugs. Her name was Cindy, but she presented herself as Cinderella. When Brenda heard that, she had to appreciate Cindy's sense of humour; that face would scare a child even on a bright day. Other than that, there was nothing funny about the woman.

12

Cinderella's friend Fatima sat on a bed, combing her hair. Smaller than Cinderella, much younger, she seemed to be in good shape. The only other inmate lay on her bed, reading a book.

The idyllic mood of the Sunday atmosphere changed when Brenda sat down at table, facing the others. Cinderella began looking at her with an ominous frown, saying nothing. The air crackled with anticipation. Brenda glanced at Cinderella and saw the menace in her eyes, so she turned her face the other way, hardly suppressing her fear. She felt Cinderella still looking at her. Another minute passed in silence. The pulsing blood in Brenda's heart faded from blue to red, morphing from fear into anger. Being bullied or abused again was, for her, worse than death.

"How old are you, Brenda?" Cinderella asked.

"Nineteen." Brenda turned to Cinderella and faced her stare with matching hardness.

Cinderella smirked. She didn't like it. "Come here," she demanded.

"What for? I'm not far away." Brenda had an urge to spit at her, but managed to hold herself back. Fighting would not be a good start for the prison term.

"I said, come here."

Brenda stiffened, not sure what to do. Cinderella turned to Fatima and said, "This sucker has to be taught rules. Nice boobs she has, ya think? Let's frisk her. Nice ass, too."

Brenda understood what "frisk" meant. She took a deep breath. There was no avoiding it now, and she accepted her fate as a warrior accepts a battle.

"Touch me, and I'll be after you as long as you live, you fucking bitch," she spat out, without raising her voice. She let all the hatred and bitterness that was overflowing from her heart pour out between them. To her own surprise, all fear was gone; instead, aggression completely clouded her mind, leaving no space for other feelings or thoughts. It was an exhilarating feeling, almost like happiness—the urge to destroy an enemy and feel free from abuse and insult.

Cinderella exchanged glances with Fatima. They nodded to each other, stood, and moved toward Brenda from both sides of the table. The other woman closed her book and watched, fear in her eyes.

Brenda jumped up and run away from Cinderella but toward Fatima. In that split second, she caught a glimpse of Cinderella's face, a mask of hatred and contemptuous confidence in the outcome.

All the dirt, abuse, despair, and anger that had accumulated in Brenda's heart and soul erupted suddenly as a volcano with energy far greater than the earth's crust could contain. It was a joy of destruction, a freedom from considered consequences, a righteous rage that neither people nor circumstances could contain. With all her strength and dexterity, she hit Fatima in the bladder with her right heel. The woman was stunned, as if from an electrical shock. A scream of pain seemed to shake the walls of the cottage. She dropped on the floor, writhing in convulsions.

Cinderella flew upon Brenda like a mad witch and showered her with barrage of punches. Her blows were hard—she was obviously an experienced fighter—but she had picked the wrong target. Brenda fought back with the euphoria of passion and fury. She might have been smaller, but she was younger, healthier, and much, much stronger. With each punch, her confidence grew. Only one thought throbbed in her mind: punish the bitch.

The fight was over in two minutes. Brenda could see that Cinderella was exhausted. Her health and physical stamina had failed her until her punches grew weaker and less focused. She tried to catch Brenda's hands and wrestle with her, to avoid the hard blows. Her face was a mess of bloodstains. Her breath was heavy, mixed with hissing sounds, as she tried to catch air with her open mouth. Meanwhile, Brenda felt a rough tide of energy, and the exhilarating sense of inevitable victory.

"Stop!" Cinderella whined in despair. "Enough! Enough!" Her grip became weak. Brenda freed herself and began kicking Cinderella with all her strength. She noticed that the woman who had been reading was gone. Fatima sat on the floor, still incapacitated, holding her stomach with both hands.

Cinderella gathered whatever energy remained in her body and darted out the door. Brenda ran after her. Outside, Cinderella stumbled over her own feet and fell to the ground. Brenda jumped on her back, grasped her hair, and began slamming Cinderella's face into the pavement.

"Please, please," Cinderella mumbled. Her voice was coarse, weak, pleading. "Please."

Guards jumped on Brenda, tore her off Cinderella, and twisted her arms behind her back. A thought crossed Brenda's mind that the woman who had read the book had run out to warn them about the fight.

Handcuffed, Brenda looked down at Cinderella sitting on the ground, bloody, short of breath, maybe having a heart attack. Cinderella looked at Brenda, but there was no menace in her stare, only fear and surprise, and admission of total defeat.

"This is not the end," Brenda hissed at her. "I'll be after you until you die, you fucking butch."

An hour later, after interrogation, she was taken to the maximum-security pod, designated for those with security risks for inmates. In the small concrete cube there was a double bunk bed, a toilet, and a small window through which a patch of sky could be seen. On the lower bed sat an aboriginal woman of about fifty; long years of suffering had left deep traces on her face.

"Wow," she said, observing the bloodstains on Brenda's clothes and face. She moved aside, inviting Brenda to sit on the bed. "Sit down. Tell me the story."

"Two bitches wanted to beat me up. For nothing." Brenda sat and looked into the eyes of her cellmate. "They started it, but I was the one they dragged here. Why not them?"

"Perhaps you did a better job," the woman remarked with a wry smile. "That's what they do. The victim is the one who lost, not the one who started things."

"What are you here for?" Brenda asked.

"For murder. Life. And you?"

"I'll tell you later."

"I'll be outta here tomorrow. They'll let me back to the normal pods. What can I do for you there?"

"Do you know Cinderella?" Brenda asked.

"Sure I do. What about the bitch?"

"Do one thing. Find Cinderella and tell her that it's not over. And say the same to her buddy Fatima."

"You fought with Cinderella?" the aboriginal woman asked. She observed Brenda with an acute interest and approval in her eyes. When Brenda nodded, she smiled, as a mother does looking at her mischievous child. "Wolverine," she said softly. "You are a wolverine."

"Why?"

"Wolverine is a very vicious animal. It's small, but attacks an animal of any size. It knows no fear. It knows to fight to the death."

16

Chapter 3

Melissa returned home at six o'clock, when the sun was rolling down from its height. The shadows began getting longer, and the mercury had plunged from blistering to balmy. The weather forecast promised an even farther drop, and a thunderstorm later, at night. The evening was nice, though, and she wanted to enjoy it in her backyard, with a glass of wine. That was the best time for chatting with her husband, Evan, and watching her son, Nick. The hyperactive seven-year-old was being his innocently exuberant self, running around and doing all wrong things: kicking a soccer ball toward the table where her glass and wine bottle sat; jumping up to grasp and tear leaves from the trees; or throwing small stones at squirrels on the top of the fence.

"Nicky, stop," she pleaded. The tone of her voice suggested no hope for victory.

A thought flickered through her mind. I spend too little time with him. But the next moment her thoughts drifted back to Edward Green. It was not the puzzles of the case that nagged her. She had investigated more complex crimes, which she eventually resolved with a solid package of evidence. She was good at her job, and she was confident that soon she would dig out the facts of this case, too. What she did not like, though—actually hated—was speaking with the victims' relatives.

She had planned to start her rounds of questioning with Edward's university friends and coworkers, but had changed her mind after studying the contents of Edward's apartment. Only one item there was of interest, but it triggered a host of thoughts, which darted in all directions like a flock of birds that had suddenly found the way to freedom after a long captivity. That was the document confirming his change of name. Five years ago Edward Green had been Lucas Kroner. That was the same time when he had been admitted to the university. And the time when Brenda had been sent to the high-security prison for violent offenders.

Coincidences do happen. Melissa knew that. Sometimes they were so weird that they seemed like convincing circumstantial evidence, good enough for indictment. However, subject to scrutiny, often they turned out to be just unrelated events, scattered by the caprice of providence. But nothing, not even a trifling thing, escaped Melissa's scrutiny. Her attention to detail had been quite remarkable since her childhood.

Even more impressive were her memory and analytical talents; professors at the law school where she studied had predicted for her a head-spinning career as a corporate lawyer, making tons of money and basking in fame. But Melissa was a woman whose idiosyncrasies did not fit into any category of middle-class thinking. For one, she didn't need money. She had been born into a very rich family, for whom her law school expenses were just peanuts. She was not a big spender or a compulsive shopper. She dressed modestly and seldom wore expensive jewelry. She was of the opinion that expensive outfits or baubles were mostly a passion for mediocre people with no virtues and talents to distinguish themselves from the crowd.

"If not for the poor pay, I'd advise you to be a police investigator," a professor of criminology had told her. She was thrilled. That was what she actually wanted to be, and where she had a wealth of God-given talent. When facts and evidences were scarce, or almost nonexistent, she was capable of recreating hypothetical scenarios that led the investigation in the right direction. Her intuition was almost inhuman. She remembered the tiniest details of every case in her charge since the start of her career. However, she discovered very soon that she was too soft, too intelligent, to enjoy interrogating abusive, rough, and often psychotic criminals. But even more repellent, almost intolerable, was the task of questioning the dead victims' relatives. Witnessing their mental suffering, often beyond comprehension, was painful. That was what lay ahead of her now.

Edward, or Lucas, had been the only child in his family. Judging by his telephone bills, he contacted his parents, who lived just two hours' drive away from him, almost every day. There were many indicators suggesting deep and touching parent-child relations.

Melissa raised her eyes at her own boy, who was chasing a large bird into the trees. What would she feel if something happened to Nicky? Oh, no, better to die than to live through that. And now, she was going to interrupt the grievance of parents, who lost their beloved, and the only child, by asking questions, which may even worsen their suffering.

Evan came out onto the patio and sat opposite to her, holding a bottle of beer. At thirty-seven, her husband was still in a great shape, a slender, six-foot blond man with charming blue eyes. He never exercised, never resorted to any diet, and stood away from sport of any kind. When asked, how he achieved such an athletic body, he said that according to his theory, muscles grow during the sleep, and good health is the result of doing and eating what you like. Not everyone appreciated his sense of humour.

"Madam investigator is at a crossroads," he said, looking at Melissa with admiring eyes. "You have that look. Perhaps I can help you with something?"

"Philosophers can't help police. But police can help philosophers," Melissa said, looking back and forth between Evan and Nicky.

"Don't generalise," Evan said with a smile. "Philosophers can help anyone, no exceptions. The sad fact is, nobody listens to us. When people are in distress or some hellhole, they go to psychiatrists, lawyers, police, church, anywhere, but not to philosophers."

"I think it's because we are all our own philosophers," Melissa reasoned. "But there is something above the life of a single individual that makes life mysterious. I doubt that philosophy will be of much help to decipher it."

"What do you mean?" Evan raised his eyebrows, and drank from his beer. "That's exactly the task of philosophy: explain the unexplainable."

Nick ran to Melissa and pulled at her sleeve.

"May I have an ice cream, mom?" he asked. Melissa hesitated.

"Okay," she permitted. "Take one from the fridge. But no more today."

"Yes!" Nick shouted, and headed to the door, jumping on one foot. Melissa turned to her husband.

"My job predisposes me to philosophizing, or general hypothesizing if you will, more than almost any other I can think of," she said. "The actions of an individual, when it comes to human relations, have a ripple effect on the lives and destiny of many people whom this individual may not even know. Sometimes, the results are so remote from the cause that you would never even guess where the whole thing originated."

"The butterfly effect," said Evan, nodding.

"The consequences of people's actions, criminal or otherwise, are often impossible to predict. You might do a bad thing to someone, or to many people, but the result could be the opposite of what you expected. And you might be kind and giving to other people, but find that they respond in malicious and nasty way, spreading misery around them. Is there a right way to behave? I doubt it."

"Real philosophical mood," Evan said. "So what troubles you, my love?"

Melissa took a deep breath. "A young man took his life. And a happy life at that. Obviously he had his reasons for that, including the fact that right before he slit his wrists he was forcibly sodomized. He was an only child. I have to meet his parents tomorrow and ask questions. I hate to, but I think it will be the shortest way to get some useful information."

"I see nothing wrong with it," Evan said.

"Right. But I hate it."

"Why?"

"For one, it's heartbreaking to barge in on grieving people. I can't get used to it. Another...reason, I feel in my gut that their son was involved in something that was not nice. My discovery of the truth may just add to their distress. From the philosophical perspective, is it still the right thing to do a good job in this case? And if not, what's the alternative?"

"Do a good job, and trash all unrelated thoughts," Evan said.

"How easy! I'm sick and tired of such things. I'll do my best, of course, as you say—I always do—but my stamina wears out. Maybe I'm not cut out for this job."

"Wow! That was said by one of the best detectives in Canada. Who, then, is cut out for the job?"

"It's more than the matter of intellectual capacity, being a good detective. You need many other qualities of mind. And spirit, too, One is being able to detach yourself from the human aspect of the case," said Melissa. "You have to deal with a case as an engineer, and solve the problem with no compassion for a particular part of a machine. I'm not good at that."

"Are you going to quit the job?" Evan asked.

"I'm thinking about it."

"Nice," Evan said. He smiled and took her hand. "I'll take sabbatical for a year. We can go to Italy for a month, the three of us. And I'll find good cooking courses for you. I love homemade food."

"Be careful, male chauvinist," Melissa said, her voice saturated with notes of laughter, reprimand, and love. "Before I retire, I'd find a good cooking course for you. In your sabbatical you'll learn, at last, practical things."

Evan took his head in his both hands in a mocking distress. "You would trust a philosopher to cook your meal?"

Chapter 4

The last evening before her release on parole, Brenda sat talking with Paula, her long-time friend. Paula had been in the narco business since she was a kid, which was a long time ago. Now, at thirty-nine, she knew all the dark facets of life: jails of different sorts, fights, murders, humiliation, deprivation, and treason, and the sporadic excesses of pleasures and sins. She loved Brenda as a mother would, unconditionally, passionately, and not requesting anything other than pure love in return.

They had met when Brenda was released from the maximum-security pod and returned to a different medium-security cottage. To Brenda's great surprise, she found out that many not-so-violent inmates were now scared of her, and spoke to her with pronounced respect. She was tentatively placed into the category of hard nuts. There were not many like that, and few newbies ever joined their ranks, as usually no one dared to mess with them—even the most dangerous and respected criminals—unless there was a compelling reason. Even the most influential cons preferred to stay away from them. Usually the only way to survive confrontation with such fierce crazies was to kill them, but that was too serious to undertake just for the sake of bullying.

The whole cottage was shocked, even appalled, when Cinderella and Fatima visited Brenda to apologize, and asked her to forgive and forget. They even gave her some coke to snort, which in prison was a very valuable commodity.

After they left, Paula had approached her. She approached any new inmate. Paula was a real gangster in skirt. She had her gang inside the prison, and even more support outside the razor wire fence. She never had to fight. If necessary, she could send one of her cronies to do a dirty job.

Brenda and Paula liked each other from the moment they met. It was a love at first sight, but without any sexual overtones. Paula had all sorts of relations, but never love. Brenda's sincere friendship, not even remotely associated with practical considerations, was something new and confusing for Paula. She was protective, like a bodyguard, and got rather jealous if Brenda talked too long with anybody else. She liked telling the stories of her life to Brenda, and Brenda was a grateful listener. But Paula knew how to listen, too. Brenda was far better educated, and Paula expressed respect for Brenda's drive to continue learning in prison.

They talked outside. It was already dark: myriad stars blinked on the sky, like blue stones thrown from a huge bucket by an almighty hand. There was no moon. All the other inmates were inside, preparing for the night's rest.

"Here's his phone number and address," Paula said, handing Brenda a piece of paper. "His name is Max, it's all there. My baby brother. He's thirty-one. Nice guy, you'll like him. Handsome, too, you know?"

Brenda knew that Paula expected some sort of a salty joke from her, which Brenda had unlimited supply of from the Internet, but she was not in the mood.

"I won't date anyone while I'm on parole," she said.

"You don't have to. But I'll let him know about you anyway. Who knows, maybe the fates will connect you somehow."

"What he's doing?" Brenda asked.

"He's in the car business," said Paul, with a grin. "He can unlock any car and turn it on without a key. He's a full-patch member of a biker gang. You know how many people used to work for him? A lot. But lately he's not that active. I don't know why. Don't dismiss him, though. I think he still has some money to support you for a little while."

"I don't need support. You know that I have proceeds from the sale of my mother's house, from after she died. I'll be okay for a few months, and I'll find my way. I'll work, for sure."

"Go to him, Wolverine. Remember: with a gang, life is simpler and better. Had you been with a gang, you wouldn't even be here for whatever you did. Everyone is afraid of gangs, even the police, because we have money, lawyers, and we don't play by their rules. Anyway, Max can help you with your plans. Know what I mean? You can't do it alone, not a chance. But the gang can do it for you."

"Thank you, Paula," said Brenda, meaning it. "If it hadn't been for you, I'd have killed some bitch in here and gotten more time. You've been like a mother to me."

In the feeble light of the stars, Brenda noticed that Paula's eyes grew wet. Paula turned aside to hide her emotions, but the next moment regained control and looked at Brenda fiercely.

"I am your mother," Paula said, in a commanding, controlled voice. "You have to listen to what I say, and do what I say. Understand?"

Brenda laughed, put her arm around Paula's shoulders. "Yes, mom."

"I'm gonna miss you," Paula said softly. "You're the only one who doesn't belong here."

"I didn't," Brenda said, correcting her, "but I do now."

"No, you don't. You always wake up in a good mood, like a kid. You look happy most of the time. How could you? How could that nice kid be a wolverine?"

"I'm over twenty. Not a kid anymore. Besides, I'm thinking about my crimes after my release."

"I met you when you were nineteen. In my mind, nothing has changed. Anyway, I know you're a wolverine. That's good; now you'll get help from the gang with whatever you want to do."

25

Brenda did want help from a gang, but not right after her release. She had read many interesting books on how to achieve success in life, and learned the importance of motivation, concentration on a goal, and dedication to the course. But to do things right, she needed time, total freedom, money, and help. In her heart, though, she was all ready to take a great risk, and put up with any fate. She was dedicated. She was motivated. She believed that she knew how to execute her plan.

* * *

Next morning, Brenda was out of the gate. The sun, so boring in the camp, blinded her and clouded her mind with heavenly happiness. A sparkling Chevrolet was waiting for her less than a hundred meters from the prison gate. Its door swung open, and Sury, dear faithful friend Sury, jumped out. She was no longer a thin, petite girl with pimples on her greasy face, as she had been almost three years ago. She had grown heavier, and her head was crowned with stylish hairdo. Now that her face had filled in, she was much better looking, but she was still her former self as she greeted Brenda with a smile from ear to ear. She hugged and shook Brenda, kissing and patting her. After a brief exchange of compliments on each other looks, they got into the car, and Sury sped away like crazy, as if she was the one escaping a dreadful place.

"You are the only family I have in the whole world," Brenda said, studying the profile of her faithful friend.

"I will always be," Sury confirmed, briefly glancing at Brenda. Then she turned her attention back to the road.

"Me, too," Brenda said. "I would risk my life for you."

"No more risks," Sury said with a frown.

"A lot has changed in these three years, hasn't it, Sury? Unbelievable! You're married, with a job, and a good husband, I suppose. And you're expecting a kid, right? Quite a different person."

"Not quite," Sury said. "In our core, we all remain the same."

"That's not true," Brenda said. "I've seen unbelievable transformations."

"How often?"

"Not often. Two that I know of personally. They both were strong characters, and had a great faith in their new choices in life."

"You also have a strong character. Are you transformed? Are you different?"

"I'm not." Brenda concentrated her stare on the road.

"Are you still bitter?" Sury asked, her voice hardly audible.

"How could you ask that?" Brenda asked. Her voice was sharp, with metal sounds clinging it. "My life was ruined for nothing. I spent years in hell. Do you think that place was a yoga retreat, where I concentrated finding enlightenment and peace of mind?"

"I know, I know," Sury said gently. "It's just...well, I don't know if this is an appropriate moment to ask you..."

"Shoot," Brenda said, getting back to her cheerful mood.

"Do you still want to strike back?"

"Of course. You know I'm a girl of my word. As you say, we all stay the same in the core of our souls." There was no trace of irritation in her voice.

"I see." Sury remained quiet for a few minutes and just drove. Then she said, "Please don't, Brenda. Life is beautiful. It can still be beautiful for you too. You have many talents, you're pretty, you can do miracles. Whatever had been is long forgotten. Everyone is not the same as then."

Brenda remained silent, waiting for Sury to continue. Sury took it as a sign of encouragement.

"And what would you gain from it? Another crime, perhaps more blood, and life in prison for you? More ruined lives. More tragedies. Who would benefit from

27

that?" Sury glanced over at Brenda, studying the effect of her words.

"You'd better watch the road," Brenda advised. "Who would benefit, you ask? I will be the first. I will achieve my goal. At last I'll get peace of mind, in prison or not. You know what mental torture is? No, you don't. Another benefit is justice. I studied law in the slammer. Justice must be served at all cost, understand? The higher the cost, the better it is for justice." She laughed, throwing her head back. "Particularly justice for what happened to me. It's worth living for such a moment. Don't you think so?"

"That's too abstract for me," Sury said with a sigh. "I love you, Brenda, so much. I want you be happy. So listen to my advice: put it behind you. My husband and I will do whatever we can to help you. I've told him a lot about you."

"Dear old Sury," Brenda said, patting her friend's shoulder. "Thank you for everything. You know…I've tried my best to put it behind me, to forget about everything and start a life, undisturbed by memory. So far, I can't picture it—me, that is—happy, forgiving, and kind. I'm bitter, angry, and hateful."

Sury gave her the longest look she could manage without running off the road. "That'll change while you are on parole," she said, and smiled. "Now you're almost free. It's not a big deal to talk to a parole officer now and then, right? But you can have a boyfriend, go to parties, dress as you like—I arranged everything for you. I rented a bachelor unit for you to start with. You can change it later. You even have a job interview already, which is a lot to start with, I know…. It's not much pay, but—"

"I have some money, you know that," Brenda interrupted her. "I'm sure I can do well. As far as parties and lovers are concerned, I'll postpone that until my full release."

"How's your studying going?" Sury asked.

"This year, I'll finish the second year of the college-level accounting program. After that, I'll go to university. All evening courses, of course, I'm gonna work, you know. I don't mind. I like to be busy."

"I'm sure that soon your bitterness will go away," Sury said, sounding confident. "You'll see. You'll have a good life. You'll have career, money, men. They'll heal you." She laughed.

"Yes, we'll see." Brenda returned her smile. "Thanks a lot, Sury, for arranging everything for me."

"Don't mention it. I'm sorry that you'll live that far away. I'd love to see you often."

"I need to live as far away from there as possible. There shouldn't be any chance of running into any of those...jerks. But you and I can meet up, sure."

Chapter 5

The bachelor flat that Sury had rented for Brenda seemed like the most beautiful and spacious dwelling in the world, with all attributes of ultimate luxury: a twin bed, nicely done, with a sparkling silver cover, a coffee table, a couch, a breakfast table, and all necessary appliances. And it was all for only one person, for her! There was even a table lamp, shedding an intimate light against the saturating darkness of night.

After Sury left, some wine remained in the bottle they'd opened to celebrate her release. Brenda poured it into her glass, walked to the floor-to-ceiling window, and stared out. The silence and quiet of the apartment enveloped her as a magic tranquilising blanket. A mix of happiness, regret, and sorrow almost brought her to tears. It took some effort and a few sips to haul her mind and mood back to her present reality. There will be tomorrow, she told to herself, and except for the parole officer, it all seemed so normal—setting an alarm clock, going to a job interview, buying groceries…and a host of other chores, the things of everyday life. The life that she had forgotten, and had to learn all over again.

The excitement of the day was too much to bear for another minute. She emptied her glass, undressed, took a quick shower, and went to bed. "So quiet," was her last thought before she fell asleep.

* * *

The days began rolling by, with unexceptional excitements and frustrations, but she liked them immensely. She was hired for the job right after the interview as a combination receptionist and bookkeeper. The pay was modest, but it was a real job where she could show off her talents, and the money was good enough to start with.

She was well received by the other company employees. A few young men tried to flirt with her, but she made it clear from the outset that she wasn't interested. She was mostly able to deflect them without effort, but once she had to be icy cold, almost impolite, to cut the attempts short. Sure, as a young, healthy woman she wanted to have a lover. She wanted parties, flirtations, exciting love affairs, and everything else that women her age had and enjoyed in those young adult years. But she was determined to postpone it until the day of her final legal release from her sentence, the day when she was completely free, without parole supervision or the obligation to report to anyone or explain her behaviour. And yes, without catching the slanted glances of those who knew her past. Only then she could get back to the day when her misery started, and make those who had caused her misery pay the full price. Consequences? Of course, there were risks, but she would take it, and accept without complaint or remorse whatever happened if she was caught. However, she would do everything as smart as it could possibly be. That's what many of her inmates did in the prison in the idle, painfully boring times: think either about smarter ways of doing crime, or revenge.

She was an exemplary parolee, with the best possible references from her employer. She had completed the last year of accounting study in the college evening courses, and gotten her diploma. She received a promotion, so her sole responsibility became keeping the company's books and most of accounting. The only parties she attended were those organized by the company. She had a few female friends, and even invited them to her apartment. The dishes that she prepared for them were the object of their delight and envy.

A few former inmates visited her, uninvited, after their release. In prison, they had thought that their friendship with Brenda would last a lifetime, and it was a disappointment for them to discover the great distance in mentality, attitude toward problem-solving, and understanding of reality that separated her from them outside the prison gates. Brenda, although held back by her past, was sure that she could do a lot in her future, in so many ways: education, career, and proper planning of activities. Her prison friends didn't think about tomorrow, at least in terms of goals. They thought that their time for education and self-development was past, and there was nothing to be done about that. For them, the only time to live was today. Whatever tomorrow brought didn't matter. If society wouldn't accept them, they would not care. After their very first meeting on the outside with Brenda, they knew at once that there was nothing, other than a few shared stories from prison, to connect them.

The parole supervisor seemed to be a nice man. In his late forties, a bit overweight, with a large, bulbous nose and round gray eyes, like coins, he had a permanent expression of surprise on his face, the look people have when they recognize a long-forgotten friend on the street and cry: "Is it you? Wow!"

He was all kindness, yet the longer she knew him, the less she liked him. It was not his fault, though. Jim didn't give her any real reason to dislike him. He didn't try to give her lessons on how to adapt to a community life, or behave in a manner customary for society; he was smart enough to understand that Brenda already knew these things, perhaps better than he.

He seldom asked her real questions, and if he did, they were seemingly harmless, natural in the course of conversations. Their meetings were just friendly talks, he explained, simply a benign mixture of a pleasant chitchat and formality. "What can I do, Brenda?' he said once. "It's my job. I'm paid for it, you know? Hopefully you don't mind our chats. Do you?"

He was smart, but his tricks did not fool Brenda into taking his tactics at face value. Jim certainly knew everything about her. He wanted to figure out if she had really put her painful past behind her, and was determined to be a model citizen. With a nice smile, he told her a few too many times that it was ridiculous to suggest that she was any kind of threat to the community. She was as peaceful and kind as a dove, and as busy with her studies and work as a honeybee. Just an ideal citizen, woman, employee...you name it. Brenda understood that her perfect behaviour was exactly what made him suspicious. She was "too good to be true," which kept him on the alert.

The day when she would be eligible for the early release was approaching fast. Half a year had been a long time to wait, but she was almost sure of getting it. Inevitably, it became a subject of discussions with Jim, and the more he talked to her about it, the angrier she became with him. He kept digging into the depths of her soul, touching the most painful inflammation spots.

"What are you going to do if I release you before the end of your time?" he asked.

"What do you mean?"

"You know, what I mean." Jim frowned, seemingly deep in thought. "Will you stay here, and advance your career at the company, or move somewhere? Look for luck elsewhere?"

Brenda made an attempt to withstand his sharp stare. The permanent expression of pleasant surprise on his face gave way to an ominous doubt.

Brenda had never been a liar. She hated lying. That was not in her nature, but Jim had put her in a tough corner, and she had no choice but to be evasive.

"If they offer me a good raise and money, why wouldn't I?" She smiled like a happy child. "I like it here. People here are so nice, so simple."

That much was true, and therefore easy to say. People were really nice and simple at this place.

"Yes, yes," Jim agreed, as if in a hurry, and nodded a few times in approval. "True, people are simple and nice here. And the company loves you." He paused. "Well, suppose you get a better offer, say, in Toronto? Would you go there?"

"Maybe," Brenda said noncommittally, shrugging her shoulders. "I'm young. I don't mind exploring the ways to move as high up as possible. I'm capable of a lot. I also want to continue my education at university, be a chartered accountant. They make tons of money."

"Excellent, excellent," Jim said, although his thoughts were obviously far away. He leaned back, pretending to be very casual and at ease with her.

"Suppose you got a good position in Toronto. You move there. You go to a bar with your friends, or coworkers, and all of a sudden you bump into someone you knew then, someone who was a witness in your case. Or a victim." He quickly threw his arms forward, palms up, as if defending himself from her possible objections. "Please, don't dwell on my terminology. I guess you have different definitions for those guys. I'm on your side, but I have to stick to formalities. Anyway, what your reaction would be?"

Brenda tightened her fists under the table. "I'd probably leave the place as fast as possible. For sure, I wouldn't want to talk with them. It's not a good memory."

"I agree, I agree," Jim said, nodding again. "Sure, it's a wise choice. But other than that… Does your past bother you? Do you think about it often?"

This was too nagging, too direct a question. She had no choice but to lie.

"If not for your questions, I wouldn't think about it at all," she said. "It's totally behind me. There's nothing I can do to change the past, but I can do a lot to change my future. Why do you ask?"

Jim straightened up, leaned forward, and put his elbows on the table. "Because I intend to apply for your early release. Before the end of your time, you know. As your parole officer, I have to. It's my duty, because your life on parole has been perfect. Exemplary in fact."

"That's nice of you," Brenda said, trying hard to calm her racing heart.

"Thanks," Jim said with a wry smile. "But there is a problem."

"What's that?"

"You know what. You are the cleverest woman I have ever dealt with in my duties. You haven't forgotten anything. You haven't broken with the past. But you know all the right answers, and that's what I have to use in my job. My gut feelings don't count."

He paused, but Brenda was too much at a loss to respond. It was a surprise ambush. She smiled wanly.

Jim took a deep breath. "Okay, Brenda. See you soon. I'll request your early release, and I'm almost certain that you'll get it." He shook his head sadly.

Chapter 6

"Philosophical attitude" means delegating problems and their solutions to the logical part of the brain, according to Evan. That's what Melissa reminded herself while she approached the house where Edward's parents lived. It would be nice if life was that simple, she thought. There is a spirit, though, that lives inside us and controls our brain. In tough moments, it kicks up our emotions, which knock out logical thinking and make life miserable.

Melissa swallowed a choking lump of compassion and rang the bell. The door opened, revealing Edward's father, Gary. She already knew something about him: wealthy developer, fifty-two, luck in almost all of his undertakings. Of average height and broad shouldered, with a disproportionally big head crowned with a short-trimmed hair, he would have conveyed an impression of intimidating strength, if not for the red rims of his eyelids, and the unmistakable cry of bottomless grief in his dark eyes.

Melissa flashed her badge and introduced herself. Gary nodded, retreated one step, and gestured for her to enter. Under less solemn circumstances, Melissa would have complimented him on the beautiful design and ambience of the first floor of the house. The open floor plan included a foyer with a floor-to-ceiling mirror, a large sitting area adjacent to the kitchen, and a huge breakfast area with all-glass walls and patio doors. Set off from that were two sets of French doors through which Melissa could see antique furniture and expensive paintings in what were probably an office and a dining room. Everything conveyed the impression of wealth, great taste, and happiness. In sharp dissonance to this ambience was Gary's wife, Karina, who sat on a modern sofa close to a window overlooking the lush front yard. She wore black. Her hands rested on her lap, and her red eyes were also filled with infinite grief. She appeared to be on strong tranquilizers.

"Sorry for my intrusion at such terrible time," Melissa said, taking the offered chair. Gary sat beside his wife and took her hand. They both looked at Melissa, tired of their grief, unable to accept the loss, bitter about her intrusion. Melissa, at last, got control of her feelings. Professionalism conquered all the unrelated emotions, giving the reins back to the logical part of the brain.

"I won't bother you for long. This is just a formality," she began. "It is in our common interest to bring any criminals in this matter to justice. Any information you can share will be useful."

"Do you have any idea about who did it? Any theories?" Gary asked.

Melissa did have some thoughts, but she was there to ask questions, not answer them. "So far we have only the results of the autopsy. There is no indication that his death was…not self-inflicted…and the circumstance remains under investigation." She quickly changed the subject. "Do you know if Edward had any enemies?"

"No," Karina said, in a cracking voice. "He had only friends. Lots of them. He was so kind, so kind…" She stopped, dabbing her eyes.

"Who were his closest friends?"

"We can't say," Gary said. "We know for sure that in his university years, he had plenty. But we didn't see them. He lived in Toronto then, you know. He visited us alone."

"I understand, sir. Did he have friends at school, before university?"

"Yes," Karina answered. "Plenty. He always had many friends. Everywhere."

"Who were his closest friends then?"

37

"In school?" Karina repeated. "Why? That was so long time ago. Five years."

"Perhaps he was in touch with some of them after he left?"

"Only one that I know of, who lives not far from here. His name is Christian."

"Why do you need the names of his friends?" Gary asked. He let Karina's hand go and leaned forward.

"Because his friends may know Edward's enemies better than parents. Perhaps they know some of his habits, things that may have complicated his life," said Melissa. "Some of Edward's connections might help us with out investigation. This Christian...do you know his last name?"

"Andersen."

"And where exactly does Christian Andersen live?"

"Not far." Karina fixed a wisp of dark hair that was stubbornly dangling in front of her right eye. She became a bit more animated, if not alert. "Near the park. His house is the second from that end."

"Who else do you know?" Melissa asked, scribbling on her writing pad. Her memory was able to absorb volumes, but nonetheless she had a habit of jotting down the most essential things, for the record.

"Other than Christian, none of his school friends still live around here now," said Gary, slightly irritated. "We know nothing about them."

Intuition never let Melissa down. She already knew that a tough moment for the three of them was not far away.

"Why did he change his name to Edward?" Melissa asked.

Karina cleared her throat and blinked her eyes rapidly. She was shaking, and seemed utterly upset. In different circumstances, Melissa would have melted with compassion, but at that moment she had to be the hunting

38

dog, on the scent of game. She put her notepad and pen on the coffee table as a gesture of understanding.

"Excuse us," Gary said, taking Karina with his left arm and helping her rise to her feet. "I'll be right back." He led Katrina to the staircase, and they both disappeared behind its steep curve. Their muffled, agitated voices reached Melissa's ears, but she could not make out a word. She took the opportunity to look around.

The bronze bust of a man in the distant corner was a fine piece of art. Melissa knew the value of things. She estimated its worth at around twenty thousand dollars. A picture on the opposite wall was no less impressive. It was a work by the Group of Seven, famous Canadian landscape painters from the twenties and thirties. Melissa had seen an exhibition of their works at the McMichael Canadian Art Collection gallery in Kleinberg, though not that particular painting. Must be worth close to a hundred thousand dollars, she decided. There were smaller things, like heavy silver candelabra, an Art Nouveau statue of a female dancer, and a sheaf of decorative brass wheat stems, with heads larger than life size, held together with golden wire. In spite of the opulence, the place conveyed the silent grief of loss, which was numb to money and influence. Death equates us all, Melissa thought. Sadness is the same at any grave, be it a small stone with just a name engraved there, or a large and showy tomb towering above all others.

On the ledge of the fireplace sat two framed photographs, both decorated with a black band. One showed Lucas when he was about seven or eight years old. Another showed him at a graduation ceremony. He looked happy, ready to step on the road toward the long and interesting years of his life. What mental torture had he endured to make him cut his veins?

A minute later Gary came back alone, and took his place on the sofa.

"Sorry. She doesn't feel well." His voice reflected a boring monotony of grief. "Perhaps we can talk some other day?"

"We can," Melissa agreed, "but time is very important in investigation. And no question goes away without an answer anyway. It'd be better if you help me today as much as you could. Unless, of course, there is a compelling reason not to do that."

"No, no, not at all." Gary was quick to protest. "Of course I'll do my best. You asked why he had changed his name. He did it when he was admitted to the university in Toronto, when moved away from here. He had been receiving threats, so he decided to hide his identity, at least somewhat, to make it more difficult for his stalkers to find him."

"He had stalkers? Who threatened him?" Melissa asked. Now you're talking.

"It was a rather stupid story." Gary was hiding his eyes, not at ease with the question. "He had a meaningless affair with a girl... I don't know the details—he wasn't too open with us regarding his girls, you know? We all have our silly romances when we're younger, and we make mistakes. Sometimes they haunt us many years." He paused.

"Yes, I'm listening," Melissa said. "Was it Brenda?"

Gary jerked his head up and fixed Melissa with his questioning stare. Apparently what he saw in her eyes convinced him that telling the truth was the best choice.

"Yes, Brenda. You know already everything, don't you?" Melissa could tell that he wanted to find out exactly how much she did know already, but she didn't oblige.

"Soon I'll know everything there is to know. Please continue," Melissa said, picking up her notepad and pen. She did not take her eyes off him. Her acute attention captured and retained in her memory with photographic clarity every change in his expression, body movements, or manner of speech. Any change. But this time she had no intention of writing anything down.

"The girl was a natural-born criminal," Gary said with a frown. "She's the daughter of a cleaning woman, single mother, so no wonder she has that set of mind.... Don't take me wrong; it's not her fault that she wasn't raised with an adequate understanding of moral values, but... Anyway, it was stupid of..." Gary stumbled for a brief moment, and then continued. "...of Lucas to have anything to do with her. In broad daylight, she attacked him with a kitchen knife on a soccer field during a game! Oh, it was terrible."

"She cut his left hand," Melissa said. She recalled a short but rather wide scar on Lucas's forearm.

"Yes, exactly," Gary said, pointing distractedly to his own left arm. "He had to run away—that's what saved him. He lost lots of blood then. Police arrested her, the knife still in her hand. You probably already know that she was put in prison for five years. The crazy girl threatened him during the court, and had insolence to pass on her threats when she was in prison."

"What exactly were her threats?"

"To hunt him until the end of his life. I think she wanted to kill him. I'm sure that she was the one who did kill him."

"It was suicide."

"Are you sure?" Gary asked.

"Yes, 100 percent sure. We don't know yet what had happened leading up to that. We'll only know all that after we've found the perpetrators—if there are any. Mind you, so far there are only speculations."

"Will you arrest Brenda?" Gary asked.

"Why should I? There is no evidence against her so far." Melissa paused, watching Gary closely. She expected him insist on Brenda's arrest, or ask questions about her whereabouts, but he didn't push the issue

41

further. He just swayed his hand in a dismissive gesture that said nothing made any difference to him anymore.

Melissa paused, giving Gary a chance to ask questions. He didn't. Instead, he cast his eyes down, examining the web of lines on his palms. Once more it told Melissa that she was on the right track. She put her notepad and pen on the table again to suggest to Gary that their conversation was now mere semi-official chitchat.

"Lucas was success with the girls," she said casually. Gary raised his eyes with a more animated expression in them.

"No wonder. He was handsome," he said. "He had his peculiar charms."

"Are you sure that Lucas had a romance with Brenda?" Melissa asked. "Absolutely sure?"

Gary shifted his eyes left and right, as if in hope to find the answer in one of the corners.

"I...I was sure," he said, without confidence. "I didn't discuss it with Lucas, of course, as he wasn't very open about such matters, but there was a mention of that at the court. Apparently, Brenda had sex with him at the party after graduation. She also had sex with someone else. Low-class promiscuous girl, you know? Someone called her on it, and she got angry, and accused Lucas and her other casual partners of rape. The case was dismissed, of course, at the court. The absurdity of it was obvious."

"How so?"

"As you said, he was a success with the girls. He had many willing girlfriends, so why would he bother with her, of all people?"

"Why did she assault him with a knife?"

"She's insane, with an impulsive criminal mind. I'm sure you can find your explanation in her court records. I'm sorry. I don't feel well. If you please excuse me..."

Melissa picked up her notepad and pen. There was no new record in it. She rose.

42

"Here's my business card," she said. "Call me if you recall anything relevant. Thank you for your time. And thank your wife for me, too. I know this must be very difficult for you both."

She left feeling far less compassion toward Lucas's parents than she'd felt when she arrived. The problem was not discovering what had really happened between Brenda and Lucas. She'd know that soon enough. There was something else going on, something vile.

Chapter 7

She knew that the news was coming, and yet, when it did come, Brenda was flabbergasted. The judge said, "Your behaviour has been exemplary. Frankly, I'm impressed. When I read your files, the question I ask myself is how such a wonderful girl got herself in such troubles in the first place. I'm sure it was just a terrible mistake of youth, a one-time error in the heat of the moment."

Brenda swallowed the huge lump in her throat. She wanted to shout, "It was about justice!" but instead she just smiled and said, "Thank you, Your Honour."

"I have no doubt," the judge continued, with a trace of a pleasant smile on his thin lips, "that you will never again commit a crime. I understand how difficult it was to be on parole: actually, sometimes it is not much better than in prison, but it depends, of course on…"

He kept talking, but Brenda was barely listening. Freedom! She didn't have to pretend anymore to be a good girl, redeemed, repentant. Not that she considered herself a bad girl, but the powerful genie who was hiding inside her was now free, able to work his creative and distractive energy.

She left the court and returned home. She sat there, doing nothing, just thinking.

How different the morning had been from her last appearance before the judge.

That day, too, she had been allowed to wear her own clothes. However, her arms had been secured by handcuffs back then. A guard led her to a small enclosure in the courtroom, a protective barrier with a lower part of polished wood and an upper part mounted with thick glass panels. To her surprise, the public benches were almost empty. Sury was there. She raised her hand and gave Brenda an encouraging smile. It was so nice to see sweet Sury! Brenda raised her manacled hands to reciprocate the greeting and demonstrate the handcuffs.

Two tables facing the judge's bench were cluttered with papers: her lawyer and the district attorney were busy shuffling them. The judge began his monotonous deliberations. He did not use his microphone, so sometimes his voice was too quiet for her to catch his words, which irritated Brenda. At one point, the judge ordered her to stand and answer his questions. She rose to her feet and said in a crisp, clear, loud voice, "I don't see the criminals who raped me."

Her young lawyer scowled at her. He could not contain his irritation, if not anger. He had instructed her not to raise this issue, at least not until the appropriate moment. He promised to deal with the "mitigating circumstances," as he called the rape, adhering to procedural opportunities. But Brenda saw no harm in pointing out something whose importance should be obvious to any judge.

To her surprise, her lawyer had been right. Her simple statement enraged the judge, who burst out, red-faced with anger, in a voice that was now perfectly loud and clear.

"You have an extreme record of violence!" he began, glowering at her. "Your conduct has escalated from bad to worse. Your unprovoked assaults, your repeated threats— these all clearly demonstrate your proclivity for violence, which can only be constrained by the penal system. I don't see any signs that you understand the seriousness of your crime or that you can live peacefully and without further menace to society."

The first judge had called Brenda a menace to society, though the jerk had been well aware that society at large was safe, and only a few guilty bastards were not. This morning, a different judge had called her a

45

wonderful girl, a child who had merely been acting impulsively then and unlikely to ever again break the law now.

Both judges were wrong.

With some effort, Brenda pushed away the memory of the past and brewed a pot of coffee. When it was ready, she carried a cup to her sofa and sat there holding a piece of paper she had pulled from the desk drawer—the scribbled name Paula had given her that last night in prison. After a few sips, she took the phone and dialled the number. A smooth, calm baritone greeted her with an indifferent greeting.

"Is this Max?"

"Max it is. Who are you?"

"My name is Brenda. Paula gave me your phone number."

"Yes, I know. Actually, she called me two weeks ago and asked if you had called. Brenda Wolverine, right?"

"It's been a long time since I was Wolverine. No one has called me that since I left that shithole."

"Wolverine is forever a wolverine. Are you going to come to my place?"

"Not right away. First, I have to settle somewhere, and then we'll meet."

"May I suggest something?" he asked.

"Shoot."

"Come to my place first. If you don't like it here, I'll help you settle wherever you wish. Paula's friend is my friend."

Brenda hesitated, but not for long. "Okay, give me your address. I'll come by."

"There's no address per se, but I'll give you directions. It's easy to find me."

"Okay. Where it is?" Brenda scribbled directions on a writing pad.

"Are you free already?"

"Yes!" she almost screamed.

"When shall I expect you?" he asked.

"In a few days. I have to finish up a few things."

"Of course, of course. Some formalities, eh?"

"Exactly. See you soon." She hung up and then dialled Sury.

"That's it!" she shouted, when her friend picked up the phone. "Freeeee! No more parole, no more reporting to anyone. That's it!"

Sury squeaked and whinnied, and screamed congratulations. "Do you want me to come to your place to celebrate, or will you come here?"

"Sury, you know I'll never go back there. But we can meet halfway. In a few days, I'll be in Toronto. I'll stay there two or three days in a nice hotel—that's where we'll meet. What hotel would you recommend? I mean, a really nice one. I have money."

"The Royal York is really nice. You leaving your job?"

"Yes, definitely."

"You said there are nice people there. They were kind to you."

"They were."

"Look, Brenda..." Sury's tone slid down from the heights of joy. "My advice to you? Drop it. Your life could be so nice."

"Thanks for the unsolicited advice. You are my best friend, Sury. I'll call you from the hotel. We'll celebrate."

"I'll come, for sure. I need to talk to you," she said. "And you know I'll try to talk you out of whatever you're thinking of doing...."

"My dear, sweet Sury," Brenda said. "I can't wait to hug you. See you at the Royal York."

Of all the administration chores that she had to do to deal with outstanding issues before leaving, the most difficult one was talking with her manager. Laura, a sweet woman in her forties, was very upset when Brenda told her about the resignation.

47

"But why, Brenda, dear?" she lamented. "I was going to promote you again after your next review. Everyone likes you here. I thought you liked it here, too. What happened? Perhaps someone was not nice to you? Maybe I can do something to encourage you to stay? Tell me. Don't hide anything. I'm your friend."

The last thing Brenda wanted was to upset this kind woman. She liked her, and indeed she liked almost everyone in the company.

"I like it here very much," she said, with all sincerity. "And I'd like to thank you for all the kind things you did for me. It's just…you know, something very important came up, personal matters, and I had to change my plans. When I'm settled, I'll let you know. We'll be in touch." When Brenda left the building, she knew for sure that they would never be in touch. She went to her apartment, packed a few of her belongings, carried them to her car, and left for Toronto.

The melodic, rhythmic music from the car radio elated her even further. She turned volume way up, vibrating the worn-out parts of her old car. She moved in time with the beat, sang together with the singer, and smiled to the rising sun.

The Royal York impressed her with its luxury and grandeur. It was the perfect place to celebrate her freedom, before starting her new, exciting life. She wasn't afraid of anything. She was ready for all the challenges fate might present.

Sury arrived the next day. They went down to a restaurant, and started with a bottle of champagne. Sury looked at the price list, but Brenda snatched it from her hands.

"My treat today," she said, with resolution. "I have money. And this is an occasion worth any expense. Enjoy. Cheers."

Sury took a sip. "Nice," she said, fluttering her eyelashes.

"Sury, tell me the latest news." Brenda swept her eyes at the tables around them, seeing people who were relaxed, confident, smiling. For them, there was nothing extraordinary about the opulence. It was an everyday ingredient of their lives, something they saw as their rightful possession.

"You know all the news," Sury said. "I've told you everything. My daughter is one year old. Some people told me that I married too early, that I should have played the field a bit longer, but I'm happy with my hubby. I don't need parties, men, flirts."

"Do you know where Yona lives now?"

The question made Sury reach for her champagne.

"No. Rumour has it he moved to Toronto. Maybe he took your threat seriously. Or, perhaps he had another reason. Not a trace of him since then."

"What do you mean another reason?"

Sury shrugged. "One guy, who used to be close to him, said Yona joined a gang. Sells drugs or something. But I don't know anything for sure. Just rumours. Brenda, you still—"

"Where's Christian?" Brenda interrupted her.

"Still lives there. Has a girlfriend. Graduated university. He's an engineer."

"Happy life, eh?" Brenda asked. She looked across the dining room at the contented faces of an affluent crowd. Perhaps Christian enjoyed that same good life with his girlfriend in a similar restaurant.

"I don't know much about him. I've tried to forget about him," said Sury. "You should too. Move on, have a happy life."

"Not that happy a life. It's not that easy."

"What do you mean?" Sury frowned in disapproval. "You're smart, young, pretty, a nice girl. You've got skills, talents. And you're free."

"Say, I meet a doctor, a lawyer, whatever. What do I tell him? That I'm a former con who spent years in

49

prison? That I cut someone with a knife? That I was raped? Do you expect anyone to take that lightly, and introduce me to his parents? Will he tell the crowd at the wedding how brave I was, and make jokes about how dangerous it can be to cross me, while every snickers uncomfortably, or laughs at my expense?"

Sury reached for the glass again, but it was empty. The waiter noticed it, and hurried to their table. Refilling their glasses, he held up the empty bottle and asked, "More champagne, ladies?"

Brenda looked at Sury, offering her the choice.

"Better yet, make it a bottle of merlot," Sury said. The waiter nodded and disappeared.

"And Lucas?" Brenda pressed on with her questions.

"He disappeared after your trial. Nobody knew where he had gone. A few months ago, my husband and I were in Toronto—he had some business here—and we went to a bar, a very nice one…a mostly professional crowd, you know. We met a few people he knows, old friends from the university. One of them was Lucas. Lucas didn't recognize me, can you believe it? I asked Rene, my hubby, how he knew Lucas. He said, who's Lucas? That's Edward. Edward Green. That's the name he uses now, the one he used in the university."

The fact that Lucas had changed his name was an unmistakable indicator that he took her threat seriously, and that some fear still lived inside him all the time.

"And Bob? You know where he is?"

"I heard that he lives in Hamilton. Brenda, please," Sury pleaded. "Don't go that way. I know that you are a dedicated fighter. I admire you. I don't know any woman who has your strength. But I believe that your mindset isn't normal. It's not good."

"What do you mean not normal?" Brenda asked. "Being strong is not normal? Are you normal to say so?" Brenda laughed, but not a trace of a smile appeared on Sury's face.

"Hold on. It's not as stupid as it seems to you. Mind you, I study psychology. Although I'm not a licensed doctor yet, I know something about the human mind. When it becomes obsessed with something that leads to abnormal efforts and risks but brings little or no tangible results, that is not normal, and in most cases it leads to disaster."

Brenda chuckled. "Many people in prison are that way. Do you consider them abnormal?"

"Well, yeah, for sure. That's why they are there. Most of them go back to prison again and again, although their thinking capacity is sufficient that they could lead productive lives. But you, Brenda..."

"It's different with me—" Brenda began, but Sury interrupted her.

"Everyone thinks about themselves as being normal and smart. Have you ever met woman who thinks of herself as stupid? She might admit that she's not tall, not thin, or even not beautiful. But not smart? Stupid? You'd insult her if you said so," said Sury. "Don't look at me like that! I am not suggesting that you are stupid. On the contrary, I think that you are exceptionally smart. But normal...? Your obsession with revenge, your determination to act, frightens me. That is not normal. If you were just out of the prison gates, I might understand it. But you've lived through your parole, and the normal life is now your way of life. You could have a great future, really nice life. You don't have to tell everyone your story..."

The waiter brought a bottle of wine and went through the tasting ritual with Sury. She nodded in acceptance and the waiter left.

"Good old Sury," Brenda said in a soft voice. "I love you. Let's drink to a great future and a nice life. But let's stop talking about that future."

And Sury complied. Their chat was meaningless and animated, with jokes, laughter, and good memories. After

51

Sury left, Brenda returned to her room, and lay in bed with open eyes, thinking about what Sury said. Not normal.

She didn't sleep well, yet in the morning she felt fresh and filled with energy. After checking out she had a cup of coffee, enjoyed the ambience of the hotel, and then jumped to her car and steered it to the Gardiner Expressway.

After a long run on highways and then scenic rural roads, she arrived at Max's trailer park. She quickly found his dwelling, pulled in and stepped out. The sun was still lingering over horizon, as if hesitant to touch it. She climbed the small porch of Max's mobile home and observed the line of similar places to the left and right. On the front lawn two trailers away, a rowdy party was raging on. A few women who reminded Brenda of her inmates in the prison were laughing and shrieking. Most of the men wore beards and bandanas; all of them looked at her as she got out of the car. Brenda was an attractive woman, and she knew it. She smiled and knocked on the door.

There was no response. She knocked again and listened. Not a sound came from inside the house, but crunching gravel under heavy footsteps made her look back. This was Max, she knew at once: tall, handsome, with large blue eyes, a large forehead, blond beard, the good posture of a proud gangster, and a hard, menacing stare.

"Brenda?" he asked, reaching the top of the porch in one step.

"Yes."

"Go on in. The door's not locked."

He followed her in, and led the way to a small kitchen.

"That will be your room," he said, pointing to one of the doors. "You can leave your bag there. Whad'ya wanna do first? Shower, eat, drink?"

"Not eat, for sure," Brenda said, settling into a small chair. "Too excited today. Got any whiskey?"

"Sure." Max nodded, and stepped to one of the kitchen cabinets. "Black Label do?"

"Anything."

While Max raised his hands to take the bottle from the top shelf, Brenda studied his athletic figure. His tight jeans and T-shirt highlighted his contours in a most appealing way. Her imagination undressed him for a brief moment. Blood rushed to her temples, and her heart raced with excitement.

Max turned around, sat opposite to her, and filled two glasses. Mesmerized, she watched his lips moving, but did not hear much what he was saying. He raised his glass.

"Cheers," he said. "Free as a bird now, eh?"

Brenda took her glass. To her embarrassment and discomfort, she noticed her hand was shaking. She emptied the glass in a few swigs, set it down, then hid her hands under the table.

"Free as a bird," she agreed. "But without a nest."

"You can live here as long as you wish," he said, observing her with insolent, lustful eyes. Brenda did not mind, and reciprocated with the same stare. Immediately the spark in his eyes ignited the flame. Max refilled their glasses.

"Paula told me your story," he said, not taking his eyes off her.

"Now, a new story begins," she said, raising her glass. She took a sip, still looking into his eyes. He did the same. At last, he smiled.

"You're beautiful," he said. "Paula told me you were, and she was right. She said you could eat men's hearts alive."

Brenda laughed. "I wish. But I don't need many."

"Is mine good enough?" He diverted his attention to the window. Now Brenda could observe him undisturbed.

"Worth trying," she said, with a shy laugh.

Ten minutes later they were in bed, enjoying each other with vigorous passion. Whiskey and love, in rapid succession, knocked Max out first. He fell asleep with Brenda in his arms. She watched him for a minute, ran her hand over his face, delicately touched his lips with the tips of her fingers, and dropped into a deep sleep.

In late morning, when the sun was already high in the sky, they woke at the same moment. His arms were still around her naked body, and his embrace tightened. Her hand was on his cheek.

"Good morning," she half-whispered and, without opening her eyes, and stretched her lips into a lazy, happy smile.

Chapter 8

The knight who saves a beautiful princess was Nick's favourite tale. He asked Melissa to read it again before he fell asleep. She was halfway through it when his eyes closed, and his breathing became slow, regular, and shallow. She kissed his forehead and retreated to the living room, where Evan sat with a glass of wine.

"Sleep?" he asked.

"Yes. The same story of the daring knight and the princess. I wonder what will become of him when he's nineteen?" She sat beside Evan on the sofa and took a sip from his glass. Evan put his hand around her waist.

"He's a good boy."

"He is. I think that Edward-Lucas—you know the kid I mean—wasn't a bad boy. However, he did something terribly wrong, something bad."

"What are your thoughts?"

"He committed suicide, that's for sure. I think he was afraid of something he thought would be worse than death."

"Yeah." Evan paused. "He likely had a weak psyche."

"True, he had," Melissa agreed. "But not so weak that he would take his life over a trifle. The thing is—and that's where unlikely merge of philosophy and investigative practice comes in, again—everything we do is recorded in our individual files somewhere. People's deeds find their way into police files, university records, anecdotes and shared memories. In this particular case, the repercussions of whatever Lucas did were far reaching. For sure, Brenda has something to do with this. I will study her files. The key to the puzzle is there."

"Criminals always find their way back to prison," Evan remarked.

"True, but Brenda is not the usual criminal. I am almost certain that if she did have anything to do with Lucas's death, money was not even a minor motivation. She earns decent money, doesn't spend lavishly, and has a comfortable life. Another thing puzzles me. She doesn't see at all afraid of police or this investigation. Yet she's not stupid enough to think that she can act without regard for consequences. I'm wondering if she thinks she's too smart to get caught."

"What do you think happened to Lucas?" Evan asked.

"I think Brenda was there before he took his life—maybe even while he did it. And I'm sure she wasn't there alone. It's not hard to conclude who helped her. She lives with a gangster, a full-patch member of a biker gang. Those thugs know how to commit crimes and get away with it. I just wonder why he agreed to help her, but I'll find it out soon. I just have to ask the right questions and find the best answers."

"Philosophy," Evan said with a chuckle. "One difference, though, is that philosophy deals with the same questions over and over again, but arrives at different answers. Or maybe that's not so different."

"I think Lucas did something wrong a few years ago, something that could now be seen as a mistake of youth. How could a good and likable boy do something so terribly wrong? What I think Brenda is doing, however, is conscious act for mature woman her age. She's taking risks that she must know will lead to her ending up back in prison for a very long time, yet she just got out and earned her freedom though exemplary behaviour. She's not stupid. It's just weird."

"Many clever criminals think that they can commit crimes and escape detection," Evan said.

"True. If she thinks that, she's in trouble."

56

Evan swayed his head in disagreement. "You have to distinguish between a miscalculation and mistake in human behaviour. When you calculate, you can come to a wrong result, but it's not a mistake. Sometimes miscalculation leads to good results from a certain point of view. A mistake, on the other hand, is a behaviour that happens under the influence of instincts and emotions. According to Freud, humans want what feels good at the time, with no consideration for the reality of the situation or for the good for others. Brenda doesn't seem to be making a mistake, as I see it. She's made her calculations, and knows the worst-case scenario. If Lucas committed suicide because of something to do with her, then he was dead scared of something. If there are any others in his same situation, then they will be even more scared now. If Lucas preferred not to go to the police, the others—if there any—are even more unlikely to now. That's the calculation. Simple, I think."

"Maybe you're right," Melissa said. "The most interesting component is the justice system will be in the picture, if the worst-case scenario plays out. Oddly enough, the scenario may play out as it does only because organized crime is involved. Wouldn't it be funny if the bandits ended up making justice accountable for its wrongdoings?"

"There you go," Evan said, grinning with enthusiasm. "You never know what cause and effect is when life plays its games."

"By funny I don't mean as a matter of amusement. I'm not a philosopher. My arms are up to the elbows in the belly of dinosaur. I'm not sure if I like opening this Pandora's box. On the other hand, I have to stop Brenda. She could do lots of harm." Melissa sighed, then shrugged.

"What are you going to do?" Evan asked.

"First, as I said, study her files. Then talk to everyone involved. I have to hurry, as I am pretty certain that she's dangerous. You know, they do call her Wolverine. That's the name the inmates gave her." She put her head on Evan's shoulder. "Perhaps it's time for me to retire. Technically, I'm more than fit for this job. Psychologically? I wonder."

Evan tightened his grip on her waist. "I suggest that you think about that later, and that we do something now for which you are well fit both psychologically and physically."

"I quite agree." She wrapped her arms around his neck and gave him a long, sensual kiss.

Chapter 9

The last day of classes in high school was over, and the sound of the bell made all the students jump in jubilation. Brenda, just eighteen, was as thrilled as any of them. Her adolescence was over. She was at the threshold of an adult life, with its intriguing love adventures and physical bliss, new friends, new challenges—plenty of good things ahead. Her life was going to be wonderful; she was sure of it.

The celebratory day had been planned well in advance. In two hours, the volleyball game between two girls' teams would start. Brenda was the best player of all. Volleyball was her obsession, almost her way of life, a channel to release her abundant energy and infinite craving for action. After the game she would go to Lucas's graduation party, along with many others from her class.

On the way home, Brenda's best friend Sury caught up with her. Petite, bony, far from beautiful, Sury was bubbly and good-humoured as usual. Her sharp tongue and nosy character often put her at odds with others, at which times faithful Brenda always came to her rescue.

"Do you feel your thing itching?" Sury asked, searching Brenda's eyes.

Brenda laughed.

"Watch your tongue, dirty mind. Why should it?" she asked with a laugh, since she was used to Sury's manner.

"Did you notice how Yona looks at you?"

Jonathan, nicknamed Yona, was one of the cool guys, tall and handsome. He was a poor student, though, who smoked pot and did other drugs, and had a reputation as a troublemaker. Some students fell for his charms and tried mimic him.

"He doesn't have a chance," Brenda said firmly.

"You should've seen how he was watching you walk by. He was undressing, and more, with those pothead eyes of his. I figured his stare was so intense you probably got all itchy-twitchy just from his leer."

Brenda laughed. "You dirty mouth!" she said, giving Sury a gentle tap with her elbow. "That's what you feel, isn't it?"

"Yes, from the cradle. But the difference is, I feel it when I watch guys, not when they watch me," said Sury. "Anyway, what are you gonna wear for the game? A skirt with no knickers? You jump pretty high."

"If I kick your little monkey ass, you'll jump even higher. You like that jerk, don't you?"

"Him...and a few others. My heart is too big for one."

"Just your heart?" Brenda asked. They both laughed, hugged, and departed to get ready for the game.

Later that day they met at the volleyball court. Sury was a spectator, and Brenda was the star of the show. She served and set the ball with mechanical precision; she saved it when the chances of returning the volley seemed impossible; she effortlessly jumped high above the net to spike the ball. The crowd yelled and cheered and rooted for her. But the three "cool" guys, led by Yona, kept up a running commentary of lewd remarks, especially whenever Brenda touched the ball. One of Yona's sidekicks was Lucas, a handsome, tall guy from a wealthy family; he had been a good kid until he fell under Yona's influence. The other sidekick was Christian, a short, muscular boy from a middle-class family. He earned some of the highest academic marks, but he was always desperately seeking the girls' attention. Being with a cool guy like Yona was the way he chose to get it.

60

For months Yona had been hitting on Brenda without success. The whole school knew it. Her rejections, even apathy toward him, tarnished his cool-guy image. Apparently he'd decided that bullying was the way to restore it, and with school over, today would be it's last public forum.

After he made one particularly loud and nasty remark, Sury walked up to Yona and started yelling at him. All three cool guys showered her with verbal dirt. Sury, who had an impressive street vocabulary of her own, fought back. She wasn't shy. The crowd roared with laughter at the show. It was innocent high-school exuberance, perfectly normal for the last day of school.

Then Yona pushed Sury, knocking her off balance. She stepped back, stumbled, and fell. The push had not been strong. There was no real harm or pain intended, just bravado and hubris. Sury quickly got up, but the game stopped. Brenda left the court, marched over to Yona with resolute steps, and gave him a hard slap on his cheek.

Yona shuddered. Lucas and Christian stared at Brenda with a mix of surprise and respect. Not saying a word, Brenda returned to the court and the game resumed. The three cool guys left, and the cheerful mood was restored.

* * *

Lucas's parents had left for Europe on urgent matters a week before the end of school, leaving their huge house to their son's care. He made a good use of it on that last day of school; the party of about thirty school graduates, left on their own, was wild and raucous.

The music, blasted by extremely expensive audio towers, made the house tremble. Pot and cigarette smoke filled every room of the two-story structure. Lucas opened the bar and set out bottles of hard liquor, and there were up beer kegs and ice chests for beer and wine. Everyone was getting high. The rooms writhed with couples twined in each others' arms, half-dressed dancers moving with the ecstasy of spirits both high and high-proof, and shouted conversations and off-key impromptu karaoke.

Brenda was in tune with everyone's mood, doing her own share of drinking, dancing, and flirting, but she kept scanning the party in search of Kenny, her boyfriend. Shy and soft, he didn't like wild gatherings, but he had promised to meet her there tonight.

Brenda bumped into Sury, who was sweating, her cheeks pink and eyes shining as she came off the makeshift dance floor.

"Have you seen Kenny?" Brenda asked.

"No. Should he be here?"

Brenda asked a few others, but got the same answer. She went into the backyard, where a group of people by the swimming pool were smoking pot. She walked over to join them and felt someone tap her on the shoulder. It was a short, unkempt guy named Bob. He reeked of cheap beer, expensive gin, and body odor.

"Hey, Kenny said for you to meet him upstairs," Bob said. "He's waiting for ya."

"He's here? Why haven't I seen him? And why would he send you?" She made it clear that Bob was probably the last person on earth anyone would talk to willingly.

Bob shrugged. "None of my business. I jus' know what he tol' me to say. Firs' door on the left."

Brenda didn't like Bob's evil grin or knowing wink one bit. She gave him a contemptuous look and walked back toward the house.

The cacophony of rock music was deafening. People's chaotically dancing bodies were moist with sweat, their eyes unfocused, their voices excessively loud and slurred. Brenda dodged between them, sometimes using her elbows to clear the space for the next step. There was no one on the staircase itself, but the dense smell of pot told her that someone had been there a short while ago. She ran up to the second floor, pulled open first door on the left, and stepped inside. There were three guys there, Yona, Christian, and Lucas. Kenny was not there.

Brenda spun around, knowing instinctively that she needed to get away from them, and ran into Bob, who had come in and closed the door behind him.

All happened quickly, as if premeditated and carefully planned. Brenda was thrown on the bed. Two of them twisted her hands behind her head. The pain in her shoulder joints incapacitated her. Her attempts to free herself were too weak to have any effect. Then the real horror began. She screamed as loud as she could, though she knew that no one could hear her over the sounds of the party.

They raped her one after another, all except Bob. He was busy photographing the rape.

The sound of someone's screaming reached her ears. Suddenly she was released. Brenda saw Sury's face above her.

"What happened?" Sury shrieked, her voice trembling with horror. "Are you okay?"

Brenda sat on the bed. Her arms numb with the pain, then rest of her burning with agony, she hid her face in her hands.

"Let's call police," Sury said, flipping open her cell phone.

"No. Stop it. Not yet."

"Not yet? What are you waiting for?" Sury was furious.

"I'll show you what I'm waiting for. Just wait. Just a few minutes."

Brenda was wracked with sobs. Sury put her arm on Brenda's shoulders. They sat a minute or two, close to each other, Sury whispering words of consolation.

Suddenly a cry of anger escaped Brenda's throat. She jumped off the bed and pulled on her jeans and tank top and ran out of the room. She thundered down the stairs and into the kitchen. Sury ran after her, screaming, but her voice was drowned in a rattle of drums of the hard rock music.

Brenda grabbed the first weapon she saw, a heavy frying pan, and rushed out to the living room. There were fewer dancers there than before, so it was easier to cross the room and see that all four of her rapists were there. Lucas spotted her first, and shouted something to Christian, the one closest to Brenda. Christian looked back, but had no time to react before the frying pan cracked across his head, sending him sprawling. Christian's scream was louder than the rattle of the speakers.

Yona was the first to recover from the surprise. He jumped toward Brenda and grabbed her wrist, wrenching her arm until the pan fell to the floor. When Brenda bent over to pick it up again, Yona punched her in the jaw. She dropped to the floor from the crushing pain in her head. Strong hands lifted her and carried to the porch. She was thrown from there down the steps to the ground, where she lay in a heap, trying to focus through the pain. She heard loud voices, angry exchanges of words, but she could not grasp who was saying what.

When the pain receded to a dull throb, she sat up and looked woozily around. There were a few people on the wide porch, staring down at her. Sury was kneeling in front of her, talking to her, but Brenda couldn't make out the words. She hauled herself slowly up, the sharp stones of the walkway biting into her bare feet, and started walking unsteadily toward home. Sury walked beside her, matching her steps, talking nonstop, but Brenda's mind refused to take in her friend's words in any way that made sense. It had simply stopped working.

"Sury, angel, leave me alone," Brenda pleaded, stumbling over her own words. "I need...need to be alone. Tomorrow. Talk tomorrow."

This time, Sury did not insist.

"Okay," she agreed. "Please, call the police. And don't do anything stupid. I'll come over tomorrow."

The chilly air of the night calmed Brenda, and eventually cleared her head. When she reached home, she quietly opened the door, and soundlessly sneaked into her room, hoping her mother would be asleep. Brenda thought in despair, If she sees me, she'll know right away what happened. Instead of a tragedy for one, it'll be a tragedy for two.

She would be in bed at that late hour. She worked ten or more hours a day as a cleaning lady for the local folks, a physically and emotionally demeaning life. Her mother kept pushing herself beyond her limits, in hopes of earning enough money for Brenda's higher education, something she'd never had.

What Brenda's mother, Rita, lacked in education, she made for up with loving attention and intuition. If she saw Brenda, she wouldn't miss a thing in her daughter's appearance—the torn tank top, the missing shoes, and, of course, the dark swelling on her jaw, among other cuts and bruises. Even if Brenda had been capable of lying, or been a great actress capable of hiding her emotions and changing her countenance, she would not deceive her mother. Her ability to read Brenda's mood was not due any exceptional sharpness of mind. She was not a clever woman by any standard. The only job she ever had in her entire life was cleaning, as though she was incapable of doing anything else.

Around town people liked to say that she'd run fast and loose with men in her younger years, and been dulled by drugs, alcohol, and all sorts of other things common to that lifestyle. At the age of nineteen she had gotten pregnant, though she didn't know by whom. She didn't care. The day Brenda was born, Rita became a different woman. The change stunned everyone who knew her. Since that day, she had never used drugs or alcohol or spent time with any man, or so the neighbours said. Every single free minute she spent with Brenda. That was not love, but obsession. Or so the neighbours said.

Even with her fairly small pay per hour, by working every day from dawn to sunset she managed to buy a small house in a decent neighbourhood so she could send her daughter to a school with middle-class family kids. Even then, thirty-nine and still attractive, she had never been seen in the company of a man.

Brenda understood the price of her love. She admired her mother for it, and loved her intensely. However, there were a few things in her mother's character that she utterly disliked. One was that her mother was afraid of everyone and everything. Anyone could verbally abuse her without her so much as a word.

"Find a new job! Find another place!" Brenda shouted at her more than once, after hearing another story of employers' abuse. "Or stay being a cleaning woman if you want, but somewhere else. There are plenty of jobs for you out there. Don't let anyone degrade you. That's the worst that could happen, to let them take you humanity. It would be better not to live than live a life of humiliation!"

Limping home and crawling into her own bed after what was supposed to have been a night of celebration, Brenda bit her lower lip, suppressing a moan of despair. Sleep was out of the question.

She sat up, staring at the wall, her mind devastated. She wept and wept, unable to control herself, unable to think clearly. After several hour she was so drained that she wasn't even able to cry. She closed her eyes and fell asleep. It was a short, but restful nap.

Her first thought after waking up was that she should go to the police and report the gang rape. Soon she dismissed it. With all investigations and court hearings, everyone in their town would know that she had been humiliated. She would not be able to survive that notoriety, and neither would her mother. Perhaps moving

66

to another town, where no one knew her, would be a better option? Her mother could find a job anywhere. Brenda could get a part-time job and study in the university. That was not a bad solution, and yet Brenda could not come to terms with the idea that the four guys who had raped and humiliated her would get away with what they'd done. Perhaps in the future she could find a way to strike back.

By the time the day had eased into noon, she had almost regained her composure, and was ready to face her mother, who was busy with her small orchard in the backyard. Following the daily ritual of their morning greetings and chat, Brenda entered the backyard from the walk-out basement. Her mother was bending over, sniffing a flower; plant health and growth had been one of her major concerns for the past three months.

Her mother turned around and rose to greet her. The smile on her face changed to a frown when she met Brenda's eyes.

"What happened?" she asked.

"Nothing. Usual crap. How are your flowers? Smell better than shit?"

"What happen to your face? It's swollen."

"I was drunk and fell off our porch. It was dark. You didn't turn the outside light on."

Her mother looked Brenda up and down. "Weird." She sighed. "You are beautiful, you know? I'm glad you're my daughter, but sometimes I think you meant to be born a man." She looked around. "You see how nice the day is?"

This was the way her mother greeted every morning, rain or shine. She was happy with everything she had.

"It's beautiful," Brenda nodded, swallowing the nauseating bitterness of the previous night.

"Something bothering you?" Her mother gave her an inquisitive look.

"Nothing."

Brenda's cell phone rang. She brought it to her ear.

"Are you home?" Sury's voice was saturated with anxiety.

"Yes."

"I'll be there soon."

"Sury's coming over," Brenda said to her mother. "I'll be in my room."

She walked inside, feeling her mother watching her. No sooner had she climbed the stairs to the second floor when she heard three nervous rings of the doorbell, in quick succession. That was fast, Brenda thought. It was no wonder. Sury was probably still shaking from yesterday's events, and still highly agitated by them. Or by something else, maybe? Maybe Sury had heard the beginning of the inevitable rumours or disgusting gossip already?

Brenda ran down and threw open the door. Sury rushed in. Her eyes were filled with fear and rage; her hair was a chaotic mess; she looked as if she had been the one running from predators.

"Let's go to your room," she hissed, and rushed upstairs. Brenda followed her. Sury closed the door of her room and sat on the bed.

"Where's your mom?" she asked.

"In the backyard. She doesn't know anything."

"Boot up your computer. Now."

"What for?"

"Now!"

"It's always on." Brenda pressed a keypad, and the screen came to life. Sury sat at the desk and pecked at the keyboard.

"What are you doing?" Brenda asked, feeling chilling waves on her back.

"Facebook." Sury frowned, waiting for the computer's response. "Here. Look."

Brenda's first reaction was disbelief, followed by shock. Sury scrolled through a series of photographs, all

68

showing Brenda, naked, having sex with someone whose face was blurred out, unrecognizable. Her own face was clear and recognizable. Her arms were stretched behind her head, but the belt that held them had been cropped from the picture. One photo, in which the click of the camera had captured Brenda's screams for help at just the right moment, so she appeared to be in the throes of ecstasy, was captioned "happy slut begs for more."

The room swirled around her. She felt an urge to vomit. Her legs did not support her; she sat on her bed, eyes fixed on the computer screen. Her bright future had suddenly dimmed to gloom and despair, horror and rubbish.

"You have to go to the police." Sury's voice reached her from another world. "I told you that last night, but you wouldn't listen. You have to go now, you hear me? I'll go with you. Or if you want, I can go for you."

Sury was saying something else, with passion and empathy, but her words merged into a meaningless droning that Brenda did not attempt to understand. A few minutes later Brenda came to her senses. The room, with Sury in it, came back into focus, and with it, a piercing understanding of the tragedy of her life. But this time, in place of despair, she felt a white-hot hatred. She looked at her compassionate friend.

"Sury, don't go to the police. Please, go home. I need to be alone."

"I can't leave you now. You might do something stupid. You shouldn't be alone, not today."

"Sury. Leave me alone. I'll call you later. I have to think things over."

She stood up, pulled Sury to the door, and led her downstairs. Sury protested, blubbering something incomprehensible, but she didn't resist. When she'd left, Brenda climbed the stairs again and shut herself inside her room.

Her mother called her from the kitchen, announcing lunch. Brenda called down that she wasn't hungry, hoping her mother would think she was just hungover, and leave her to her misery. Better her mother think she had just been drinking too much than to admit the truth. Soon her mother left for work. Brenda burst into a violent crying fit, wiping endless stream of tears. After an hour of heart-crunching emotional stress, she suddenly fall asleep.

When she woke up, her first thought was that she should kill herself. Her life was ruined. There was no place she could go, proud, self-confident, and pretty, with a reputation of a strong girl who knew her worth. Now she had been disgraced in front of the whole world, portrayed as a wanton slut and not the victim of a brutal attack. She would carry the burden forever, until the end of her days. How could she study in the university when all the students would know, or think they did, what happened to her? How could she get a job and work with people who had seen her naked, having sex with at least three different men? She could never erase those photographs from the Internet.

Suddenly the thought crossed her mind that committing suicide would make her even more of a victim, someone even weaker than her mother. That made her shudder. A host of emotions made her jumpy, and she began pacing the room like a wolf in captivity. To die would mean letting those bustards live happy lives untarnished by and unpunished for their violence and aggression. She would leave this world in shame, in disgrace, for what? For nothing! Wouldn't it be better, when she left, to take with her the lives of those jerks? To make them pay, and to make them and their friends, their parents, and maybe everyone who stood idly by shudder in terror and respect her for the rest of their lives?

Her heart was racing, craving action. Her throbbing energy was back. Her mind, all logic scrambled by bitter emotions, concentrated on one, and only one thing: find them, and make them pay. Kill them, as they had killed her.

She went to the kitchen and took one of very sturdy, short steak knives. Without any specific plan of action, she began walking in the direction of Yona's house. The knife was tucked into the belt of her jeans, and hidden behind her blouse. She knew that what she was going to do was crazy, but no acceptable alternative flashed in her mind.

Between her house and Yona's was the soccer field in the community park. A game was in full swing, with cheering spectators, the dull sounds of the kicked ball, and the kaleidoscopic shuffle of colorfully dressed players. Brenda was halfway along the edge of the field when she spotted Lucas and Yona, both a head taller than the surrounding players. Both were fully absorbed in the game, gesticulating, shaking fists above their heads, and shouting.

Yona, who stood behind Lucas, was the first to notice her. He touched Lucas and nodded in Brenda's direction, a trace of concern flashing across his face. Yona had many lawless friends, and some experience in rough street life. That he smelled trouble was written on his face, but he didn't look especially worried. After all, what harm could come to him in public from one eighteen-year-old girl?

Lucas turned his head, and saw Brenda when she was only a few steps away. He frowned, but only for a brief moment, and then curled his lips into an insolent smile. If he wanted to stage a show of his bravado, it didn't last long. Brenda yanked the knife from under her belt and darted toward him with all the speed and dexterity of the athlete she was. Struck with horror at the sight of the glinting blade, he lost a precious moment he could have spent running away and was left to try to defend himself. He stretched out his left arm to try to fend her off, but Brenda's knife flashed out, making a long, deep cut on the

71

tender inside, from his wrist to his elbow. Lucas screamed and belatedly tried to run away across the soccer field. Blood poured from his arm, scattering scarlet spots on green grass. The players stopped, as if struck by lightning, watching the inconceivable, surrealistic scene. No one dared interfere.

Lucas looked back and saw Brenda running after him. He continued to scream like a wounded animal in anticipation of imminent death. He kept running, yelling, pleading for mercy, along the deserted summer street of the bedroom community. It was as though they were the only two people left, with no one else in sight, just Lucas was running and screaming, and her running a few steps behind him, still clutching the knife.

Lucas was not weak. He could have endured a long run, if not for the profuse bleeding. But Brenda was athletic, too, and determined to run as long as necessary to catch him. Get the son of a bitch. The thought consumed her, and throbbed in her temples.

Lucas was at the crosswalk of the busy street when the traffic light turned red. He dashed across the road. Brenda followed. There was a screech of tires stopped by brakes, the metallic crumpling of collided cars, but she didn't care. She ran and ran after Lucas, her confidence growing that the bastard was near collapse. They ran to the other side of the street, the distance between them diminishing by the second. There was another screeching of tires, this time very close to her, but she didn't stop.

Lucas's screams were growing hoarse from weakness and despair, and he looked near collapse. She was nearly upon him when someone tackled her legs from behind. She went flying forward, her face scraping along the macadam and the knife skittering away toward the curb. Her hands were deftly twisted behind her back, and handcuffs locked onto her wrists. The rough, searing asphalt burned against her road-rash-bloodied face and arms. She tried to catch her breath. Strong hands yanked her to her feet, and threw her into the back of a police car. Her mind blacked out.

Chapter 10

It was late afternoon when Max hit the brakes of his Ford and came to an abrupt stop a few inches away from the wall of his house. The tires of the car screeched in complaint.

"One day you'll crash into it," Brenda said, holding her breath.

"Cars are my way of life," he said. "They obey me even better than my women do." He opened the trunk and began pulling out the dozens of bags and boxes that held the new clothes and accessories for Brenda, things they had bought at the mall during a five-hour shopping spree. Max had paid for everything, saying it was his gift to Brenda. The two-hour drive to Toronto was the first time that week they had ventured past the yard.

"If you want to, I'll obey you even better than your cars." Brenda already knew how provocative she could be. She took as many bags as she could and carried them inside. Max carried some more, following her.

"Another word, and I'll throw you in bed. I'll shred those old clothes right off you." His eyes meant it. He put his load on the floor. "Drop it here." He pointed at the bags in her hands. "I'll bring the rest."

His last load was almost as big as the first one. Among the other packages was a small red bag carrying something that Max had bought when Brenda was busy trying on an outfit. He had refused to say what was in it, which intrigued her, but for now she was content to sift through the clothes, belts, scarves, and other things she had dreamed of during those long years in prison and on parole. It was all hers. It made her head spin. The things were even more beautiful and exciting in reality than they had been in her fantasy.

"You're crazy, Max." She observed the cluttered floor. "It'll take years to wear all this. And it cost a fortune."

"Not years." Max took a beer from the fridge, settled into an easy chair, and twisted off the bottle cap. He looked Brenda up and down, as though she was a statue he was about to buy. "Try everything on for me. Now."

Pleased, Brenda looked into his insolent eyes. They glowed in lust and anticipation.

"What's in this small red bag?" she asked, starting to pull off her shirt.

"Hold your horses," he said with a chuckle. "So far as money is concerned, it comes and goes. I used to have plenty, but lately things have gone the wrong way."

"How so?"

"Stop chirping and go about your fashion show."

Brenda picked up a few bags, and stepped toward the bedroom.

"Here," Max growled. "I wanna see you change here. You want me to miss the best part of your act?"

"Bastard," Brenda laughed. "I'll do what you say, but I'll make you do the same for me."

She took her clothes off piece by piece, in deliberately slow motion, watching Max from the corner of her eye. He opened another beer. Brenda thought he would ask her to take off her underwear, but he didn't. After an impressive swig from the bottle, he rested his eyes on her. She pulled a pair of jeans from the shopping bag, along with a white blouse, and a pair of low-heeled shoes for everyday wear. When she put them on, she turned slowly, like a model on the runway. With her back still toward him, she asked, "How's this?"

"Tailor made," he said.

"The jeans or the blouse?" she asked, making another turn.

"Your ass!" he roared in delight. "Your boobs. Custom made to my specs. You're not in the car business, but I bet you still know what that means, made to my specs."

"Watch it now," she said, removing the clothes for another round of demonstration. She picked up another outfit: a green long skirt, an elegant matching jacket, a pair of high heels. Once again, she spun and posed a few times. "How's that?" she asked.

Max cleared his throat.

"You look like a lady. Like a movie star. Fuck, if anyone hit on you, I'd slash his throat."

A loud, confident knock on the door startled them both. Neither of them wanted guests, or even a minor disturbance.

"Sit. I'll get it," Brenda said. She unlocked the door and flung it open. She saw a young woman standing on the porch. She was good looking, but the deliberately chaotic arrangement of hair, the puffy face, and general dishevelment from overindulgence in drinking told the tale of her lifestyle. The tattoos on both arms and shoulders screamed ex-con.

"Max home?" the woman asked, measuring Brenda with a jealous, contemptuous, and hostile stare.

"What do you want?" Brenda asked.

"None of your business. Lemme in."

Brenda blocked her way, all anger.

"Lemme in, ya fuckin' bitch," the woman demanded, almost screaming. "I'm his girlfriend."

Suddenly, the second language Brenda had acquired in prison came back to her fluently.

"Beat it, ya fucking cunt." Brenda knew already what she'd have do. That type of woman would come to her senses only under hard blows. "He has no girlfriend."

"Shithead," the woman shouted. "And who are you, ya fuckin' twat?"

"I'm his wife."

The woman stood there, speechless a moment, absorbing the news.

"Wife?" she yelled at last. "Wife? He ain't got no wife. Get outta my way!"

She pushed Brenda with both hands, confident that someone dressed as Brenda was could be easily subdued. But Brenda was a fraction of second faster. She hit the bitch in the bridge of her nose with all her force. The woman collapsed to her knees, holding her face with both hands. Brenda grasped her by the hair and shoved her down the steps. The woman hit the ground hard, and roared in pain.

"Come here again, and I'll break your legs," Brenda shouted. "Got it?"

She slammed the door so hard that the whole house shook.

"Girlfriend," she repeated through heavy breathing, while resuming her place for the show. "No more girlfriends here."

Max leaned back in the chair, and observed her with an approving smile.

"Wife, eh?" he asked. She heard happy notes in his voice. A warm wave travelled from her heart to her crotch and back up. Her anger suddenly dissolved, like smoke in the wind.

"You heard it. Back to show biz," she declared, taking off the jacket.

"Skip those outfits. Try the red bag."

She took the first package that her hand found, unwrapped it, and held up two pieces of black lingerie. It was a dream outfit for a seductress. She gave Max a long look and began taking the dressy outfit off, piece by piece. When she was naked, she locked her eyes with his and, in silence, walked a few paces back and forth, as much as the small space permitted. After slowly turning around a few times, she stopped in front of Max, proudly pointing her breasts at him. Then she held the mostly see-through bottom part of the set up to her eyes and winked at Max through the material. Then she slowly, slowly slid the bikini bottom down her body, its silky blackness stark against he white skin, and slipped into it. Max watched. She put on the matching bra top, which hid nothing, just emphasized her curves and attracted attention to the places it half covered.

Max's jaw dropped. His stare wandered around her hips and legs, held a few moments on her waist, then moved up to her breasts. When their eyes met, Brenda winked again.

This was too much for both of them. She began unbuttoning his shirt. He helped her with his clothes and boxers, then deftly unhooked the bra with one hand and flung it. She pushed him back into the chair and hopped on his lap, straddling him. Face to face with him, she felt his strong hips against the tender skin on the inside of her thighs. His strong hands cupped her bottom and they merged in a powerful, violent embrace, hungry for each other.

His grip was strong and yet gentle, communicating the passion that consumed him. His heavy breathing sent out invisible, powerful waves of his biological craving for sexual union. Her breasts rubbed against his hairy chest; her restless, searching lips were all over his face. In the fits of a joyful spasm Max grasped a handful of her thick hair, and pulled it down: it did not hurt, only took her breath away. She closed her eyes. The whole universe shrunk to the final tide of bliss, which struck them at the same moment. It manifested in her gentle, feminine, and melodic moan, and his growl of a bear. They sat for a minute, holding each other, catching their breaths, still enjoying their closeness, but in a different, more tranquil way.

"I have to lay down," Max mumbled, loosening his embrace. Brenda stood up and let him go, observing his figure with delight. But the next moment she sensed that something was wrong. When she lay down beside him, she noticed how pale he was.

"What happened?" she asked. Apparently the expression of her face told him the full depth of her concern.

"Don't worry, hon," he said with a faint smile. "Sometimes I have this pain in my stomach. Nothing serious to worry about. You see, it's almost gone."

"Tell me what it is," she insisted. "I'll take care of you."

He lay on his side and ran his large hand over her bottom, up and down, and from side to side. She recalled Paula's lessons in prison about men. "If a man, after being with you for a while, still grabs your ass, he loves you." At the time Brenda had laughed. Having had almost no experience with sex, and none with romance, she was puzzled and bewildered. Why my ass? Now she understood.

"How many women have you had before me?" she asked.

"I had my share. What about you?"

"I was with two guys before I was sent to prison. Nothing like this. They were just kids fumbling around, trysts, not that crazy joy that I have with you. And I don't count the bastards who raped me. That wasn't sex." She paused. "They probably forgot all about it. I'm going to make sure to refresh their memories."

"You know what you're gonna do?"

"Yes. I've thought about it a lot. I plan to put them through the same hell they put me through. Although I might need a little help."

"Can I help you?"

"Maybe." She ran her hand over his cheek. "Do you know any guys who'd like to fuck those bastards good and hard, rough? Real thugs?"

"Most of the guys I know are real thugs. Tell me more."

"I want to videotape them when someone fucks them in the ass. Then I'll upload the beautiful video on all the social networks I know. It'll take some preparation, as I have to find out who they work with, their Facebook friends, how to get to their darling grannies and stuffy old uncles, anyone who knows them."

Max chuckled. "It's not for nothing they nicknamed you Wolverine. You know they'll call police, right? You thought about that? You'll be back to the can."

"I thought about that too. Not that simple, Max. I'll tell each one of them that I'll take them to the court for raping me if they go to police. I still have all the evidence. Sury, my friend, saved all the photos they uploaded onto the Internet. She'll testify, and some others will, too. I already know a lot about law. I'll have enough money to hire a good lawyer. This time they won't be able to bribe attorneys or a judge, as the court will be here or in Toronto, where I will live by then. The publicity would ruin their lives. In the end, they'll be in the slammer a few years for raping me—and for bullying me in the media. What a treat for journalists!" She looked into Max's eyes. "What do you think?"

"Swell." He leaned back, to observe Brenda with renewed interest. "I can help you with this. It must be fun."

"You know someone who'll fuck them?"

"Sure. I will."

"What?" Brenda propped herself on her elbow, giving him a bewildered look. "Are you gay?"

"No. I'll strap on a dildo. Buy a nice, big, sturdy, studly rubber dong in a sex shop. We'll make sure they look back on the experience with a fond memory." He laughed.

Brenda fell onto her back, deep in thought.

"Why would you do that?" she asked. "You could end up in jail, too, for a long time."

"I think you're right that none of them would go to the police. What straight man in his right mind would admit that he was butt-fucked...on camera...while a woman he raped is right there? You think any of those uptight dudes would want to say that out loud in court, everything that happened? No, I don't think one of those entitled douchebags would admit in front of a jury, or judge, that he raped a girl and got away with it. And even if he did, they'd think he got what he deserved, and he'd be right. And there's another reason...." His hand stopped moving. After a few moments of silence, he mumbled, "Because I love you, dummy."

Brenda almost choked. It was the first time in her life she had heard words of love from a man. She rested her head on his hairy chest to hide her tears. After a minute, when the ability to think and speak came back to her, she said, "No. I can't let you risk your life. I love you, too."

He played for some time with her thick hair. Then he began speaking slowly, as if in deep thought.

"If it hadn't been for those jerks, what would you be doing now? I mean, what would you do for living? What would your life be like? You know, I wasn't brought up to be in an outlaw biker gang. I wanted to be engineer. My parents were very educated people. All my dreams and plans fell apart when they died in a car accident. Even later, when I joined the biker club, I planned to drop this car business and go to university."

"Me, too. That is, I'd continue my education in the university. I like it. It's easy for me. I have a good memory, a good brain. But before that, I have to establish myself."

"Do you know how you'll do that?"

"I have some plans. I'll open my own business and, I hope, earn enough to make a living. I have some money to get started. When my mother died, our house was sold. Whatever's left from the sale is mine. I'm a good accountant, you know? Whatever I do, I do well."

81

"That's damn true in bed," he said with a smile.

"I try. You may laugh, but it's very important to me. Such strong, wonderful feelings and sensations, so why shouldn't it be? What a joy to make my lover as happy as I am!"

"Agreed, agreed." He ran his fingers all over her body. "Good life, isn't it?"

"Yes. Don't you think so?"

"I do. So, back to your plans. There's still a chance that something might go wrong, ya know," he said. "People do stupid things when they're afraid. Witnesses could talk. The police might find out something by a sheer chance. You'd be a repeat offender, so your chanced in court wouldn't be great."

This time Brenda paused. His points were too strong to ignore.

"I was in deep shit because of those spoiled jerks." She was speaking more to herself than to Max at that moment. "I felt such shame. You know, I was about to hang myself. And then prison…I think my mother died of a broken heart. All because of them. I can't live knowing that they are living happy lives, that they got away with everything. I want them to go through hell. I thought about it almost every day in prison. I can't let it go."

"Sure," Max said.

"I thought about the worse case," she said. "I know that no matter how you plan things, something can go wrong in the most weird, unpredictable way. I know it too well. But if some random act of unkindness takes me down, at least I'll go back to prison without remorse. And I'll pull a lot of people down with me. I just don't want you to be one of them."

Max slid from the bed, went to the kitchen, and came back with a bottle of beer.

"Without that determination I wouldn't be able to do much," she said. "Before you take your first swing in a fight, you have to decide if you can accept total defeat or not. Calculation and common sense don't work in such a game. My motto is that I need to accept any outcome, and move on."

Max smiled and patted her head. "Real wolverine," he said, and sat beside her. Then he took a swig from the bottle.

"Let's do that. Fuck them with a dildo. Videotape them. But instead of putting this video online, sell it to them. Take their money, a lot of it. Give them a choice. Explain what'll happen if they go to police. You'll have all money you need for your education, and more, eh?"

"You don't understand, Max. It's not about money. It's about principle. Justice, if you will."

"Justice. Principle," he repeated. "You didn't learn a thing in prison. Anyway, you can count on me. Don't worry about me ending up in prison, either. My guys'll scare the shit out of them, show what would happen if they testify. They will be in deep shit whatever way they go. Don't forget that there is no one who is not scared of the gang. Even the police don't mess with us. And there's something else, but I'll tell you later." He sat on the bed and took a pull from the bottle. Then he kissed away her questions.

They lay side by side, smiling.

"When we finish with your jerkwads, I'll leave the gang, set up my own car repair shop. I have the money. By the way, did I tell you I have a house in Toronto? It's under a different name, but it's mine. We can move into it this winter. You'll like it; it's nice. And I'll introduce you to a guy, quite a guy, later on. After." He regarded her in silence, with a smile in his eyes.

"What guy?" Brenda asked, with a sleepy smile. He was so sweet, her Max.

"I wonder, what would you do if I fucked another woman? Would you kill me, Wolverine?"

"Don't call me that. No, I'd just leave you. If you ever hit me, I'd kill you. What about you? If I fucked another man, what would you do?"

"I'd kill you. Don't ever fancy that you'd get away with that."

She gave him a long, sensual kiss, and closed her eyes with a happy smile.

Chapter 11

The local jail had allowed her to visit with Brenda in the afternoon, so Sury had been busy as hell all morning with preparations. Eager to bring some good news, or at least something encouraging, to keep her friend's mood up and give her hope, Sury had drafted a plan. But to make things happen, she needed to discuss it with Rita, Brenda's mother. Talking to her was on Sury's mind anyway; the woman was devastated and needed some support. Rita had no relatives, no friends, anyone who would care for her. Now Sury hoped to kill two birds with one stone: to cheer up both women, and explore ways to find money for a good lawyer.

Brenda's lawyer, provided by legal aid, was not up to the task. Young, inexperienced, and apparently not enthusiastic, he did an obviously sloppy job. Sury, with her fiery temperament, was all fury. She tried convincing other girls, ostensibly Brenda's friends, to raise money to hire a better lawyer, but didn't get too far. Instead of money, they offered Sury the words of sympathy, compassion, and explanations that money was in a short supply. Sury took all her savings—about a thousand dollars, spared from summer jobs—and went to see Rita, as had been agreed the day before. Perhaps Rita had some savings, and together they could do something about money.

Sury was well prepared for the conversation. Rita was a poorly educated woman, of very low intellectual capacity, and understood little about financial matters, and even about legal ones. But she had a big heart. Rita's love for Brenda was unflagging, and her daughter was the essence and purpose of her life. Rita would sell her house and slave herself forever to get money, as much as needed, for the release of her daughter.

Sury had seen her a few days earlier. Rita had looked ten years older. She had cried nonstop, and implored Sury not to leave her alone, as she was incapable of doing anything. Sury did her best to calm her down. This time, while driving to see Rita again, Sury had rehearsed the words she intended to say.

When she pulled in the driveway, the day had just started. The old, ten-year-old Ford, the car Brenda and Rita shared, sat in the driveway, sparkling clean as usual. The rising sun cast dark shadows from the trees. The air was cool and crisp. In better times, Rita would not have missed such a fine day for working outside the house: raking leaves, cutting grass, and taking care of her plants and flowers, or whatever the fall had left. Now the browning blanket of colourful leaves covered the small front lawn and the interlock path to the front door. She was likely at home, as her car was there, but there was no sign of her. Sury climbed the steps to the porch and pressed the doorbell, then knocked on the door. No response. She pounded the door hard enough for Rita to hear the noise, even if she was fast asleep, but there was still no response. Concerned, Sury tried the door, but it was locked.

Perhaps she's out in the orchard. Rita was growing all kinds of vegetables in her small backyard, and excelled at it. Her salads were delicious, as were her vegetable soups. Even eaten raw her produce was a delight. She often talked about her plants as if they were human, living beings that shared with her their sacred secrets. More than once, when friends came over, Brenda had had to interrupt Rita's orchard stories and asked her to leave them alone.

A wooden fence surrounded the backyard. Sury pushed open the narrow door built snug to the side wall and went into the backyard. Rita was not there. There

86

were no fruits or vegetables, as the season was over, but some flowers still hung on, although their colors were dull and fading. Rita adored her flowers: she often cut them into bouquets for Brenda's friends or the neighbours. At that moment though, Sury felt that the spirit of human presence, which she usually felt in the garden, left it for good.

The feeling suddenly made her aware of how silent the neighbourhood was.

There was a sliding patio door at the back of the house. Sury tugged at the handle and the door easily slid open. Sury went into the kitchen and stopped. The kitchen was clean, but a few dirty dishes were in the sink, which was unusual for Rita. The house was quiet. Sury walked through the downstairs and, seeing nothing amiss, climbed to the second floor, where the two bedrooms were. She opened the door to the Rita's bedroom and found her there, lying on the bed, fully dressed, with even her shoes still on.

"Rita?" Sury called, and grasped her hand. It was warm. Rita was alive. Her eyes were open, but she didn't seem to recognize Sury.

"Rita? Rita!" Sury called again, frightened out of her wits. Rita seemed to be dying. Sury had never before been in a situation that required a life-or-death decision. "Are you okay? Should I call ambulance?"

"No," Rita said, gasping for air. Sury tried to calm herself. Hearing Rita speak was encouraging. The woman was half-conscious, maybe in pain. Maybe she'd had a heart attack or a stroke? Her cheeks were devoid of any color. Something had to be done right now, not a second later. Sury pulled out her cell phone and dialed emergency.

"A woman is dying. Please send an ambulance," she pleaded, speaking fast, giving the address. When a female voice at the other end assured her that an ambulance was on its way, Sury fetched a glass of cold water from the kitchen, and then lifted Rita's head to make her drink. Rita did not respond. Sury had never seen the death before, but she knew for sure that Rita was dying.

Paramedics were quick to arrive. Sury ran downstairs to let them in. "She's upstairs," she said, pointing at the staircase. "She's dying. Please, please, this way."

She led the way to the bedroom and stopped outside the entrance, as the room was very small. While one paramedic examined Rita, the other was asking questions, and Sury gave him as much information as she could, although that wasn't much. The paramedics placed Rita on the stretcher and carried her to the ambulance. Sury closed up Rita's house and followed behind the ambulance in her car.

At that time of day, traffic was not dense, but there were repairs on the road, so she couldn't keep up with the ambulance. It took almost half an hour to sort out the bottleneck of the traffic jam, and it exhausted her more than physically demanding work would have. When she arrived at the hospital, she left the car in a No Parking zone and rushed inside the ER.

She quickly found the gurney on which Rita lay. One glance told her that there was no more need to hurry, only questions to deal with.

"I'm so sorry. Is this your mother?" a nurse asked.

"No. My best friend's mother."

"I'm terribly sorry," the nurse said. "There was nothing we could do. Apparently she died of heart attack. An autopsy will confirm."

After Sury left the ER, she sat in her car and cried until the parking attendant knocked on the window.

"Please move out," he said, with a stern face. "You cannot park here."

Sury nodded, started the engine, and steered out to the exit. A glance at the clock startled her. It was 1:30 p.m. She would barely make to the jail in time to meet with Brenda.

Deep breaths, deep breaths, she told herself, trying to stay calm. I can't show up in tears, or in distress. It will make things worse.

At some point her mind disassociated itself from reality, which was beyond comprehension. At the gates of the local jail, she showed up calm and composed, as she usually was. A guard met her at the entrance, and led her to the visitor's room, where a few tables with basic easy chairs were set up in a seemingly chaotic manner. Brenda sat at one of them. When Sury appeared, a happy smile brightened Brenda's face. That's how close friends greet each other, Sury thought, and tried to smile back. Brenda, of course, was looking forward to an interesting talk, some local news and, of course, some moral support and encouragement.

Sury settled across the table from her and forced a smile.

"I'm so glad to see you, Sury," Brenda said, and touched her hand. A jail guard, a burly woman who stood by the door, swayed her head in disapproval. Brenda hid both of her hands under the table and leaned forward. "Such misery is here," she continued in a half-whisper, rolling her eyes left and right to make sure that no one was listening to their talk.

"Are you okay in here? Do they harass you?" Sury asked.

"No, it's not that. The people are actually not that scary, not like you'd think. Most of them are just people, not all bad, but people who did one bad thing...or had bad things happen to them, you know? And anyway, I can take care of myself. I can stand up against anyone, you know?"

"Yes, I do," Sury said, nodding. At the back of her mind a frightening thought made her guts tremble: eventually Brenda would ask about her mother. Oh, God, help me, she pleaded. Dear God, please help Brenda. I can't just come out with it. My heart would stop.

"Something's wrong," Brenda said. Her stare became probing, penetrating into Sury's heart. Sury took a deep breath, then another, then swallowed the choking lump that was blocking her throat.

"Say it," Brenda demanded in a strong voice, one that conveyed strength and the confidence of a person who can cope with anything. "You know, nothing can scare me now. I don't give a shit."

"I went to see your mother today..." Sury began, then stopped.

The blood had drained from Brenda's face. Her wide-open eyes filled with torment, but she said nothing, waiting for Sury to continue.

"I called the ambulance, but...but...it was too late."

Brenda remained silent. The news was too big, too terrifying to comprehend. Sury didn't know what to say, either, so she said nothing.

"Dead?" Brenda finally asked, her voice was hardly audible. Sury nodded, and looked down at her hands. It was impossible to look into Brenda's yes.

A few moments later Brenda crossed her arms on the table, fell on them face down, and began shaking with violent sobs. Sury began crying as well, although she tried to suppress the sound of her sobs. It seemed to her that time stopped. At some point the guard came up and said, with surprising compassion, "I'm sorry. Time's up."

Brenda stood up and turned around, not even glancing back at Sury. She shuffled away, and disappeared through the door.

As if in the drunken stupor, Sury lumbered out, crawled into her car, and drove away. When she arrived at home, the day was still bright, although not as warm as it had been at noon. The breath of the late fall brought a crisp, chilly air. She went inside the house, filled a glass with wine, and went to the backyard, where she settled on the patio and took the first swig. It relaxed her a bit. She recalled faces of guys who had raped Brenda.

"Goddamn you all," she cursed. "I hope you all go to hell. I wish you were dead."

She began crying, as violently as Brenda had cried. When her tears ran dry she drained her wineglass and gazed around the backyard, barely seeing the blue sky with its few tiny white clouds, and the huge maple tree, towering above the fence. Its leaves were blood red, as beautiful in death as they had been vibrant in life. A sudden gust of wind tore a large scarlet leaf from a branch and carried it away. The leaf, twisting and turning in the air as it fell, circled gracefully on the currents until it settled to the ground, where a carpet of other fallen leaves awaited it. Sury traced its fall, and then tried to find it among other leaves. She could not. They all looked the same: beautiful, dry, and dead.

Chapter 12

The front stretch of the house on Truman Crescent could serve as an idyllic illustration to a romance novel with happy ending: neatly cut grass, a tasteful but colourful flower bed, fresh interlock walkway, and a big tree casting shade. On the porch sat a young woman, reading a book and gently bouncing the baby stroller close by. When Melissa pulled up to the curb, the woman put the book on her lap, and watched Melissa with curious eyes. The sun blinded her. She shielded it with her hand, and rose to her feet.

Melissa introduced herself, and offered her business card. "Sury?" she asked.

"Yes." Sury took the card. "I've been waiting for you. This is my daughter, Ghana. She's sleeping. Please, come in." She opened the door for Melissa. After moving the stroller to the middle of the room, she gestured Melissa toward the sofa.

"Tea, coffee, a drink?" she asked, as if Melissa were a friend with whom she was about to share some intriguing gossip during a long and lazy chat.

"Nothing, thanks," Melissa said. "I need to ask you a few questions about Brenda Rorke, your school friend. You still maintain contact, don't you?"

A shadow ran across Sury's face. She settled in a chair at the opposite side of the coffee table, and crossed her legs.

"Not much. We call each other once in a great while, just for the sake of old memory. We don't have much in common anymore, you know? I have a family, and she's single, far away, with a different lifestyle. I don't know much about her these days. Why? What do you need to know? Is she in trouble?"

"No, not yet, but she might be involved in something I'm investigating. Actually, right now, what I'd really like learn more about is the details of the crime committed against her. She was raped. You were a witness, is that correct?"

"Yes. What exactly do you want to know?"

"Everything you can remember. Every detail, whether or not you think it's significant."

"Are you finally going to indict them? I don't think she's interested in that anymore. I think she's put it all behind her."

"You think so? Why? It was a great injustice that those boys were not put in prison."

"True," Sury said. She nodded. "But it was long time ago. I doubt that she wants to go through all these court proceedings again, questioned by unscrupulous defence lawyers who try to convince the court that the sex was consensual, that she was some sort of promiscuous tease. And the photos…exposing her naked body all over again, showing her being raped by those guys… It'll be another trauma. Did you ask her if she wants it?"

"No, I didn't. And the prosecution may not be as dramatic as you think. It could be settled without all of that. And what pictures you are talking about? There were none presented at her case."

"Of course not." Sury's eyes lit with flames of rage. "The prosecutor had them, but she didn't even mention them in court. A girl with no experience in life, no relatives, and no money—Brenda was defenceless against them and their high-priced mercenaries."

"That's true. Let's get back to pictures. What pictures you are talking about?"

"Those guys took photographs while she was being raped. They had fun. For good measure, they uploaded them onto Facebook. They blurred out their own faces,

93

but made sure that Brenda's face and body were crisp and clear. I saved these pictures before they took them down after Brenda's arrest. I still have digital files, and screen shots as well."

"You did the right thing." Melissa felt like a treasure hunter on the trail of a valuable find. "May I have them?"

Sury shrugged. "If you wish. I can send them to you by e-mail."

"Good. Now, can you tell me, please, everything you remember about what happened?" Melissa produced her writing pad and a cheap ballpoint pen. She never used expensive accessories in her fieldwork.

"Brenda had a boyfriend, Kenny. He was sweet—a shy, timid boy, a striking contrast to Brenda's strong character. Brenda was always on fire. Strong physically, with an iron will, she never let anyone bully her, or treat with contempt. She always stood up for me, too. She had a rather sensitive pride, I think. Her mother was a cleaning lady, you know, and Brenda never even knew who her father was. I don't think even Rita knew. She had a bit of a reputation when she was young, you know? It was a pain Brenda carried in her heart. But people said Rita changed after Brenda was born. She gave up drinking, drugs, running around with men, and worked around the clock to make a decent life for Brenda. She didn't make much, but she grew most of her own fruits and vegetables, and saved every penny. Rita was afraid of everything, even her own shadow, but she was a wonderful mom. Brenda never let anyone humiliate her. Any insult made her fly off the handle. In fury, she was scary."

"Had she had sex with Kenny?" Melissa cut in.

"Yes, she had. Somehow it was not a secret. Then Yona, one of the coolest guys in the school, started hitting on her. Brenda shut him down, which made the other girls laugh at him, which really pissed him off. At the end of school, there was a big party at Lucas's house. His parents had gone on to Europe for some reason and left him alone in this big, beautiful house, and he threw a huge party. Lots of people were there. Then the party got really rowdy, with lots of people drinking, smoking weed, doing drugs, dancing. When I noticed that Brenda had disappeared, I set off looking for her. When I was looking upstairs, I heard a weird noise behind one of closed doors and I burst in."

Sury stopped to pour two glasses of water. Melissa got the feeling that she wasn't thirsty so much as unsettled, and need a way to compose herself.

"What I saw made me sick. Brenda was stripped naked on the bed and her hands were yanked up over her head. With a belt, I think. Yona was raping her. One of his hands covered her mouth, to muffle her screams. Lucas and Christian held Brenda. Another guy, I forget his name, was taking pictures. I yelled at them and pulled Yona off the bed by his hair. They threw me on the floor, but soon they all came out. I think they sobered up when they saw how angry I was, and they kind of slunk off down the stairs.

Brenda was on the bed, crying, covering her face with her hands. I asked her what had happened, and she said that they'd told her Kenny was waiting for her upstairs. Kenny wasn't there, of course. For four guys, it wasn't that hard to rape one woman, even a strong one. The music was deafening, nobody heard her screaming."

"And what did you do? Did you call the police?"

"She asked me to wait a few minutes. As soon as I started trying to console her, she got control of herself. She became the Brenda that I knew. She stood up and ran out of the room. She grabbed a heavy frying pan from the kitchen and found the boys down in the living room. She was on a mission, and I didn't dare to stand in her way. Christian stood with his back to doorway. Yona saw her coming and tried to warn him, but when Christian turned around, Brenda hit him on the head with the pan.

Christian fell on the floor, and those three cool guys, Yona, Lucas, and the photographer, jumped on her, and wrung the pan out of her hand. Brenda kept fighting—punching and kicking—but Yona punched here and they beat up and threw her out of the house onto the front lawn. I went over to where she lay on the ground, groggy from the blows. Then she stood up and left, like she couldn't hear a word I was saying."

"Were there any other witnesses of the rape?" Melissa asked.

"Yes, a couple of guys walked in and out of the room while it was going on, and they told other people at the party. They were all laughing."

"Were any of them ever asked to testify?"

"No. There was never any investigation of the rape. If you had been in the court, you wouldn't have believed it! A young woman, a kid really, up against an experienced gang of rich lawyers who made it sound like she was violent psycho who was trying to ruin a bunch of honourable young men from good families because she was jealous. She didn't stand a chance."

"Okay." Melissa scribed a few words on her writing pad. "We'll come back to that later. So, she left the party. What happened next?"

"Next day I called Brenda. She asked me not to come, but I'd seen the photos of the rape on Facebook. It was so degrading. I called her and insisted on coming. When I showed her, she was devastated. She asked me to leave her alone. I didn't want to…I was really afraid she might kill herself. But instead she took a knife and found some of the guys playing soccer field. Lucas was just lucky that he was a good runner. She just wounded him, and that was all. Everybody was in shock. The next day the boys pulled the photos down off Facebook, but I had saved them all on my computer."

Sury fell silent, frowning.

"Anything else?" Melissa asked.

"Well, not much. She was arrested, as you know. All those brave guys were scared out of their wits. That's why Brenda wasn't released, as she should have been until formal charges were laid. But they and their rich mommies and daddies were afraid that Brenda would go after them. Right they were."

"You say 'right they were.' She was angry, and she went after them. Would it be reasonable to suggest that Brenda would go after them now?"

Sury shrugged. "I wouldn't suggest anything. I have no idea what her intentions might be. As I said, we're not that close anymore."

"Did you visit her in jail?" Melissa asked.

"Yes, I did." Sury took a deep breath and paused. "We met in the room for visitors. We sat at that plastic table, opposite each other, and I had to tell her...I had to tell her that her mother died that morning of a heart attack. She sat a few moments in silence, then hid her face in arms and burst into tears." Sury was crying silently now. She stopped to dry her eyes, and cleared her throat. "Excuse me. It was so...well, words just can't explain how awful it was. She just sat there, shaking and crying, until visiting time was over. Then she stood up and left. She didn't even say goodbye. I never saw her cry once after that. She became again her usual self, merry and optimistic, in good times and bad times."

"Did you visit her in prison?"

"Yes."

"Did she ever complain about her life there?"

"Never."

"Had she ever threatened these guys?"

"I never heard her threaten them in person, but it sure seems that way. All of them, except one, left town soon after she was sent to prison. One changed his name. Brenda did say in court, though, that none of them would ever die in peace, and she wished she could make their lives a living hell, as they had done to her. But I'm sure all that is in the records."

"Have you ever talked to any of the guys since?"

"No. I ran into Yona once at the plaza, but I didn't speak to him. As I said, they all left the town. They were afraid of her, because they knew what they'd done was evil." Sury paused, looking at Melissa, expecting another question. Melissa kept quiet. Sury could not tolerate the awkwardness of long silence.

"Is something wrong? Has something happened?" Sury asked, concern in her voice.

"Did you know that Lucas committed suicide recently?" Melissa asked.

Sury turned pale.

"What…what does that have to do with Brenda?" she asked, hardly moving her lips.

"Lucas was raped before he slit his wrists. Did you know that?"

"I knew he was dead. I didn't know any details. Do you suspect Brenda of something?" Sury's hands began tremble.

"Whatever she did or didn't do, she couldn't be accused in his death. It was a clear-cut case of suicide. It was his decision to take his life. Can you tell me anything else you think might be relevant?" Melissa picked up her writing pad again, but didn't expect anything interesting to write down.

"About Brenda or Lucas?"

"Lucas."

"Actually, I didn't think he was such a bad guy." Sury raised her shoulders, as if in surprise. "But he wasn't stable. Once he had a sweetheart at school. There was another guy, a bigger, stronger guy, who kept hitting on her. He began bullying Lucas to humiliate him in front of his girl. At some point it became too much. Lucas started a fistfight, but it didn't last long. The guy knocked Lucas down with the first punch. Lucas couldn't even stand up without help, and everybody laughed. His girlfriend told me later that Lucas cried all that evening, literally cried, like a hysterical girl. She had to console him, like a mom. That just seemed funny back then, but it made Lucas want to be a cool guy, a hero, someone other guys wouldn't mess with again. There was a model for that: Yona. That's why Lucas smoked pot with him, probably did other drugs as well. He tried to look like a movie hero, but after a few minutes of talking to him you'd realize that it's just a show, a soap bubble, you know what I mean?"

"Yes, I know what you mean. It's important. Anything else you can think of?"

"It was weird how the attorney and judge behaved. They completely ignored the fact that Brenda had been gang raped. They claimed that her sex with those guys was consensual. That was a blatant lie. No wonder Brenda lost her faith in the system."

"Is that why she took revenge?" Melissa asked.

"I'm not saying she did, or even wants to. Not at all. I think she wants to start a new life. She wants to forget about the past."

Melissa picked up her notepad and pen and put them into her bag. Rising to her feet, she said, "That's not true. You know it. I know it. Thanks for your time. You have my card. If you think of anything important, please call me."

She left, feeling Sury's stare on her back.

Chapter 13

The car windows were made of tinted glass. From the outside, it was impossible to make out who was inside, even if it had been bright daylight. It was late evening, when the dusk began saturating into darkness, and no one could see Brenda and Max in the front seats.

Hunching over the steering wheel, Max turned to Brenda.

"Stop worrying, hon," he said, watching the street. "Why would you care?"

"I don't want another death." Brenda didn't take her eyes from the door to Christian's house. They were about hundred meters away from it; the deepening dark, they might miss him when he came out.

"There won't be another death. That last joker was cuckoo. People don't kill themselves just like that. By the way, you didn't listen to me when I told you that he had to pay money for what he did. If you told him, 'gimme money or else,' he'd have had a chance to get out of it. Everyone would be happy—you, me, and even that creep, what's-his-name."

"Lucas. Edward. Whatever."

"Right. Lately my memory fails me. Now, we're not gonna make the same mistake. I want his money, and I'll get it. It'll be damn good for what he did, trust me. An eye for an eye, a tooth for a tooth, you said so the other day. So, you go to the dentist, and he'll tell you a tooth costs big money." Max laughed at his own joke, then leaned back and put his hand on Brenda's thigh. "This guy ain't gonna kill himself, as he'll have a way outa this mess: money. Get it?"

"Maybe you're right," Brenda sighed. "I'd prefer, though, for him to have to live through what I did."

"What he'll get is still pretty damn good," Max insisted. "Not the same, but pretty damn good. He'll live with it till the end of his fucking life."

The darkness crept in, and few streetlights went on. Christian showed up when the stars and the moon moved into the sky, and the last pedestrian disappeared from the street. He held the leash of his dog, which tried to free itself with sudden pulls and tugs.

"There he is," Brenda said. She sneaked out of the car.

They quickly caught up with Christian, Max at his right side, and Brenda at his left. A small black poodle raised his head at Brenda, wiggling his tail in a friendly welcome. Christian shook, in the grip of fear, and quickly looked right and left, his eyes wide in the yellow light of the half moon. He made a half-hearted attempt to free himself, but gave up when Max pressed the stainless steel pistol at his nose. The barrel of a gun just an inch below his right eye, the firm, painful pressure of its cold tip, the depressing darkness of the night, and Max's sinister grimace must have scared him into surrender. Brenda took the leash of the dog from his hand. The dog didn't mind, and adjusted his walking speed to Brenda's.

"What's all this?" Christian muttered. "What do you want?" His voice was cracking, on the verge of tears.

"Shut up," Max growled in a low voice. "Don't say a word, until I let you. Do what I say, or I'd kill you, like a pig."

The entrance to the park was a few hundred steps away. They walked to it in silence, along the deserted street, ghostly lit by a few lamps positioned high on their posts. When the last one was behind them, Christian began shaking in fear. Holding his upper arm, Brenda felt his trembling flesh, shuddering at the prospect of his seemingly imminent death.

They reached a small gap between the bushes, through which a narrow, winding path lined with dense

101

forest sloped down into the ravine formed by a small river. The leafy crowns of trees blocked the moon entirely. The chilly darkness sucked out whatever strength remained in Christian's body and his knees buckled. If Max and Brenda hadn't supported him, he would have fallen to the ground.

"It's not far now," Max said, holding him firmly. "We won't kill ya. Just do what I say. Understand?"

"Yes," Christian said. He began sobbing, shaking as if in fits of malaria, and groaning in despair. The anger and hatred that had consumed Brenda for the last five years suddenly vanished. She felt nausea, pity for Christian, and the revolting feeling that she was doing something terribly wrong became unbearable. When Christian stumbled over something on the path, she propped him up and said, "We won't kill you." The tone of her voice was almost conciliatory.

"Where are you taking me, and why?" Christian asked between sobs.

"You'll know in a minute. Just be quiet," she advised.

Her manner of speaking calmed Christian. He was still crying, but the force of his shakes and sobs subsided.

Max turned his flashlight on, and pointed it down to the ground so they could descend to the bottom of the slope. They turned left and came to the public toilet.

"Hands on the wall," Max commanded. Christian obeyed. Max handed Brenda the gun. She took it and pressed the barrel between Christian's shoulder blades.

"If you move, we'll shoot you," Max warned matter-of-factly. He removed some tools from his pocket and began working on the lock, as the building was locked after sunset. Max and Brenda had found that out in the course of planning.

Max was fast and efficient. After all, picking locks was a part of his criminal profession. However, the minute it took him to work felt like an eternity to Brenda.

She suddenly realized that even if he ran, she wouldn't be able to shoot Christian. She didn't feel any hatred for him. She didn't see in him anything of the young guy at the school, the one who had been part of causing her such misery. This was a stranger, a grown-up man devastated by fear, who had no idea why he had been abducted in this beautiful night. But when Max opened the door, her ever-present drive for action took control.

"Go in," Max commanded. Christian entered the toilet building without any attempt to protest. His will, and thinking ability, were totally paralyzed. The only thing he could do was to obey his captors.

Max closed the door and put the flashlight on the floor. Its beam hit the ceiling, and bounced back down from its white surface, shedding dispersed light over the space. The floor was wet with urine, and stench of human excrement hit Brenda's nose and lungs.

Brenda tied the dog's leash to one of the pipes. The dog sensed danger, and began whimpering, his tail between his legs.

"Take off your clothes," Max said.

"What for?" Christian asked between sobs.

"Do it!" Max roared, angry. It seemed to Brenda that the whole building shook with the thunder of his voice. The dog began barking. Max gave it a powerful kick, and the poor animal screamed in pain.

"Okay, okay," Christian mumbled, and began taking his clothes off. "Where shall I put them?"

"Throw them on the floor, asshole," Max said. "All of it. Fast."

Christian removed all his clothes except his shoes, and stood naked, his body trembling, his eyes wide open in horror. He seemed about to faint.

"Put your hands on the wall and bend over," Max commanded. Christian did. Brenda shoved the pistol under her belt, took her video camera from her shoulder, turned on its flash and pointed it at Christian. All her anger and bitterness were back.

Max pulled down his pants, strapped on the dildo they had bought in the sex shop, and began raping Christian. Christian screeched in pain like a tortured animal. Max turned his face away, while Brenda videotaped the morbid scene. The dog barked, Christian screamed, and the whole thing seemed to Brenda like a horror movie in which she was a player. She shut off the camcorder.

"Enough," she said, in a voice suggesting unquestionable obedience. "Stop it."

Max removed the dildo and pulled up his pants.

"Look at me, Christian. Do you recognize me?" she asked.

Christian was in trance, incapable of recognizing anything.

"I'll help you, Christian," she continued. "I'm Brenda. Do you remember me now?"

Christian froze. It was difficult to guess what was on his mind, as his face was distorted with horror and pain. At last he said, "Yes, I remember you. I'm so s—"

Max cut him off. "Look at me, asshole," Max said. "You need to get fifty grand together by next week. I'll send word how to get it to me. If I don't get the money, all of it, on time, I'll place this video online, and make sure everyone you know, from your boss to your mommy, sees it."

"I don't have that kind of money." Christian began crying again. "I'll have to sell my house. It's impossible. Where can I get such money?"

"You want me help you with finances?" Max asked. "Maybe I give you a loan?" Max chuckled.

"Either you find the money, or you'll see yourself on every social network out there," Brenda said. "This will be a lesson for you, free of charge. If you don't pay, you'll know even more so how I felt when you did the same to me. We'll be in touch."

"Make it a month, please! I can sell my house." Christian began picking up his clothes from the dirty floor.

"By the way, something else," Brenda said. "If you go to the police, you won't get off the hook this time. All evidence of your raping me is still there. Sury will testify, and you won't be able to bribe anyone this time. All the world will know what you are, a filthy rapist—and now you're a rapist who's been fucked, at that. Everyone will know: your wife, coworkers, the mailman…everybody. A month, you say? Okay. One month. By the way, do you know where Yona and Bob live?"

"No." Christian wiped his tears with his sleeve. "I know that Bob is somewhere in Hamilton, but that's all. Last time I saw him was three years ago."

"What about Yona?" Brenda asked.

"Nothing. I know he was in jail for a short time, something to do with pot. After that, I have no idea. I haven't seen him in years."

Max picked up the flashlight from the floor and turned it off. "If you fancy the idea of calling police, you won't live long," Max said. "I'll find you and kill you, got it?"

Brenda turned around and left the washroom. Max followed after her.

"He's ruined." Brenda broke the silence on the way back. She was looking at the round beam of the flashlight, which Max pointed at the pathway.

"All assholes are the same, when it comes to death," Max said in a calm voice. "Show them a gun, and they'll do whatever you want them to do. Don't worry, though. He'll do whatever he can to survive, and get out of this shit. Fifty grand isn't beyond him. The sucker understands that the other choice is the end of life for him. First, everyone would know he got fucked. What a treat for his coworkers to see his fat ass in Technicolor, eh?" Max laughed in delight, opening the car door. He turned the engine on and made a U-turn. "And then," Max continued, "If he goes to the police, he'll be in court for rape. His wife would know what he did, and so would everyone else, the whole world. This time he won't jump off the hook, and he knows it. All hell will break loose for him. Fifty grand is your mercy for him. You made a mistake with Lucas—I told you so even before we went to him, remember?"

Brenda remembered. "Let's see what happens," she said with a sigh. Exhausted, she closed her eyes, but that gave her no peace. Her memory brought back the night with Lucas with a vengeance.

Max had asked her to blackmail Lucas. "Don't do it for nothing," he insisted. "His old folks have tons of money. He'll pay whatever you wanna get. You need money, I need money. Stupid not to take it."

But Brenda was adamant. "This is not the matter of money," she insisted. "He, and all other brats, have to go through the same things I did."

Max arranged surveillance of Lucas's building, tracking his comings and goings. There was a stable pattern to his behaviour, which made things easier. Luca usually arrived home at about six o'clock, give or take ten minutes. Often his girlfriend arrived one or two hours later. Sometimes they went out, and occasionally she stayed overnight.

Max checked out the lock to the apartment, and found that picking it was pathetically easy.

On the day they chose to execute the plan, Max went into the building alone. Brenda remained outside, awaiting his call to let her know that he was inside the apartment.

Brenda lurked around, waiting for Lucas. She dressed like a man, including a small beard and moustache, figuring that only someone who was very suspicious and attentive would recognize her in her disguise.

As expected, Lucas pulled in a few minutes before six. Brenda caught a glimpse of his face through the front window. Like many happy, healthy young men for whom life has always been easy, he was absorbed in his own thoughts and didn't pay much attention to anything around him, and certainly not Brenda, who stood by the bus stop. He went straight into the garage.

Five minutes later her phone rang.

"Come," was the short order. Brenda went into the building and took the lift to the twelfth floor. She pulled the door open and went in.

Lucas was sitting in a chair, pale as a dead man. His lips were twitching, hands trembling, eyes not blinking, as if the horror froze his eyelids. He stared at Brenda, and then at Max, who held his gun pointed at Lucas.

"What is this, guys?" he mumbled. "This must be a mistake. You must have the wrong guy."

"Oh, no. You're the right guy. Now, do what I tell you. That's your only chance to survive. Understand?"

Lucas nodded.

"Stand up. Take off your pants," Max demanded.

"My pants...what for?" Lucas asked, bewildered. Max stood up, his eyes as menacing as only gangster could make.

"Yes...yes," Lucas mumbled and unbuckled his belt. Max leaned him over the table, then pulled down his own pants and slipped the dildo into the harness while Brenda taped Lucas's mouth. She stepped back, took out her video camcorder, and pointed it at Lucas. The ugly rape began. It disgusted her, but she kept filming, clenching her teeth. Lucas made no attempt to resist or protest. His will was crushed.

"Enough," Brenda commanded, shutting down her camera. Max removed the dildo and tidied himself.

"Get dressed," Brenda told Lucas. He was crying, tears streaming down his cheeks. He pulled up his pants and sat in the chair, horror and pain in his eyes. Brenda took off her disguise and confronted him.

"Recognize me?" she asked. It took a moment. Then his eyes opened wide in surprise, followed by a look of even more intense horror.

"Brenda?" he breathed out.

"Ah, you do remember. I told all of you shitheads that I'll come after you until the end of your lives?"

It was the moment she had dreamed about for the past five years.

"I apologize," Lucas wept.

"Awwwww, me too. Does it help? Tell me, does my apology help? You feel better?"

"It was a long time ago. Please, Brenda."

"It was a long time ago. And I'm still suffering because of it. Now you can share my pain."

"How much do you want, Brenda? My father is a rich man, you know."

"I know. That's why I was sent to prison and not you. You know."

"What do you want, then?" Lucas asked.

"I want my life back. But since I can't have that, I want to ruin yours. I will place this video on every social network there is. You'll be famous, just as I was! You'll see yourself on Facebook, and so will your friends, your family, your coworkers, and even your girlfriend. After I edit it, I'm sure they will enjoy the movie."

"Brenda, Brenda…" Lucas moaned. There was a moment when Brenda wanted to step back from her plan. She might have, had it not been for Max, who looked at her with approving eyes.

"Now, you could go to the police, tell them who fucked you. But if you do, I promise that my case will be reopened. This time, your father's money won't do any good. You and those other jerks will do time, God knows how many years. I don't care what will happen to me, but this time going to court would be much more fun. Don't you think so? So, enjoy the movie when it's released, and keep your mouth shut."

Lucas fell on his knees, begging them to accept money and forget everything. "Any amount," he cried. "Name your price."

"Money. You think that's the answer to everything." Brenda glared at him with disgust. Then she walked out the door.

"He won't go to the police," Max said, smiling, when they left the building. He was right about that. But it had never occurred to her that Lucas could commit suicide. She hadn't wanted that. She didn't want them to die, only suffer as she had.

A gentle push of Max's hand brought her back to reality. She could still hear Christian's cries echoing in her head, and smell the acrid stench of the bathroom even though they were in Max's car, and had just pulled into the driveway.

"Come back to me, honey." His smile was from ear to ear. "You were great. Real wolverine. I won't dare mess with ya. Now he'll go through hell, probably run away as far as he can. Still better than being in the can." He paused. "And in a month, maybe we'll have money. Anyway, you were great. Just great."

Chapter 14

"We're going to Mississauga," Max said. "It'll be fun for you to know him. Very few know who he is, but he knows everything about everyone."

"Who is he?"

"Anything you want. An artist. A lawyer. Rather, a former lawyer. He was indicted once, but never served a term. He won't be pleased to see you—he doesn't usually take to our girlfriends or ol' ladies— Max used the biker word for a wife or a permanent girls friend — but he'll like you." He darted a quick, benevolent look at her. "I'm one of the most trusted. We're friends, as a matter of fact."

"Why doesn't he like women?" she asked.

"It's not a matter of like or dislike. He is one of the pillars of our gang. Women are the least trusted and reliable folks in a biker gang. It's not only his opinion. Only a few people know what he does. Those who find out are either dead or trustworthy. He's weird, but he's a good guy, when you get to know him."

"What does he do that's so dangerous to know?"

"Officially? He's a translator. He translates not only documents and texts, but also does synchronic translations at courts, law offices, whatever. He's a genius in whatever he does."

"And unofficially?"

"Forges documents of any kind, which only experts with best technology can detect. Finds information on anyone and anything. Gives top-notch legal advice. Some other stuff that I don't want to talk about, and never will. Has connections everywhere."

110

"Weird," Brenda shrugged. "Why he is your guy? If what you've said is true, he could make good money without you."

Max nodded, yes. "Sure. He does. But he's with us. You'll understand why."

He pulled into the driveway of a small bungalow. It was in immaculate condition, as if it had been built days ago rather than decades. Not a single speck marred the perfection of the cream-colored garage door. The stucco finish of outside walls looked as fresh as if it had been applied that morning. The small lawn was as neatly kept as a golf course, without a single weed or fading flower. The interlock leading to porch had been laid with a precision of a clock master.

"Is it a new house?" Brenda asked.

"No." Max stepped out of the car and led the way to the entrance. "He lives this way. He maintains clinical neatness and order in everything in his life. Come on, he's waiting for us."

Max jumped on the top of the three-stair porch and pressed the button. A few moments later the door swung open to reveal a man in his fifties standing just behind the threshold. He was casually, but neatly dressed in a custom-made blue shirt, matching trousers, soft moccasins, and a wide belt with an elegant, stainless steel buckle. His shortly cut beard glistened with threads of silver-gray hair. With watery-blue eyes, he scanned Brenda with lightening speed and, it seemed, quickly lost interest in her at the same moment.

"Please, come in," he said, speaking to Max, and stepping back. There was no hint of a welcoming smile on his face.

"Good day, Bogdan," Max greeted him, shaking his hand. "This is Brenda, my ol' lady."

Bogdan nodded almost imperceptibly in welcome, and gestured them inside.

111

"Please, sit down," he said. He settled into a cozy chair in front of a large sofa. Brenda sat face-to-face with him, and swept her eyes around the room, taking it all in: expensive modern furniture, elegant and very comfortable, with off-white colour prevailing; slim, sparkling crystal chandelier; golden hardwood floor, shining like a mirror. There were weird pictures on the walls, faces of men and women—not portraits, but something between a mask and an ancient sculpture— white, like gypsum, like death masks, clearly indicating that these were dead people. However, some tiny red or brown spots on their skin or a glistening spot in a dark space where the eyes should be indicated that some life still remained. The impression was strong, frightening, and nauseating.

"Coffee, tea, something stronger?" Bogdan asked, looking between Max and Brenda. "You know, Max, I only have the best."

"Later," Max said. He turned to Brenda, "You?"

Brenda shook her head. She regarded Bogdan with growing interest. His straight and model-perfect nose, noble longish face, nicely outlined lips, and stylish haircut made him look like a first echelon Hollywood leading man, the one who plays the hero and gets the girl in the end. His forehead was large, a bit disproportionally for his face, more befitting a noble philosopher than someone connected to gangsters. Women must love him at first sight, she thought, except for... For what? She couldn't explain what it was, but the man was scary. She suddenly felt that she was inside a supervillain's private lair. She did not like it.

Bogdan pointed his stare at Brenda and narrowed his eyes. She thought he was angry with her for something, but he said, sounding friendly, intelligent, "Make yourself at home. The coffee machine is there, in the kitchen. It'll make you whatever you want at the press of a button: cappuccino, latte, whatever." He turned to Max: "You

112

know where the bar is. Whenever you feel like it, help yourself."

He took a sturdy board from a side table, and placed a large white cartoon sheet over it.

"Excuse me," he said, speaking with the trained, soft voice of an accomplished public speaker. "If you don't mind, I'll keep drawing while we speak."

"Sure, no problem," Brenda said. Max did not comment.

Bogdan produced a large pencil, placed the board on his lap, and began moving his hand across the paper.

"What brings you here?" he asked, not taking his eyes off the drawing.

"Brenda spent a few years in a crowbar hotel," Max began.

"Uh huh," Bogdan uttered, his head down. "High security."

"Yeah. There were four guys who should've been there for rape. Instead, she was there."

Bogdan nodded in understanding. "She's done something, has she?" he asked.

"Yeah." Max practically wriggled with delight in the sofa and chuckled. "She cut one sucker's arm with a kitchen knife."

Bogdan threw a fleeting glance of interest at Brenda, and then quickly returned to his drawing.

"After them now, is she?" he asked Max, as if Brenda was not there.

"Yeah." Max cleared his throat. "We became friends with the two of them already. As much as we liked them, one of them is no longer with us."

Bogdan raised his eyes to Brenda. "What's his name?" he asked.

"Edward Green. A few years ago he was Lucas Kroner. He thought that way I wouldn't find him." Brenda needed a break. "May I have a cup of coffee?"

113

This time Bogdan did not look at her. "Sure," he nodded. "As I said, feel like you are in your own home."

Brenda stepped into the kitchen, where she found the sophisticated coffee machine with two rows of buttons. She had no idea how to use it, but rejected the idea of asking Bogdan for help. The kitchen appeared surgically clean: white walls, off-white marble counters, white kitchen cabinets, stainless steel appliances. Everything spotless, precisely arranged, aligned.

"Cups are in the cabinet above the coffee machine," Bogdan said. Brenda took one, a snow-white porcelain piece of art, and placed it in the cup-sized opening in the coffee machine. She pressed a button and the machine came to life, letting the brown liquid flow into the cup. She heard the conversation in the living room flowing uninterrupted.

"We found the third guy, the one who photographed the whole thing, in Hamilton. We'll meet him soon. But there's a fourth one. No one seems to know where he is, but he's the most important for Brenda, you know."

"I see."

When Brenda returned to her seat, Bogdan was still bowed over his art.

"Tell me more about him," Bogdan requested.

"His name is Jonathan Freeman. Yona he's called."

"Was he mentioned at Brenda's court appearance?"

"Yes."

"Tell me everything about this case. The court date, location, the names of the judge, prosecutor, lawyers, witnesses." He met Brenda's eyes. "Tell me." He raised his head; his wide-open eyes transmitted the keen interest of a sadist. Then he cast his stare down.

While Bogdan hunched over his drawing, Brenda reported all the details. Bogdan nodded, but didn't ask questions. When Brenda finished, she turned her glance to the art on the walls. It seemed that the faces there, the almost-dead people, were trying to scream, but lacked the strength to utter a sound. The room was silent but for the sound of Bogdan's pencil moving on the paper. To break the awkwardness of the moment, she said, "You have a bit of an accent. I can't place it."

Bogdan raised his head. "I'm from Serbia, and fluent in four languages. As a result, I have a slight accent in all of them."

As Bogdan once more returned to his art, Brenda took advantage of the moment and studied him with a hungry interest. She had once read a novel, a love story set against the background of the civil war in Yugoslavia. Had Bogdan been a part of that? Was he a war criminal who had participated in genocide, and was now living in a safe refuge in Canada? If so, the sophisticated devil had already wiped out all traces of his original identity.

"Would you be able to find him?" Brenda asked. Bogdan smirked the way some smart people do when they hear something they find appallingly stupid.

"People never disappear, even after death. Unless they are burned." He looked at Brenda and smiled with real joy in his eyes.

"Just to change a subject for a sec...I gave you a licence plate number the other day," Max said.

"He's in Lake Nipigon, swimming with the fish."

"I see." Max stood up. "Thanks, Bogdan. We've gotta go."

Bogdan also rose to his feet and held out his drawing for Brenda. She took it, but at the next moment had an urge to drop it like a hot pan in a bare hand. It showed her face, snow white, without wrinkles, like a mask, her mouth stretched in a grimace of pain. There were no eyeballs between the wide-open eyelids, but a red spot between her teeth indicated the presence of life.

"Thanks," she said without strength in her voice.

"If you think people can't see the pain in your heart, you are wrong." He smiled. "There is only one cure for it. Have fun."

Brenda did not look at Bogdan, and did not shake hands with him. When they back in the car, she said to Max, "I want to throw this drawing in the garbage."

"Hold on," Max said. "Don't rush. You don't like the guy, do you?"

Brenda just looked at him, saying nothing.

He navigated the car to the highway, and glanced at Brenda. "He's a genius," he said. "He remembers everything that ever happened to him, and to other people. He remembers everything he's ever seen, heard, or read. You wouldn't believe what that kind of head he has. I don't think he's human."

"Did he kill somebody?" Brenda asked.

"No one knows. I think he did. Did you look into his eyes?"

"I did." Brenda swallowed a choking lump at recollection. "Is he gay?"

Max threw at her a quick and sharp glance. "How'd you guess?"

"Intuition."

"Well, he's bi. That's as much as I know. The less I know about him, the better."

"With his talents, why does he deal with you?" Brenda asked.

Max chuckled. "He's from another world. From our world."

"I think he's a sick man," Brenda murmured.

"Who of us isn't?" Max asked. "We're all screwed up, each in our own way. You think you're normal? Eh? After those years in the hellhole?" He laughed. "Let's go to a bar and have a drink."

"Do you know how he'll get the information?" Brenda asked.

"Not specifically, no. But he has his ways. He knows everyone, and has connections everywhere, with police, lawyers, judges, even the government. He meets with connected people almost every day. I have no idea how he

116

can make use of it. I know that he has lots to do with finances, flies to Europe often, deals with offshore banks, big shots. Sometimes he needs our help, sometimes we need his. That sort of thing, you know."

"What kind of help does he need from you?" Brenda asked.

Max chuckled again. "You guess. There are many things that we do for each other. Let's talk about something else. You'll sleep better."

Chapter 15

It seemed to Melissa that Christian did not sound surprised when she presented herself to him over the phone. "Would you mind if I drop by to talk to you?" she asked, as casually as she could.

"Where?" he asked.

"At your home."

"Eh...well, of course. What time?"

"Tell me what time is best for you."

"Eh...let me think. Is seven okay with you?"

"Yes."

Christian cleared his throat at the other end of the line. "What's this about?" he asked in a hopeless voice.

"See you at seven." Melissa hung up and turned to Larry. "We'll visit him tonight," she said, and then added, "He almost seemed to be expecting my call. Perhaps something happened."

After a long and boring drive, Larry pulled into the driveway of a small townhouse at the end of the street. A single lamppost was already lit, but was not bright enough to compete with the fading day. Melissa took in the view of the park entrance, just a short walk away, and the quiet of the neighbourhood, with no human beings in sight. Larry did the same.

Christian opened the door almost at the same moment as the bell rang. Stocky, with hunched shoulders, bluish bags under his eyes, and a grim frown, he wasn't the example of a young, careless man as his age might suggest. He gestured them inside, not paying attention to the badges they proffered.

The first floor of the house was tiny: just a living room, overcrowded with cheap furniture, a kitchen, and a plastic table in the breakfast area.

"Please, sit down," Christian said, pointing at the two worn-out easy chairs.

"Where's your wife?" Larry asked.

"I asked her to visit her mother for a few hours. She's pregnant. I don't want her be here, you know, when you…"

"When we investigate the death of Edward Green. Lucas, as you knew him at school."

Christian nodded without a comment.

"You know about his death, don't you?" Melissa asked.

"Of course I do. His father told me he committed suicide."

"Yes, he did. But there is more to it than that. Do you know if he had any enemies, or someone who threatened him?"

Christian shrugged his large shoulders and shook his head.

"So, you don't remember Brenda? Another old schoolmate?"

"Oh. Yes." Christian blinked a few times, and swallowed a large lump in his throat. He straightened up, as if anticipating a blow.

"Five years ago, you raped her, along with three other guys."

Christian lowered his head, watching his trembling hands.

"Yes. It was terrible. I still don't understand how it happened. We'd had a lot to drink that night, done some drugs…You reopening this case?"

"Not necessarily. But you didn't just rape her. You also made obscene photographs and placed them on the Internet."

Christian jerked his head up. "Not me!" He raised his voice with emphasis. "That was Yona and Bob. Bastards. When I found out, I beat the shit out of Bob. Lucas didn't like it, either, but he was a weakling. No guts to stand up to them."

"If it comes to that, would you be willing to testify?" Larry asked. Christian frowned and shrugged again.

"I guess there's not much choice," he said, looking at Melissa, not at Larry. "You have enough evidence anyway, I guess."

"Brenda hit you with a frying pan after the rape. You testified about that, though you failed to mention the rape."

"No one asked me about it," Christian said. "We all were dead scared about that. We were scared of prison. We were scared of Brenda. She was so mad, like a devil. We thought that if she was released before the court hearing, she might use some weapon more serious than a kitchen knife. A rifle, a gun…you know. Even Yona, Mr. Cool himself, was afraid of her."

At this moment Larry interrupted.

"Looking back, do you really think she would have done something? That she was really dangerous?"

"For sure. She would've started with Yona, I suppose. She had no boundaries."

"She's out now, free," Larry went on. "Do you think that she might be capable of doing something like that now?"

"I don't know," Christian mumbled. "That was long time ago." He turned to Melissa. "May I ask you a question, though?"

"Sure," Melissa agreed.

"Is it Brenda who wants to reopen this case?"

In any other circumstance Melissa would not have answered this question, or any question for that matter. Her duty was to ask questions, not to answer them. But she had some tactical reasons to deviate from the rules.

"No, she didn't. Does it matter?"

"It does. If she doesn't want it, why should you?"

"One reason is that justice has to be served, whether anyone wants it or not."

"Justice!" Christian blurted, hardly suppressing his anger. "Why wasn't it served then? I'd rather have faced the charges then, and done my time for my part in what we did. But now..." He grasped his chin with his right hand, as if in an attempt to shut himself up. "Now, I'm an engineer. I have a career. My wife is pregnant. What kind of justice is that? It's a knife in the back—no, straight into my heart. It's the end of the world. My world. You don't understand it, or don't care."

Melissa didn't interrupt him; she had had the same thoughts.

"Now, it's a disaster not only for me, but for others who had nothing to do with what happened then. I doubt that Brenda wants your kind of justice, if you call it that."

Now he clasped and squeezed his hands in a nervous spasm. He was on the verge of tears.

"It's not only about what happened then," Larry cut in. "It's more about what happened, or what it is happening, now. Mind you, we are working on Lucas's case. It may be that Brenda had something to do with that. Do you think so?"

"I don't know. Maybe. She threatened all of us in court. We all took it seriously. But too many years have passed since then. She should have cooled down, but maybe she didn't."

"Look at it from a different angle. What if a man...say, one of you...was raped, and his photographs put on the Internet? Would he ever cool down?" Melissa asked.

Her words made Christian shudder. His face got red, as if he was experiencing dangerously high blood pressure. Hands trembling, arms moving chaotically, he mumbled, "That's different."

"Different? I don't see—" said Melissa, but Larry cut her off.

121

"Do you know where Brenda is now?" Larry asked.

"I have no idea."

"You sure?" Larry pressed.

"Yes."

Melissa knew he was lying.

"I haven't spoken to Lucas, to any of them, for years," he said in a trembling voice. "How am I supposed to know?"

"This isn't just about Lucas," Melissa said, watching him closely. "It's about Brenda, too. Have you seen her lately? Has she been in communication in any way?"

Christian began coughing. For a few moments, he was short of breath. Obviously, he was utterly disturbed, thinking hard and fast about what to say and what not to say. Finally, he seemed to regain his composure.

"I haven't seen Brenda since that day in court. I know nothing about her."

"Have you been in contact with Yona? Or Bob?" Larry asked.

"No." Now Christian spoke with confidence. "After that time, particularly after the court, I never wanted to see any of them again."

"What do you know about their whereabouts?" Melissa asked.

"Nothing for sure. I heard that Yona became a biker, or so people say. I don't care where they are, and I don't want to know anything about them."

Melissa stood up and handed him her business card. "Call me, if something new comes up."

Larry stood up, too.

"You lie," he said flatly. "But it won't help you. We'll know everything."

Christian raised his shoulders in a gesture of "what-can-I-do?" and said nothing.

When Melissa was out the door, Larry asked, "What do you think?"

"The same as you," she said. That was not entirely true. She thought about a lot more.

Chapter 16

Max pulled up his sleeve and glanced at his watch. "Hurry up," he said with a frown, rolling down the passenger side window. "Bogdan is meticulous. He'll be pissed off if we are even a minute late."

"That freak," Brenda said. "The world won't collapse in a minute."

"That's the way he is. His time is worth a lot. He's doing us a big favour, though."

"It's not for free."

"True. Hurry up. Do your best."

Dodging traffic and breaking a few rules, Brenda pulled into the parking lot of the Starbuck's with two minutes to spare. She followed Max's quick steps and got inside. Luckily, a small table by the window was vacant, and they took it right away. At precisely three, Bogdan came in, grabbed a chair from another table, wiped it off, and sat down.

"Good afternoon," he said, and then faced Brenda. "Just regular coffee," he said in a commanding manner. He sees me as the lowest one in the hierarchy, here to serve him, thought Brenda. She stood and went to the order counter. As she placed three large cups of coffee into the paper tray, she looked back at Max and Bogdan. Their heads were tilted toward each other in a conspiratorial manner; they talked with serious, concentrating frowns. Maybe she was wrong, and Bogdan merely wanted to discuss something with Max without her hearing.

She was deliberately slow to collect sugar packets, stirring sticks, and milk. When she approached the table, the two of them stopped talking, and turned their attention to her.

Bogdan took a cup, brought it to his lips, and savored the first sip, staring into infinity through the window. It began raining outside; the whole sky was draped over with black, heavy clouds. Coffee in such weather was a good mood booster, she thought, after the first swig of the hot liquid.

"I have found something about your friend Yona," Bogdan began, locking his eyes with Brenda's. Butterflies began fluttering in her stomach. Bogdan knew how to add suspense to his speech, not raising his voice.

Brenda was not a coward, she was quite sure about that. She could face danger, if she understood it and the extent of its associated risk. But Bogdan was a man who could surprise anyone with his actions. He would be the kind of adversary against whom it would be impossible to build defences in advance, as his actions were logical and yet unpredictable. She felt the flame of sick cruelty under his cool, detached manners.

"Good," she said, flushing her throat with coffee. "Do you know where is he now?"

"His health card is issued for an address in Scarborough, but his driver's license is for another, in Newmarket. He is with the Punchers. A small gang, but very efficient—don't underestimate them. Very fluid, no official clubhouse, but people in the narco business know them and don't like them, though they are in no rush to clash with them. The gang selects its people carefully. The police know almost nothing about them."

"Where can he be found?" Max asked.

"There are a few bars in Scarborough where they sell their stuff. I'm not sure if you'll find Yona there. But I am sure that he is not the type of man you will be able to capture, manipulate, and let go. He will retaliate, quickly and with force. If you have such something against him, you would be better off to just finish him. It's unlikely that his gang would suspect the two of you. Too many things happen in their business, you know. Likely, they'd suspect someone else, someone from their rivals."

Brenda exchanged glances with Max, but said nothing. She was waiting for more.

"If you want him alive before you're ready to bury him, you can count on me," said Bogdan. He looked at Max. His mouth smiled, but his eyes did not. They became watery, pale, wide open. Brenda felt sick to her stomach. "You know me, Max. I like talking to other predators." A frown appeared on his face. "You can just arrange things, to make life simple, you know. It's not your specialty, Max, but it would not cost much. You pay, and then you can sleep well."

What Bogdan said made sense, Brenda thought. She should either agree to have Yona killed, or drop her plan entirely. Neither of those options was to her liking. It would be intolerable to just walk away, to know that the pig would continue to get away with what he had done to her. But killing him...that was out of the question. She was of the opinion that God gives life, and only God can take it. What should she do? Her life since prison, especially since Max, had been a happy one. Why not just let the whole thing go? And yet...

As if reading her mind, Bogdan resumed his monologue. "Yes, it's probably too late to just let it pass," he said. "I imagine he knows what has happened with his friend Lucas. He might even suspect it's something to do with you, but until he can connect another dot to the first one, he will just be a bit more alert. Still, if he gets wind of something that you have done to the others, it will be a whole different ball game. Yona is no dummy. I would not be surprised if one day he appears at your doorstep, Brenda, in a pre-emptive strike. If you don't intend to stop in your tracks, get rid of him. The sooner, the better. Just prophylactics, you know. I mean, he wouldn't know

126

anything about you, Max, that's not likely…but he for sure will go after Brenda."

"Would his gang help him?" Brenda asked.

"Most unlikely." The corners of Bogdan's mouth went down in a contemptuous grimace. "I doubt that he would ask them for help, as that would imply fear of a woman. Most likely he would either do something himself, or hire someone—if, of course, he knows someone reliable. But who knows what a frightened man will do?"

"Right," Max agreed. "We should think about that."

"Good," Bogdan nodded. "I'll bring my car to you the day after tomorrow. Okay?"

"Yes," Max nodded.

Bogdan stood up. "Have a lovely day," he said, and left.

"What he will bring his car for?" Brenda asked.

"He wants me to build a hidden compartment box into it, something only experts could find."

"What for?" she asked, then bit her tongue. Such questions should not be asked. "Sorry, it's none of my business," she said in an apologetic tone.

"It's okay," Max said. "I have no secrets from you. He needs, or, rather, his people need to carry different things across the border. Money, coke, whatever. I don't care."

"He must trust you a 100 percent," she commented.

"We've known each other for a long time. There's been a lot of back and forth."

"I see." She sank into deep thought, staring out the window.

"What he said about Yona makes sense," Max said. He was in tune with her thoughts.

Brenda gave him a long look. "Which part, exactly, do you mean?"

"I mean, we have to kill the sucker," Max said. "I'm sure that he'll be expecting you to come after him. He can hire someone to kill you as easily as we can hire someone to kill him. I regret now that we didn't ask Bogdan about him before we started all this."

"Would it have changed anything?" she asked.

"One thing, at least. We would have done him first. No one would suspect a thing. And then deal with others whatever way you wish." He ran his palm over his head. "Well, it doesn't matter now, does it?"

"It does. I don't want any more deaths."

"What about your death? Your head is on the line. And I want your head for my own selfish needs." He laughed. "There's no other way, honey. We should do it. Like he said, the sooner, the better."

"We?" she asked, her voice almost trembling.

"We won't do it ourselves. But we'll have to narrow down his whereabouts. I have no idea what he looks like, so you'll have to help me with that."

Brenda looked out the window, watching drops of rain bombarding pools on the ground. A shower of thoughts, cruel as a swarm of stinging angry wasps, attacked her. Life had taken an unexpected turn. If this had all been happening right after she'd left the prison, she probably would have moved ahead without a qualm, without caring about the consequences. But life had treated her well over the past year. She was happy, in love, and content with what she had. Now she would be risking it all. The worst of it was the knowledge that she was putting Max at risk. He was her love. He was willing to sacrifice himself, but for what? Not for her life or happiness, but for her obsession, her blind need to hunt those who had harmed her.

It complicated things that Lucas and Christian had both seemed to feel real regret over what they had done to her. With what she knew now, maybe she should just settle the score with everyone except Yona. Except that Yona was the one who deserved punishment more so than the others. And he would be the most dangerous to deal with. But kill him? No, murder was out of the question. Risking Max's life? Intolerable. Stop everything right now? Bogdan was right; it was too late. What then?

"Everything'll be okay, hon," Max said, putting his hand on her shoulder. "I've dealt with much worse."

"Perhaps," she said, touching his hand with her cheek. "But now you want to leave the gang and become just an ordinary family man, with a wife and maybe a kid or two. Murder is not a good start for that. Even if we could get away with it, it would haunt me until the end of my life. And if something goes wrong, it would be the end of our lives. Our happy lives."

Tears began welling up in her eyes. She had not expected such an outburst of emotion from herself.

"Let me sleep on it," Max said, and then added, with a smile, "With you."

Chapter 18

Nick took Melissa's hand and led her to his bedroom. It was nine o'clock, his usual time for bed, and he wanted his mom to read him a book.

"What story do you want to hear tonight, dear?" Melissa asked. His soft, warm hand was transmitting through its skin that invisible substance that made her melt in delight, as if she were under influence of narcotics.

"Something like mystery," he asked. "Scary."

"Scary isn't good at night," she said, arranging his pillows. "You may have bad dreams."

If he had been older, she would have told him that life often is more frightening than any tale. She had been in the center of scary world for too long. Her profession was dealing with human ills and suffering, both physical and mental. One wrong step, and anyone could be forever outside the borders of law and order, of normal life, which also had its many traps and causes for fear and suffering.

"I don't have bad dreams," Nick insisted, cozying himself in the bed.

"I think I should read you a fairy tale about a beautiful princess who gets saved..."

"No," Nick protested emphatically. "No princess stories. Too boring."

Melissa laughed. In ten years or so, a beautiful princess would likely occupy his mind most of the time, and tales about her, tales from his own imagination, would be anything but boring. As long as nothing scary happened in the meantime.

"What are you laughing at, mom?" Nick regarded her with disapproving eyes.

"Never mind. What story you'd like?"

Nick jumped off the bed and ran to the shelf, taking down a big book with laminated thick covers, and gave it to Melissa. On its front cover there was a picture of a dragon, a sword, and a warrior on a horse. Nick jumped back into the bed, and pulled the blanket over himself.

"Read it," he commanded with confidence. He had no doubt that his mom would obey his orders.

After five minutes of her singsong reading, Nick fell asleep. Melissa quietly sneaked out and went to her bedroom. Evan was already in bed, with his electronic reader in hand. He glanced at her, smiled, and went back to reading. When Melissa undressed and lay beside him, he put his reader on the night table and turned his face to her. They both liked pillow talks. Very often it was the only time when they had an opportunity to socialise.

"Any need for a philosopher?" Evan asked, running his palm over her cheek and hair.

"Always," she said, and kissed him. "It might be nice to be with my husband and make sure he's behaving day and night."

"I hear too often lately that you are thinking of quitting. What's bothering you this time?"

"This case. Brenda. Wolverine. Remember, I told you about this one?"

"Of course I do. What's wrong?"

"Nothing. As a matter of fact, it's moving along quite well. That's the problem."

Melissa sighed, lay on her back, locked her hands behind her head, and stared at the ceiling. Evan put his hand on her stomach, a gesture meant to divert her attention from the ceiling back to him.

"Paradoxes of profession," Evan said. "What is it this time?"

"There's no direct evidence yet, but I'm pretty sure I'll get it soon. Brenda is behind this. She's a clever young woman, and she can be vicious sometimes."

"How come that there is no evidence? The guy was raped, was he?"

"He was. But there wasn't a trace of a struggle. There was nothing material found: no sperm, not a single pubic hair, no fingerprints. Nothing. But I know for sure what and how it happened. It won't be the first time that my conjectured crime turns out to be almost identical to what really happened. In my profession, once you have an exact picture of what happened and who the players of the drama were, you eventually nail them down."

"That's a prelude, darling." Evan kissed her elbow. "What's the essence?"

"The essence is that I like Brenda. The more evidence I find, the more I like her."

"Sounds like a case of revenge. What about the victims?"

"It's tricky. They deserve compassion, but they also deserve punishment. Brenda is clever. Indicting her would open Pandora's box. There would be more than a few people dragged into it who would be both victims and criminals."

Evan chuckled. "That would be fun, wouldn't it?" He put his palm on her cheek and gently turned her face toward him. "That's how it happens in nature, and more so in social life: one event triggers another, starting a chain reaction. The result is a strong disturbance that is hard to quiet down."

"Nice observation, Evan, though it doesn't make my choices easier. So far, the guys who committed the crime, the ones who gang raped Brenda and posted pictures of themselves doing it are, in many ways, different people now. They have professions, families. If I put them in prison, their lives, the lives of their kids, wives, and even parents, would be destroyed." She turned on her right side, facing Evan. "Sometimes I don't think I'm not cut out to be a homicide detective? Is it because I'm a

132

woman? It's not easy to do a good job when it causes so many tragedies."

"I think it's because you are a thoughtful, intelligent, complicated human being, capable of seeing not just the skeletons and flesh of everyone involved, but also their characters, and maybe their souls. And that's doing your duty, isn't it?" Evan asked.

"It is. However, if I were sure that Brenda would stop now, I'd find the way to just close this case. Too many people are involved, you know? I can smell it. It's not something that I have to do by the book, but sometimes we face terrible dilemmas. The concept of justice doesn't always help us know the right way to act. However, all other ways are against the law, at least in theory. Are we supposed to serve humanity, or the justice system? Your thoughts, my dear philosopher?"

"The first thing that comes to my mind is the conversation between Krishna and Arjuna. Indian philosophers have always fascinated me with their attitudes, and this is just one example. Arjuna, being of the warrior caste, had to fight against his cousins and kill them. Not an easy mission for a good person, which Arjuna was. Krishna convinced him to fight. His argument was that there was no good or bad for the one who was merely doing his duty. I think it make sense. Otherwise any job description would be meaningless, and execution of duties would be up to the interpretation of individuals."

"Sounds very smart on the surface, but not when on second thought," Melissa said, after a short pause. "I'm not a follower of any Indian philosophy. I'm a Christian. I believe that there is a superior judge, and we supposed to know his moral values, and these must guide us through our lives. Take, for instance, war criminals, or Nazi criminals. Many claimed that they could not be held responsible for the atrocities of their superior officers, as they were just following orders and executing their duties. In some cases, that was true, you know?" Melissa turned to her side and looked into Evan's eyes. "But they pulled the trigger. They flipped the switches. They herded people like cattle. They took part in crimes against humanity," she continued. "They knew that what they were doing was participating in the crime of murder. They—"

"What nonsense you are talking about?" Even sat upright on the bed. "Your job is to fight against crime."

"I'm not comparing my job with theirs. Don't take me wrong," Melissa said calmly. "I just extrapolated your argument to its absurdity. My point is, sometimes your conscience elevates your mind above considerations of duty. The easiest way to live is just to dismiss them."

"Hmmm, that's worth thinking about," Evan said. "Different dimension of reality. But quitting the job is not the solution."

"Frankly, I don't want to see Brenda in a high-security prison again. However, her nickname speaks to her character. When a wolverine hunts, nothing can stop it except death."

Evan lay back and rested his head on pillows.

"If you have sympathy for her, that means she has fine human qualities. You probably appreciate them more than the law permits you to consider. From the outside, you look like an iron lady. Inside, though, your humanity is your greatest weakness—if you can call it that. I happen to think it's a virtue. But maybe this Brenda has some weaknesses too. Find them, and use them to settle things."

Melissa kissed him on the lips and gave him a long, loving and meaningful look.

"Love you," she said. "Good night, darling."

Chapter 19

At lunchtime, Brenda started the coffee brewing and made herself a sandwich. When she settled at her desk, the door to her office opened and, without knocking, Max came in.

"Go ahead with your lunch," he said, and sat in a chair. He looked smug and relaxed, a familiar sign that he knew something important and was ready to act. "Finding Bob was easy." He leaned back and crossed his legs.

An invisible hand tightened on Brenda's throat. She put her sandwich aside and reached toward the coffee machine.

"Want some?" she asked, hiding her face. Lately she had been seriously considering dropping her plan of revenge and living in peace. So far, the tormenting memories had driven her more pacific emotions away, but it was a struggle. Which, she wondered, was worse to live with? Having her life ruined by a pack of heartless beasts...or ruining her own by becoming as heartless as they?

"Sure. I'd love to." Without turning back, she felt Max's stare. "You know, Max, I've been thinking a lot about what we...about what I'm doing. I love you. So, it's weird, but the better we live, the less I want to risk losing every—

"It's not much risk," Max said, interrupting.

"But it is, it is!" she insisted. "Bob's strange. You never know what kind of idea will strike him after we do him."

He took a cup of steaming coffee from her and savoured the first sip.

"I read your mind before you even said it out loud."
His countenance exuded confidence and strength. "I
thought it over for you. We won't touch him, okay? But
we'll make him live in fear for the rest of his life. Like
it?"

"Not bad. How?"

"Everything is set. My guys found him. I know where
he lives and where he works. It'll be simple. He rents a
basement in a private house. His car is always in the
driveway. He goes out at about 8:30 in the morning every
weekday and drives to work. We'll go to his place and
wait. Of course, you need to recognize him, just to make
sure it's the right Bob, although I'm 100 percent sure it is.
He'll drive to work and park his car about a hundred
meters from his office building. That will give you a
second chance to make sure there's no mistake."

"And then?"

Max laughed. "You're gonna love this."

* * *

For driving to Hamilton, Max chose his sparkling
Harley-Davidson. He and Brenda put on helmets with
face-protecting shields. Brenda sat behind Max and,
holding tight his strong torso, enjoyed the fast ride. The
morning was fresh, a bit on a chilly side, and bright.
Streets and roads were bustling with cars and people. A
busy daily life, with its routine succession of problems,
solutions, frustrations, and successes had begun. When
they arrived at the small parking lot between two rows of
town homes, two of Max's friends were waiting for them.
Both rode Harley-Davidsons, and sported club insignia,
bandanas, and long hair, leaving no doubt about their
status as outlaw bikers. Their proud postures and heavy
stares suggested the tough confidence of gangsters.

Max brought his bike to an abrupt stop, and shook
hands with them. He introduced Brenda as his ol' lady,
and they nodded to her with respect.

"This is the house," one of them said. "See that car, the old GM?" He pointed. "He should be out soon."

Brenda remained seated on the bike, still wearing her helmet with its protective shield down. It would be impossible to see her face through it. She observed the street while the bikers exchanged jokes in their peculiar jargon.

A woman with two kids went out of her house. When she noticed the bikers, fear sparkled in her eyes. She pushed her kids into her car and drove away.

A man came out of another house. His reaction was the same. He hurried into his car and left, eyeing them fearfully in his rearview mirror.

At exactly 8:30 a.m., Bob came out. Brenda recognized him at once. His cheeks had become puffier, his hair longer, and he had different glasses, but it was Bob. He stopped at his car and unlocked its door, and at that moment noticed the group of bikers. His stare lingered over the group, and then stopped on Brenda. He couldn't see her face behind the shield, but he could guess, Brenda thought. All the bikers looked back at him insolently. It must have been obvious to Bob that their menacing looks were meant for him, as he dove into his car, started it, and sped away. All three bikers followed Bob's car at a short distance.

Half an hour later, Bob pulled into a parking lot, but at the bikers passed him, heading for the office building entrance and stopped. Max got off his bike and said, "Wait here. I'll come soon."

Brenda followed him with her stare. Max confronted Bob halfway from the parking lot. He said something, and then pulled a cigarette out of the pack. Bob flicked his lighter for Max. Max said to him something else and began smoking. He was clearly not listening to whatever Bob was saying. Bob shrugged and began walking toward the building. Max followed him, a few paces behind.

137

When Bob was close enough, Brenda took off her helmet. Bob looked at her, met her eyes, and started to shake.

A dense flow of people streamed into the building. The passersby threw curious glances at the bikers and at Bob. Indeed, the scene was unusual: gang members, sinister with their outfits and insignia, talking to an office worker. Bob was about to say something, but then thought better of it, sped up his pace, and entered the building. Max turned back to Brenda.

"Happy reunion," he said with a rough guffaw. "He'll spend the rest of the day in a toilet."

"I think his friends at the office will be asking him a few questions," Brenda said. "After all, it doesn't happen every day when a biker gang engages you in conversation, right?"

Max hopped on his bike and turned the key. All three bikes moved with a growl of powerful engines. On the way home, the other two bikers peeled off and went their separate way, and Max drove Brenda to her office. He stopped by the rear door.

Brenda took off her helmet and climbed off the bike. "What did you say to him?" she asked.

Max chuckled. "Nothing fancy. First, I asked if he was Bob. He said yes, scared, like a rabbit. Then I asked him if he had a lighter. His hands were shaking, all right. He was blubbering. 'Who are you? What do you want? Why are you following me?' and stuff like that. I promised I'd see him again soon. That's all." After a short pause, Max said, "Come here."

She did. He took her by her waist and kissed her. Looking intensely into her eyes, he said, "Trust me, we scared the shit out of him. He'll spend the next few years always looking over his shoulder. You won't find anyone who's not dead scared of a biker gang. For sure, he won't go to police. You can take him off your mind."

She returned him the kiss.

"I won't be late tonight," she said. She began walking toward the building, feeling his eyes on her. She opened the door and looked back. When their eyes met, she said, "Love you, Max."

He started his bike after Brenda went inside.

Chapter 20

Brenda's case file was not as voluminous as Melissa had expected. Her criminal behavior was well documented: she had assaulted Christian with a frying pan at Lucas's house; she had assaulted Lucas with a kitchen knife, cutting his arm enough that he required stitches; she had issued threats in court and after, when she was in the federal prison. Evidence of physical violence and witnesses' testimonials, as well as Brenda's own testimony, confirmed without reasonable doubt that she had committed the violent crimes. Obviously, the conclusion that she could be dangerous was justified, especially in the context of her threats to down hunt four people: Yona, Lucas, Christian, and Bob, the guy who had taken pictures of her rape. What she meant by "hunt," and what she intended to do when she found them was open for speculation. Melissa read every page of the case, giving her usual close attention to the details.

The prosecutor's name was Pamela Salazar. She was, no doubt, a professional with good experience, knowledge, and sound judgment. The judge was Adam Price. Melissa had never met him. She knew, however, that he was a man of good reputation. The hearing had been without a jury. That was set up with Brenda's consent, perhaps it was even her choice.

Brenda was not on bond before the trial. There was no one to put up the money for a bond on her anyway, as her mother had died very soon after Brenda's arrest, and there were no other relatives. But even if there had been, the state demanded that she be kept in jail until the trial, as Brenda was, they said dangerous a criminal to release on her own, and a risk for society outside the jail gates. The judge agreed. The subsequent court proceedings confirmed the rightness of that decision: when the court was adjourned prior to the verdict, Brenda pointed in the direction of Yona, Christian, Lucas, and Bob, and yelled, "I'll hunt you 'til the last day of your fucking lives. You won't find a safe place on earth."

Well, that's as far as the proof of her guilt was concerned. A remarkable contrast was the absence of facts pertinent to her rape. The prosecutor said that Brenda had been seen having sex with some of the witnesses, which was obviously consensual, and that she had been drinking and most likely under influence of illegal drugs. Such behaviour of Brenda and her sex partners was in the domain of morality, the prosecutor said, not a criminal issue, and therefore should not be a subject of discussion in the court.

In her conclusion, Pamela Salazar said, "It is clear now how dangerous this criminal is. After being seen having sex with her schoolmates, she accused them of rape. Very convenient to justify her immoral behaviour. Then she assaulted them with intention to kill. As if that's not enough, she threatened their lives in this very court. I have no doubt that she means it, and likely will try to carry out her threats after her prison time. She is dangerous, and must be isolated from society."

Right you are, Melissa thought. However, how acceptable would your arguments be had you told the truth about Brenda's brutal rape? She obviously was raped. Why, madam, did you not mention the degrading photographs of her rape that were floating around on the Internet? Was it that not a hideous crime? How is that no one investigated the rape, the beating afterward, the pictures? How could that the eighteen-year-old girl, with no one standing by her, be so badly treated by the so-called justice system?

The judge, His Honour Adam Price, in his final speech, expressed anger with Brenda. As he stated, not only had she threatened witnesses in the court, which by itself was a criminal offence, but by the virtue of her behaviour had not admitted her guilt or remorse. The most despicable part, in his opinion, was Brenda's attempt to justify her criminal acts by accusing the witnesses, all boys of good character and from fine families, of wrongdoing.

According to court records, Brenda interrupted him, shouting "dumb asshole!" and other names, for which she was held in contempt by the judge.

Now the fun begins. Melissa gathered as much information as she could about Pamela Salazar and Adam Price. There was a limit, though, to what she could get, as she could use only open sources. Still, there were many bits and pieces that a sharp mind could collect and put together to assemble them into the mosaic of a real picture.

Just to make sure that she was on a right track, Melissa drove through the neighbourhood where Pamela Salazar lived. In that upper-middle-class bedroom community, every house had a neatly manicured front lawn, some with flowerbeds, and some with trees and shrubs. Pamela's house was more than three thousand square feet by Melissa's estimates. Decorative stones lay along the pathway to the roofed porch; brown driveway interlock and a cream-painted stucco wall completed the impression of harmony, designed by a professional.

She glanced left and right. The street, with its sharply trimmed evergreen shrubs, perfectly aligned fences and gates, trickling fountains, and formal statuary, seemed surrealistically lonely and uninhibited.

Melissa drove home, smiling at her own thoughts. Over the next few days, she gathered up information about the prosecutor and the judge's family members, their overlapping connections, and particularly about their finances. This took some effort, as no judge would grant her access to private information without solid reason, but there was a lot to be found in public records. Melissa had

142

no intention of alerting anyone that she was looking into their backgrounds, however. She had a different plan in mind.

After weighing all the pro and con considerations, Melissa opted to start with Pamela. She dialled her phone number; after the second beep they were connected.

"Pamela Salazar," came the businesslike response. The voice was calm, confident, with ominous notes in it—the manner in which people of power speak.

"Good day, Pamela," Melissa said, and introduced herself. She tried to induce a friendly smile in her tone when she said, "I'm a special unit investigator from Toronto. How are you?"

There was a moment of static noise. "Oh, hi," Pamela said, with the same friendly manner. "What can I do for you?"

"Would you mind meeting with me? Perhaps today, if at all possible?"

"I'm busy most of the day." Pamela did not sound very confident. "Something urgent?"

Melissa smiled again. "I'm flexible. I can meet you after your round at the golf club. Just a few minutes to chat."

Pamela cleared her throat at the other end of the line. Melissa read her mind. Obviously Pamela was not pleased that Melissa knew when and where her golf game was. If Melissa were in her shoes, she would try to find answers for herself to few unpleasant questions, like why there was an investigator so interested in her that she knew her golf schedule. To know that, the investigator would have had to contact the club. That meant that she was likely to have the list of members of the club. And a lot, lot more. As a professional, Pamela would assume that the investigator was very well prepared for their "chat."

"Ah, sure, after the game," Pamela agreed. "Is six o'clock okay?"

"Yes." To add some more poison to Pamela's mood, she added: "There's a nice veranda at your club house. Let's chat there over coffee."

There was no need for two professionals to let each other know what to look for. They recognized each other the moment Pamela appeared on a huge patio. Melissa was already there, sitting with a cup of coffee at a table in the far corner, bordering the lawn, where it was unlikely that anyone could eavesdrop on their conversation.

Pamela approached with a broad, almost sincere smile, and stretched her hand over for a handshake.

"Good afternoon, Melissa." Pamela settled across the table, and dropped her bag on the ground. "What brings you here?"

Pamela's countenance was almost what Melissa expected it to be. Close to fifty, her face was tanned, wrinkled from the sun, probably from so much time spent on the golf course or vacationing. Otherwise, she looked healthy and in a good shape, with a slim, strongly built figure; bleached, short-cropped blond hair; blue, cold eyes; and thin lips. On her forehead she wore a bandana, as people do to absorb sweat.

"I need your help to clarify a few things." Saying that, Melissa noticed a sparkle of concern in Pamela's eyes. She must have connected a few dots during the day: Melissa was investigating the death of Lucas and had already talked to Gary; Gary was a member of the Pamela's club; the Lucas case, in all probability, had something to do with Brenda's case, in which she had been the prosecutor.

"Sure. Something to do with Brenda? Gary told me about your visit to him. Terrible tragedy, isn't it?"

So, Pamela has decided not to play stupid games. Good for her.

"Right." Melissa sipped her coffee, letting Pamela fill the silence.

144

"Looks like Brenda is behind it, don't you think so?" Pamela was quick to ask, directing the meeting onto the track of a friendly discussion between professionals. Melissa didn't mind. "Looks like it," she agreed. "So far, no other theories make much sense."

"Do you have any evidence against her?" Pamela asked.

"In terms of material evidence, no. Nothing on the scene. And it was a suicide. No one slit his wrists for him. The only consideration is Brenda's possible motive. I'm thinking maybe revenge. As you were the prosecutor in her case, I thought you might help me with that."

Pamela put up a mask of an impassive diplomat, but Melissa was sure that she did not like at all where the conversation seemed to be heading.

"At the court, she threatened the witnesses, saying she would 'hunt them until the rest of their lives.' This is the material evidence."

"That is hardly enough to make a case," said Melissa, in a tone that added as you well know. "And that is not a motive to commit a crime, only a threat. So if she was involved, what would be her motive?"

"That is the motive. She was in prison because of the witnesses testimonies."

Melissa took a sip of coffee, to swallow a lump of brewing anger. "No. She was raped by three of those four boys, while the other took pictures. That's why she threatened them. You know that, don't you?"

Pamela forgot for a second that she had no authority over Melissa. She moved her shoulders back and looked at Melissa with menacing anger of a prosecutor.

"I know she said in court that she was raped. But Brenda Rorke had consensual intercourse with those boys. When she found out that it was no longer a secret, she accused them of rape."

This was not the first time in Melissa's experience when she'd encountered a person in the legal profession who, while being questioned, behaved as stupidly as an inexperienced criminal. Usually it happened when they had no clue how much Melissa already knew, and what it was possible to keep hidden. In any case, the ones being questioned didn't know Melissa's strategy and tactics, so it was difficult for them to avoid making mistakes or looking stupid.

"There were witnesses to the rape. You knew that, and yet you didn't prosecute the criminals. Instead, you made them witnesses."

Pamela tightened her lips. "I dealt with the material of investigation. There was nothing about the rape."

Melissa gave her a look that would have frightened even a hardened criminal. "There was. Brenda offered you the evidence. Sury, her friend, was willing to testify."

"It was a long time ago. I've had hundreds of cases since then. I don't remember the details. What's your point, Melissa?"

Melissa ignored the question.

"I'll remind you of the details. The boys who raped her also took obscene pictures of the rape. They blurred their faces out, leaving Brenda's face clearly recognizable view, and put the pictures online on Facebook."

"I never saw any photos. I don't know what you're talking about. Probably it was Brenda's fantasy."

That was a huge mistake. It didn't matter, though. Mistake or not, Pamela was in a tough corner, but still hoping to find a way out of it.

"Wrong again. Her friend printed the screen images—they show the dates, times, everything—and saved them on her computer. True, the pictures were only on Facebook for two days. Someone gave these boys good advice to take them down. You do know that nothing ever really disappears from the Internet, though, don't you? As it happens, I have copies of those images with me right now. Do you wish to see them?"

146

Pamela shrugged. "Again, what's your point, Melissa?" she asked in a tone that now lacked any self-confidence.

"As a prosecutor, you knew how despicable it was to put up pictures like that on the Internet. How a teenage girl would take it, knowing those pictures up there for everyone to see? I think she'd see it as the end of her life. These boys should've been in prison...but they were just 'witnesses.' You knew it, and the judge, Adam Price, knew it, too."

Pamela's hands began trembling. She hid them under the table.

"What's your point, Melissa?" she repeated a third, this time in a weak voice.

"With the proliferation of cell phones equipped with photo cameras, handy in all occasions, this type of crime gets more and more popular among youth in many countries. You know that, don't you? They rape a girl, photograph the scene, and then threaten to put the photographs on social networks if she goes to the police. For most girls, that notoriety is as great or an even greater horror than the rape, and worse than having to sit in court and talk about the rape. The shame, Pamela. They're made to feel ashamed, though they are the victims. In many cases, if the rape case even makes it to court—which far too often it does not—the lawyers turn things around and present the pictures as evidence of consensual sex, and accuse the girl of lying. So she's a victim all over again: raped, shamed, and made out to be a liar. But you know all that."

Pamela cast her eyes down. She was close to defeat, but not quite there yet. Melissa took another sip of her now-cold coffee. Then she went in for the kill.

"You have son and daughter, Pamela. Right?"

Pamela raised her eyes, which were filled with suspicion and fear. "Yes."

"Your son graduated from a private school. How's he doing?"

Pamela's cheeks got pale. "Do you mind if I fetch a cup of coffee?" she asked. "I'll be right back."

"Sure, sure," Melissa said, with friendly warmth in her voice. She did not expect Pamela back soon. She would likely make a few calls under the pretence of buying coffee. Let her.

Melissa watched the people around her on the veranda. Most of them were middle-aged or younger, with money and a high place on the social ladder. They had no idea of the drama that was unfolding with one of their club members right now.

Pamela came back ten minutes later. Her face was grim. "Sorry, there was a line."

Melissa was fairly certain there had been no line, but she nodded. "No problem. How many years did your son attend the private school?" Melissa was relentless. Melissa was sure that Pamela was getting the message: Private school is expensive. You have two kids and a sick husband. You do not have sufficient income to afford the private school.

"Three years," Pamela said, taking two nervous sips from her coffee cup. "We had to cut back on many things for his education."

"Yes, sometimes sacrifices are necessary," Melissa agreed, making it a point to look slowly around the veranda and out at the golf course. "I understand. I also have a kid."

"How old is he?" Pamela asked, relieved to have a break from the stressful "chat."

"Seven."

"Will you send him to a private school?"

"Not sure," Melissa said. A flicker of hope began glowing in Pamela's pale blue eyes. But it was extinguished when Melissa added, "You have a very nice house."

Pamela did not respond with words. She stared at Melissa, no longer hiding her hatred and fear. After a short pause, she said, "It doesn't mean anything."

"Maybe not. As long as it has no link to Gary. In spite of complicated accounting and hidden cost, I'm sure I will be able to prove that Gary did substantial financial favours for you and Adam Price. Actually, I won't need to work very hard. I'll just ask Gary to confess that he bribed you and the judge to save his son from a rape charge and prison."

"You sure you could?" Pamela's lips hardly moved.

"Yes, I'm sure. And I'm sure that I can make you and Adam confess as well. I suspect that you'd all rather make a deal with me than trigger a full investigation. Don't you?"

Pamela turned her face toward the links. She didn't cry, but the rims of her eyes reddened. Melissa did not interrupt the woman's silent conversation with herself.

"It would be a disaster for many, many people, Melissa. And what would it accomplish? Lucas committed suicide, you know. There's nothing we can about it."

"What do you suggest?"

"You know, Gary is a big developer, very well off. There are ways, you know…"

Melissa interrupted her with a laugh. She was tempted to say that she inherited enough money to afford anything, but thought better of it.

"Any suggestions other than trying to buy me off, too?" she asked icily.

"Can't you just arrest Brenda Rorke? After all, she is dangerous. There is circumstantial evidence that—"

Melissa again interrupted her. "Consider this. She is no longer a helpless child with no one on her side. Toronto is a different city; it's not your town. No judge will give you any favours there, and no one would accept ambiguous threats or slanderous comments about her character as grounds for her arrest. You know that, don't you? There is nothing, literally nothing, that we have that would allow us to lay charges against her. There is also another, very significant consideration. She has connections with a criminal organization. Let's say that they commit crimes, not her. They have lawyers, money, connections of their own, and all manner of resources. If, by chance, we found any evidence or witness against them, then a full-blown court hearing would be unavoidable. That's when all hell will break loose around you, and rain down on anyone connected to Brenda's rape."

Pamela's eyes got red.

"These boys are different people already," Pamela mumbled. "They're young men with educations, professions, families. Kids. There are so many lives that would be ruined! Isn't there any way to settle this?"

"If I close the Lucas case, there are still others out there. I agree that she is obsessed, and dangerous, and that she considers that since the rape and the pictures on the Internet, she has no future worth worrying about. Unless…"

"Unless what?" Hope flickered again in Pamela's eyes.

"Never mind."

"What do you want from me?"

"Cooperation. I'm going to try something, but it may not work. If it doesn't, then we can all expect the worst. Then you'll have to cooperate with me, no matter how painful it may be."

Pamela gave her a long look and slowly nodded in consent.

"What's on your mind, Melissa?" she asked in a rather submissive tone.

The veranda was filling up with golfers. "Let's discuss it next time we meet." Melissa stood up, and so did Pamela. "I'll contact you."

150

That was all. Melissa did not say a polite "good-bye." She did not offer her hand for a farewell shake. She knew that Pamela would understand her meaning: investigators do not shake hands with criminals. Melissa picked up her bag and left, feeling Pamela's stare on her back.

Chapter 21

The aroma coffee began its luscious spread through the kitchen as Melissa poured her first cup of the day. Her phone vibrated, and she pulled it from her pocket to see the icon that indicated a new text message. Since the breakfast hour was a sacred time for her family, her first impulse was to ignore it. After all, lately there had been many urgent matters that eventually turned out to be not that urgent after all. When she noticed that it was from Larry, however, she retrieved it. It said, "Jonathan-Yona in hospital, bullet wound. I arranged a private room for him."

"Damn it," she said.

Evan, who sat at the breakfast table with his cup of coffee, chuckled. He looked at her with loving, understanding eyes.

"See you later?" he asked.

"I'm afraid, so, yes. You'll have to take Nick to school."

"Of course. Another homicide?"

"Not exactly. But related. I've got to rush." She added, "This job! No private life."

Evan stood up and kissed her. "You enjoy it. It's your vocation. Don't complain; you were born for this."

"I have the second thoughts about that. Anyway, I love you, my oh-so-understanding husband." She returned his kiss and dialled Larry's number as she headed to the bedroom. He picked up at the first beep.

"Hi, Melissa," he greeted her before she uttered a sound. "Our friend Yona is in hospital. Bullet wound in the left thigh. I think he'd love to speak with us."

"You bet. Which hospital? Oh, I see. And you're already at the hospital? Good. I'll be there soon."

With quick, but well-coordinated movements, she dressed, picked up her things, went to her car, and drove through the dense morning traffic. While manoeuvring through the rush hour mess, she tried to guess what could have happened. According to police files, Yona had no criminal record, although since he was a member of a bikers gang, crime was undoubtedly a way of life for him. As his gang was dealing with narcotics, he was almost certainly involved in the gang's drug deals. He was an anomaly, though. Usually outlaw bikers do not become criminals in an instant. They begin with petty crimes in childhood, and continue into their adolescent years. By the time of their adulthood, they are usually well known by the police, and may even have spent some time in jail or prison. Not Yona. Not much was known about him. He had studied economics in college, but dropped out after his second year. He didn't own any property. Not much to go on so far.

Now he had a bullet wound, the first serious grounds for the police to dig out more information about him.

Larry met her at the entrance to the hospital. They walked a few steps away, to distance themselves from any listening. "He came in with a nine-mil slug in his leg," he began. "It happened close to midnight, near The Rooster. Quite a place, I tell you. We found a gun on the road not far from the bar. No valid prints on it, maybe because there was hell of a lot of rain, may be some other reason, but the gun had been fired."

"Any idea whose gun it might be?" Melissa asked.

"Hard to say." Larry raised his right brow. "There was a shootout at the bar. Two shots fired, according to the neighbours. The sounds of shots were mixed with the roar of a powerful bike. Yona came to the hospital on his bike, and told the responding officer—you know, hospitals immediately red flag all gunshot cases—that he had no idea who shot at him. BS."

"Anything illegal on him?"

153

"Nothing. He's too smart to bring anything to the hospital. I'm surprised he went in at all. Usually these guys just do their own amateur surgery, but he was losing a lot of blood, and apparently he was about to die. Coming in probably did save his life."

"Nobody else came in with bullet wounds?" Melissa asked.

"Nope. Regretfully." He grinned.

"Stop it." Melissa frowned.

"I mean, it would've been easier to make them spill the bins," Larry said, justifying his cynicism.

"We have other ways." Melissa paused, looking through Larry and thinking. Has Brenda had something to do with it? If so, the matter would spill far beyond her personal vendetta. One shooting would follow the other, and eventually an innocent bystander would be hit. In any case, shooting and deaths, even among criminals, was not good. Too many complications, and something to be averted at all costs.

Larry shook his head. He led the way through long corridors, where visitors and medical personnel hurried back and forth, their faces reflecting the absorption of their purposes and thoughts. Larry stopped at a blue curtain hung in the opening.

"Here," he said, and slid the curtain to the left. Melissa stepped into a room with one hospital bed, on which Yona lay. His long hair was in disarray. He was fairly handsome, with a longish face, very white skin, nicely formed lips, and a heavy chin that gave an impression of strong character. His large blue eyes left no doubt that he was a gangster. They exuded that peculiar image of menace that distinguishes people who live in danger and defy it. He must have felt really bad, perhaps on the verge of passing out, while driving himself to the hospital. When he saw Melissa and Larry, he did not

154

blink, but as far as Melissa could tell, he understood who they were.

She introduced herself and Larry, flashed her badge, and settled on a small plastic chair, facing Yona. He watched her with hateful eyes, and rolled them from her to Larry and back. Melissa noticed that he had no tubes attached to his veins, and no oxygen lines over his face. His left leg was wrapped in a thick bandage.

"Police already talked to me," he said. "What else do you want to know?"

"How do you feel?" Melissa asked. His lips curled down in a contemptuous smirk.

"Better. What do you want?"

"We want to know what happened. Do you know who shot at you?"

"No idea. I was driving home. There was no one on the street. All of a sudden I heard a shot. The bullet hit my thigh, and I almost lost control. I drove to the closest hospital, to the ER, and passed out. That's all." He directed his stare to the ceiling.

"From where were you going home?" Larry asked.

"From a bar."

"What bar?"

"The Rooster." After a short pause, he added. "The barman knows me. He can confirm."

The guy was on defensive, Melissa noticed. He had no experience dealing with investigations. He had long way to go.

"Right. Did you have a row with anyone there? Perhaps an enemy of yours showed up?" she asked.

"No. I have no enemies. Everything was okay."

"Maybe you had a bitter enemy in your distant past?" Melissa asked. "After all, this looks like an obvious attempt to kill you. It didn't happen in the bar or the parking, where a fight might start on the spur of the moment. It happened on the street, where only you and your attacker were."

155

"No, I don't think so. I told you, I have no enemies."

"We found a gun at the scene," Larry said. "Is it yours?"

Yona, it seemed, was prepared for the question. He kept staring at the ceiling, as if his life continued to be as boring as it was for anyone else in the hospital.

"No. You think I had shot myself?"

"No. But the gun had been fired. Only one bullet was missing from the magazine. There were two shots fired."

"Perhaps there were two guys firing at each other, and I got in the way. How am I supposed to know?"

"We'll find out soon," Larry said. "After we receive a report on fingerprints."

Yona remained unperturbed. If he'd worn gloves, which made sense for a premeditated assault, then he wouldn't be worried about fingerprints. Of course, many bikers wore gloves routinely, so it could still have been self-defence.

"Do you suspect me of something?" Yona asked with a contemptuous sneer. "If so, I'd like to have a lawyer before I talk to you about whatever it is."

"As it stands at the moment, you're the victim of a crime, and a witness. We'd like you to tell us as much as you remember."

"If I'm a victim or a witness, why did you ask me about the gun?" He watched Melissa with glowing hatred in his eyes.

"Exactly because of that," she answered calmly. "You were shot at. You may know important details that would lead us to who shot at you."

"That's all I can tell." He turned his attention back to the ceiling. "Now, get the hell out of here. I'm tired. I wanna rest." To make a point, he closed his eyes.

"I have one question, related to your past. Nothing to do with this shooting," Melissa said. Yona remained silent, his eyes closed. "You remember Brenda, don't you? The girl you and your friends raped five years ago?"

Yona opened his eyes and shifted them from Melissa to Larry. "We didn't rape her," he said. "She was a slut. Anybody could have her, anybody who wanted."

"Who put the photographs of the rape up on the Internet?"

"That was Bob, the guy who took pictures. Son of a bitch, no one asked him to do that."

"No one? We have different information. We have evidence that you organized the rape, and that you and Bob displayed the photographs. So far as Brenda being a slut, we know that to be a lie."

"What's this all about?" Yona raised his voice. "Are you investigating a shooting, or reopening some old stupid shit? I don't give a fuck about that whore, and no one else will either. Get the fuck out of here."

"Watch your mouth," Larry said in a tone that could frighten a tiger. "It takes almost nothing for me to take you to the police station. You could enjoy our hospitality there for quite a long time while I find new reasons to hold you."

Yona gave him a long, hateful, and defiant look, but said nothing. Melissa leaned toward him and asked in a very calm, quiet voice, in a way that sounded almost like a confidential talk between her and Yona: "Have you seen or heard of her lately?"

"No," he said curtly.

"Have you talked with any of your old friends lately? Lucas? Christian? Bob?"

"No. I have no idea where any of them are, and I don't give a damn."

"When Brenda threatened to hunt you and your friends for the rest of her life, did you take her threat seriously?"

"No. She's just a stupid chick. I don't give a shit what the slut said."

"You don't," Melissa repeated, as if agreeing with him, and paused.

157

"Why do you ask?" Yona said, showing a genuine interest in the conversation the first time.

"Because I'm thinking that this shooting has something to do with your past. We know that the gun is yours. We know you fired it. We can reopen the Brenda's case at any time, and this time, you won't get off. I know that it's useless to tell you that. I have little chance of convincing you that it's in your best interest to cooperate with us. But you'll learn it eventually. The hard way"

Yona looked again at the ceiling, and whispered: "Fuck you all." He closed his eyes.

"We'll meet soon," Larry said. "Trust me, joker."

Melissa stood out and left the room. Larry followed her.

"Do you think it was your pet Wolverine?" he asked.

"Not her personally, but maybe her biker friend."

"We can arrange an indictment," Larry remarked, angling his head to indicate Yona.

"I know. Let's wait. A lot will be clear soon."

"What do you mean?" Larry asked.

"We'll see. Surprising as it seems, we have no material evidence so far against Brenda. We have no incentive to reopen her case regarding the rape. Does she want it? You know the answer. She does not. Even if we push it, she won't cooperate. It may... Never mind. You know, what I mean."

"What do you want to do next?" he asked.

"Work," she said, avoiding the direct answer.

Chapter 22

Brenda's one-room office was on the eighth floor. Its large window let in a flood of light on a sunny day, and offered a tall building's urban scenery of the street below. It accommodated a desk, a file cabinet, a small shelf for binders or books, two easy chairs for clients, and a small table with a coffee machine and supplies. There was little space to move about, but she didn't want to spend money on a larger office for a business that had barely started. "This is crazy," she told Max, when she deposited payments for the first and last month of the lease. "We'll lose money if the business doesn't pick up." But Max was unperturbed.

"I'll get you lots of clients. I know a lot of guys who have legit businesses and need bookkeepers, especially honest ones they know they can trust. They, and their people, need help filing personal income taxes, which you know how to do. You even know how to do business income taxes, right? You'll have plenty of work, trust me."

He was right. The success, which she had virtually from the start, made her head spin. With the help of a webmaster, she developed a website that, quite unexpectedly, brought in new clients as well. Very soon she had more work than she could handle during normal business hours. She had to spend lots of time during the day on the phone; to catch up with the backlog, she often worked until late evening. Although Max didn't like that last part, Brenda was happy nonetheless. She liked the work, and she liked making money. Sometimes, when she was driving home, she thought about plans for the future. As the daily drive to the rural mobile community became almost impossible, she and Max moved to his house in Toronto. It was not big, but it was cozy and nice inside. The furniture was not expensive, but it had been well selected and was in good condition.

Usually, when she returned home from work, Max was already there, waiting for her. They had supper together, and it became the most enjoyable time of the day for both. Brenda was a good housekeeper and managed to find time for meal preparation and all other household chores. They never had guests in the house: Max did not want anyone to know about the residence.

He was no longer involved in car theft, but he was still busy with something. He never told Brenda what he did, and she never asked questions. Max was clever; he knew what he was doing. Her concern was his health. Something was very wrong with his stomach, but he stubbornly avoided answering any questions in that regard.

Sometimes he dropped by her office, when he happened to be anywhere close. She was always delighted with his visits. They drank coffee, exchanged jokes, and discuss things of common interest.

A week after they had met Bogdan, Max came to her at noon, when she was about to take a lunch break. With a toothy smile on his face, he sat in front of her and asked, "Are you accepting any new clients?" He was in a good mood; she had no doubt about it.

"Is it you?" she asked.

"No. Yona."

She found nothing funny about it.

"Look, Max. We have good life. And it's getting better every day. The more I think about all this...the less I like it. Maybe we can drop it?"

"A friend of mine, a full patch in our club, told me where Yona sells his stuff. He actually doesn't like him or his gang, the one Yona belongs to. My buddy wants to help us, but he has never seen Yona and has no idea what he looks like. There aren't that many secrets in our world, you know. Most of their stuff they sell directly only to those they know personally. But still, they sell in bars, and who knows where else. They don't have a clubhouse; they don't pretend to be big-time bikers. Very secretive, strictly business. Which means that it's not simple to deal with them."

"We are not going to deal with a gang. We're after Yona." Brenda tried to avoid Max's eyes.

"True. But his gang'll back him up in a time of trouble. Anyway, it's on us to locate him. Change your face as much as you can when we go to these bars. After we spot him, the rest won't be difficult."

"Max, like I said, I don't want to kill him."

"Don't be stupid, Brenda. For sure he already knows what happened with Lucas. Soon enough he'll know what happened with Christian. He knows how to add two plus two, right? He'll want to come after you. Besides, now my gang wants to help me. What do I tell them? Thanks but no thanks, we've decided to go legit?"

A chilly wave ran down her spine. She believed that she had thought everything over and knew what she would do in any possible circumstances. But now she was confounded. On the one hand, she still hated the guys who had ruined her life and indirectly caused her mother's death. She would never forgive them, nor would she forget it. The wounds were too deep, and there was only one way to heal them. On the other hand, she couldn't go along with murder. Not just because the danger was enormous—although she did like her new life too much to want to risk it—but because it was wrong. She felt like a traitor to her mother, and to herself as well.

"You don't know for sure where he sells the stuff?" she asked, looking out the window.

"As I said, likely one of three bars. I've been to one of them once, Rooster."

"When did you want to go?"

"Tonight. Why wait? C'mon, cheer up, Brenda. You started it, and now want to chicken out? That's not like you. As I said, I don't want him to be forever behind our backs. Prophylactics, as Bogdan says. You just need to recognize him, point him out. That's all. You don't even need to know what happens afterward."

There was no need to ask what would happen to Yona afterward. Blood began pulsing in her temples.

"Think of your mother. She's in a grave, but Yona doesn't give a shit. He doesn't give a shit about what you went through. He wouldn't give a shit after he kills you."

Brenda cleared her throat. "Okay. Let's go tonight. I'll try my best to change my face, maybe do something different with my hair. I could add some padding, dress like a biker chick. But all this makes me sick in my stomach. What if he recognizes me?"

"I doubt it," Max said. "Lots of time had passed since then. He doesn't expect to see you. You might not even recognize him at first. But even if he does recognize you, he won't do anything right away. We'll just leave the place, that's all. Don't worry, it won't happen. Just make yourself as inconspicuous as you can. Okay?"

One her way home, Brenda stopped at the drugstore and bought a pair of reading glasses, cheap plastic sandals, and a bottle of temporary hair coloring to darken her brown hair, which she pulled back into a thick, messy single braid. At home, she put on a pair of old jeans, one of Max's oversized T-shirts, and aged herself slightly with makeup, adding shadows under her eyes, thinning her cheekbones, and slightly reddening her nose. When she threw on the drugstore reading glasses, and looked like a frowsy factory worker stopping off after her shift for one too many beers. Even she didn't recognize herself. When they were about to walk out, Max stuffed his SIG Sauer under his belt and buttoned up his jacket to cover the gun.

"What's the gun for?" Brenda asked. Max looked into her eyes and said, after a short pause, "Dangerous place, the Rooster. Don't worry, babe. I take it sometimes, just in case. I've never used it." He even kissed her, to make a point. Brenda darted a suspicious glance at him, and went out. Max pressed a remote, and the garage door began its slow slide up.

"Move your car out of the driveway, and park over there, by the curb," he said, and went into the garage, where a small Honda stood.

"Whose car is that?" she asked.

"Ours. For tonight. One-time use only." He climbed into driver's seat and started the car while Brenda moved Nissan to the street. Max backed Honda out, and Brenda got into the passenger seat.

"I'll return it to its legitimate owner tomorrow," he said. Max always resorted to funny expressions when he spoke about stolen cars.

"Okay," Brenda said, observing the interior. "But today you are the legitimate owner of this car. With a gun," she added half-jokingly.

"I brought it just in case. I don't like fighting with tough dummies. It's insurance. Guys get rowdy, you just show them a piece, that's all. It soothes nerves better than any drug. Besides, you've seen it before."

"Hope I don't see it tonight," she said.

"You won't. Now, we'll park in a small lot a block away from the bar. It's free after eight."

The first large drops of rain, carried by wind, began drumming the front window.

"We better hurry," Brenda suggested. "Thunderstorm is coming."

"Yeah," Max agreed. "I'll go to the right. This is the shortest way to the other side of the parking lot. I know this place."

Most of the parking spaces on the lot were vacant. No guard sat in the kiosk. Max pulled in to the place closest

163

to the exit, and they hurried on foot to the bar. The rain was picking up.

The Rooster was already filled with the drone of many conversations and loud music from a jukebox. Max grabbed a chair by the only vacant small table. It was too close to the bar, but there was no other free table.

"Sit here and I'll fetch a couple of beers," Max said and went up to the bartender. Brenda sat and surveyed the place. In the dim light she saw people drinking and laughing in groups of two and three, and a rowdy group standing around a pool table. The patrons were not a pleasant lot; their manner of speaking and laughing showed quite clearly that they were trouble. Max was speaking with a bartender, a man in his thirties, with a round face, puffy cheeks, and a constant, but rather unpleasant smile. Placing two mugs on the counter, he nodded, winked to Max, raised his thumb up, and turned to another client. When Max turned his back on him, the bartender's eyes followed to Brenda and immediately lost interest. Good.

"What did you tell him?" Brenda asked, watching the entrance. She caught a glimpse of a few tall blond guys, who would have fit Yona's description, but none of them was Yona. It might be not be that easy to recognize Yona after all, she thought.

"I asked him if I could buy some weed," Max said. He was also examining people around. His stare lingered briefly on the rowdy group around the pool table, and then he directed his attention back to Brenda.

"What for?" she asked again.

"Yona sells it. It'll give me a chance to look him in the eye, you know? Just to make sure that I know the sucker. There should be no mistake, you know. Very important."

"What did the bartender say?" Brenda propped up her right cheek on her right hand, resting her elbow on the table. It distorted her face, and she thought it would make her even more difficult to recognize.

"He said that he'd give me a sign when the dealer's here."

Brenda had an urge to say "I'm scared," but suppressed the impulse. Max knew her as a tough girl, and liked her that way. She didn't want him to ever see her as weak.

People came and went through the entrance, but none of them looked like Yona. The time dragged on and on, very slowly, in a very stressful and boring way. They bought another round of beers and looked around at the people, the rowdy, deliberately unkempt riffraff, including a plump woman in a very short black dress, one the rear of which was printed "SOFISTICATED. POLITICALLY INDEPENDENT."

Many of the women in the bar were of the sort Brenda had seen in prison: loud, vulgar, fighting for attention. She felt a great distance separating her from those folks. She was no longer one of them. She stood away from them while on parole, and didn't meet them after release, in spite of living with a gangster, or former gangster. Her clients were different, and she had already grown used to their different manners and behaviour. As a former con, though, she thought she understood what was in their heads. They saw any stranger as a potential enemy, someone who might be aggressive for no reason. But anyone who didn't "belong" could be abused without risk, which was also a good open option. These were stupid and dangerous people, and a conflict with any of them could lead to many unpredictable complications.

"I think it's time to go," Brenda said. Max nodded, but the next moment he stood up.

"Hold on. The bartender's signalling." He said it to Brenda, but his attention was directed toward the bar. Brenda followed him gaze, and it stopped on Yona. He stood among people who were around the pool table, and he was watching Max. When he glanced at Brenda, she casually but quickly lifted her beer, hoping the mug covered enough of her face. She couldn't tell if he'd even seen her, let alone recognized her. But he could have seen her long before she noticed him.

She recognized Yona at the first glance. He seemed even taller, with round, powerful shoulders, and a menacing face of a tough guy. He wore a leather suit, and indeed looked like an outlaw, but without insignia.

Yona caught a signal from the bartender and walked up to Max. They exchanged a few words, and then left the bar through the back exit, which also led to the restrooms.

That's how Yona got in, thought Brenda. I would have seen him if he'd come in through the front door.

Tense all over, she listened to the monotonous drone of voices, expecting to hear the short, dry, angry bark of a gunshot. There was none. Max came back and sat in front of her.

"Everything's busted," Brenda said, searching nonchalantly for Yona.

"What do you mean?" Max also looked around.

"Yona saw me."

"You sure? Did he recognize you?"

"I think so. Actually, I'm sure. Where is he?"

"No idea. He sold me some pot. We didn't talk much. He left first, that's it."

"I think we should get out of here. I don't like this place, or the guys over there. I don't see Yona, and I don't like it."

Max took the last sip from the beer mug.

"You're right. We have better things to do tonight. Let's go, and discuss it at home."

They left the bar and went into the wet, chilly night. The street they turned onto was dark, without a single streetlight. There was no traffic, no pedestrian in sight. Oncoming wind threw rain droplets in Brenda's face; she squinted and quickened her pace. She stumbled over a

166

pothole on the road, and would have fallen if not for Max, who grasped her hand and held her up. She cursed, wiping her wet face.

"Watch your step," Max advised.

"I can't see a thing," she said, irritated. "Why's it so fucking dark here? Max, what if he smells something? Would he do something?"

"Don't know."

At that moment, the quietude of the street was torn apart by the growl of a powerful bike. Brenda looked back. A dark figure on a motorcycle, rolling toward her at high speed, triggered a wave of horror in her chest. At that moment, she felt a powerful push. Max pushed her away from him with such force that she fell on the wet, cold asphalt.

The reverberating roar of the engine did not muffle the crack of a gunshot. At the same moment, Brenda saw a flash. Max uttered a choking sound and fell on his knees. In the darkness she saw his arm, stretched in the direction of the running away bike. A shot flashed from Max's gun. The bike made a sudden twist, then another, then wiggled a moment, and then stabilized and quickly disappeared along the twist of the road.

Brenda jumped up and grasped Max's shoulders. He sat in a puddle, holding his chest with both hands. His gun lay beside him.

"Max, Max," she said. "Are you hurt?"

"Take the gun and run to the car. Fast. Pick me up, if there are no police. If there are police, beat it." He stretched out his hand with the keys, and raised his voice. "Now! That way!"

She yanked the keys, picked up the gun, and darted toward the parking lot. It was just half a block away, but she had to cross a pile of debris from a new construction. One shoe slipped off her foot. She picked it up, removed the second shoe and rushed forward. A few steps over the debris made her scream in pain, but then she stepped on a lawn, and then on the paved ground of the parking lot.

Only a few cars were there, their wet roofs glistening in the yellow light of a single lamp. She rushed to the car, threw her shoes and the gun onto the rear seat, turned the key, and moved in reverse. The tires screeched when she stepped on the gas pedal. She crunched the steering wheel to the left. One sharp turn, then another, and one more, and the beams of the car slid over Max, who still sat on the asphalt, leaning back against the wall.

Brenda slammed on the brakes, jumped out, and helped Max into the passenger seat.

"Straight," he commanded, his voice a rasp. Brenda swallowed hard, but her mouth was dry.

"I have to get you to a hospital," she said, shaking all over.

"No," Max said, his voice weak but resolute. "We're going home. I'll show you the shortest way."

"But…" Brenda said. In her peripheral vision she watched Max. He removed his cell phone from his inside pocket and dialled.

"Whom are you calling?" she asked.

"Bogdan," he answered curtly. A second later, when a connection was established, he said into the phone: "Send him right now." There was a short pause. "No, not there. My house. What? No, I'll be there in ten minutes. Fifteen minutes max. Okay." He turned to Brenda. "The surgeon will be there soon. Keep going."

A faint but fast-approaching sound of a siren made her push the pedal gas to the floor.

"Slow down and do as I say." Max was short of breath. "Give me the gun."

"What for?"

"Give me the gun," he repeated. Brenda picked up the gun and gave it to Max. He took it from her hand, rolled the window down, and tossed the gun out into a ditch. "Take the second turn to the left." She did that, touching the brakes. The rear wheels complained, the car wiggled its tail, but the next moment its tires reclaimed their grip with the road. Max was thrown to the door by the force of the sharp turn. He groaned, and then said, "Good girl. Now straight. Yeah. Crazy girl, you've done it. Now move slow, here we have to move quiet, normal. Don't attract any attention."

The police siren was approaching at frightening speed. Brenda was thinking hard and fast. If the police stopped them, it would be the end. She was in a stolen car, with a wounded gangster inside, and he was known as one of the best car thieves. He was carrying drugs. She was a former con, recently released. Yona could be in the hospital as well. Bloody police! Did they know where their car was? At night, in the maze of the city streets, it seemed impossible.

"Don't rush here," Max rasped. "They won't find us. Right turn here. Easy, girl. Ouch. Here we are."

Indeed, their house was a hundred meters ahead. Brenda dropped the speed to a crawl, attempting not to make any noise. When she pulled in on the driveway, Max took the remote from the glove compartment, and pressed the button. The garage door slid up, and Brenda rolled the car inside through the opening. The space brightened in the headlights. Max pressed the remote again, and the door slid down.

The dim garage door lamp stayed lit for a minute. She hoped it wasn't visible from outside. She slipped out from her seat, struggling in the small space between the car and the garage wall. She opened the passenger door and grasped Max under his armpits. He was losing consciousness, breathing with hissing sounds, but still struggling to help her.

"Hold on, Max, hold on," she repeated, over and over again. "Please, darling. Hold on."

Her mind was cold. She felt no fear, no panic, only determination. She was focused on one thing only—save

169

Max. When they passed the door leading from the garage to the house, Max's legs let go. With a strength Brenda didn't know she had, she tightened her grip under his armpits, and hauled him to the dining room. Turning on the bright ceiling lights was out of the question. Although the house had only small windows on that side, she didn't want anyone to be able to see in. She brought a table lamp from the living room, plugged it into an electrical outlet and turned it on. She pulled the shades down.

She looked down at Max, who lay on the floor, his face distorted in a grimace of pain. He had not lost consciousness yet, but his face was pale gray. He seemed about to die. His jacket was unbuttoned and bloody. Blood covered his shirt and pants. His hands were covered in blood, too.

Brenda wasted no time. The first thing to do, she decided, was to remove his clothes and see where the wound was. She pulled his arms out of the jacket sleeves, and tore his shirt in the front. The bloody mess on his right side almost stopped her heart. At that moment, the doorbell rang. She sprang up, shaking all over. Fearing it was the police, she turned off the table lamp and tiptoed to the door that led to the small foyer. She closed it behind her, slipped close to the entrance door, and peeked through the glass pane of the side window. A dark figure stood there. A car was parked on the driveway. The doctor.

She flung the door open. Not saying a word, the tall man came in. She opened the foyer door, rushed to the dining room, and turned the table light on. The man was already behind her, with a huge bag in his right hand. About forty years old, with an athletic figure, a mane of dishevelled hair, and a face wet from rain, he looked grim and angry. He put his bag on the floor with such care that it might have held some fragile treasure. He took off his raincoat and threw it on a chair.

"Help me to get him up on the dining table," he commanded in a voice better suited for a bear. "Hold his legs." With ease he lifted Max and placed him on the dining table. "Bring a pillow," he growled. Brenda darted upstairs, tense as a spring. When she returned with the pillow, the doctor held a syringe in his hand.

"Anaesthetic," he grumbled. "Stay here. You'll assist me."

"Can you save him?" she asked in whisper, watching the needle penetrating Max's vein in his left arm."

"Seems so," he said. "Call me Peter. He has a dipnoous wound, likely from a nine-mil bullet. I think no vital organ was touched. Now all depends on luck and how much blood he lost." Peter gave her two transparent bags filled with liquid. "Hang these from the chandelier," he said, attaching the ends of narrow tubes from the bags to a port in Max's arm. After that he plunged into work, all his attention directed to the Max's wound.

Max was either in a deep sleep or in a coma. It seemed to Brenda that he did not breathe, although she knew that wasn't true, or the surgeon would stop working.

She tried to follow his occasional curt orders with the precision and detachment of a nurse, suppressing all feelings and thoughts. Her life and destiny were in hands of providence and this doctor. She glanced at the surgeon's face from time to time. It showed seriousness, but not worry, and not a trace of anxiety. Why did he come here, risking his professional licence, and perhaps even his freedom? What ties him to the biker gang? And how is it that this whole network exists—these outlaw bikers, Bogdan, and Peter, if that's even really his name?

Peter was moving on to final touches: stitches, salves, and dressings. He wrapped Max's torso with a bandage. When he was done, he went to the sink to wash his hands and instruments. It was nearing dawn.

"I'm sure that everything'll be okay," he said, not looking back at her. "Apparently the shot was at close

171

range. By the way, I saw a police car was cruising around here." He used a piece of paper towel to wipe his hands. "I'll visit him later, in the evening. In case of emergency, call Bogdan; that's what he told me. I'll come as soon as I can. Now, let's get him to the bed. Where's the bedroom?"

"Upstairs."

"Okay." This time Peter did not ask her for help. He picked up Max as a mother picks up a child, and walked with ease through the living room and up the stairs. Not turning the light on, Brenda yanked the blanket off the bed, and Peter placed Max on the white linen. "There you are." She couldn't see his face clearly, but detected a trace of a smile in his voice. "Cheer up. Everything will be hunky-dory."

At that, she had an urge to burst into tears, but held her ground, playing the tough woman.

"Hope so," she said matter-of-factly.

Peter ran downstairs, and then to the dining room, where he quickly picked up his belongings.

"By the way..." Peter paused a second. "I'm sure that he'll be okay. But...you know, anything could happen. If he dies, don't call police. Call Bogdan. You know his number, don't you?"

"Yes." She nodded in confirmation. Peter put two small plastic containers of pills on the table.

"These are pain-killers," he explained, pointing to the first. "He'll need them, I'm sure. These are antibiotics, to fight any infection. Don't worry too much, though. I'm sure everything will be okay. But there is always a chance of complications. If he was in the hospital, he'd be hooked to machines that would measure his pulse, blood pressure, oxygen consumption, you name it. Not to mention nurses and doctors, ready to take care of him any minute. But we have to live with whatever we have. Ciao."

172

He raised his hand in a farewell gesture and rushed out with quick and confident steps. Brenda heard a crank of the starter and a quiet purr of a powerful engine. A few seconds later, a deafening silence settled throughout the house. Brenda turned off the table lamp and ran upstairs to the bedroom where Max lay. In the gray light of a dawn, he looked awful, almost like dead, but his chest heaved in a slow but steady rhythm. Only a few hours before he had been a man of steel—fearless, full of energy, and…and a good lover. Was it worth risking his life over a jerk like Yona? Wouldn't be better just to send a hired gun to finish him off and be done with it?

She lay beside Max, weeping softly. The last time she had shed tears was five years ago, when she lost her mother. Since then her eyes had been dry, in sorrow and in joy. There was nothing worth crying for, she had believed. But now there was a different world and a different life. Max was her first and the only love in her life. As if in attempt to catch up with the lost time, she loved him with all vigour and devotion of youth, when the object of love personifies the beginning and the end of the world, the only source of future and happiness. How stupid it was to risk it, just to avenge five-year-old humiliation at the hands of a thug! Was there any other way? Could she do it alone? Certainly not. Could she leave it as it was? If she knew where it would lead to, perhaps yes. Anyway, right now only one thing matters, she thought. Max must live. She would devote her life to him. After he got his health back, she would work from dawn to dusk, making money for their good life. Max wouldn't need to steal cars, and would leave the gang world. They would travel, have fun, perhaps even have a kid. If he survived, life would be beautiful. It will, yes.

Brenda wiped her tears and looked at Max. His lashes began trembling, and he opened his eyes.

"Max, Max," she whispered, shaking with joy and fear for his life. "How do you feel?"

A weak smile stretched his lips. "Shitty. But alive. Everything okay?"

"Yes, honey. Want something?"

"Water."

Brenda jumped off the bed. "Yes, darling."

She darted downstairs, filled up an empty bottle with water and rushed back. "Here you are. Want a pain-killer?"

"Yes." He took a pill and downed it with a swig. "Everything will be okay, Brenda. Don't worry. Things happen, that's what our life is about."

"I don't want such things ever happen again," Brenda said. "I don't want you ever help me with it. You are worth more to me than life itself. I love you, Max. This is the end of it."

"End of what?" he asked, making an attempt to raise his head.

"End of my revenge. End of chasing Yona. End of chasing Bob, or anyone."

Max took another swig from the bottle and looked at Brenda.

"Whatever you say, Brenda, but with Yona it's just the beginning."

Chapter 23

The sound of the telephone ringing pulled Brenda back from the tall stack of papers to the reality of the day. The caller ID was not displayed, but Brenda picked it up anyway and responded with her usual, businesslike "Brenda speaking." There was silence on the other end, and then the short and frequent beeps of a disconnected line. She glanced at her wristwatch. It was almost seven o'clock, time to leave behind the troubles of the day, and relax. Max was still not in the best shape, and needed her care. He had expected a few friends to visit him that afternoon, which gave her some time to catch up with the backlog.

Brenda stretched her arms and back, and looked out the window. The shadows had gotten longer, and the day was fading away. Time to go, she decided, and pushed papers aside.

There was some unexplainable charm at the border dividing the dry business hours and the time of personal life, she thought. Something romantically sad was in the dying day, but at the same time intriguing and promising in the approaching darkness. There should be a nice dinner, a soothing ambience of home, lover's arms and lips, and the cozy warmth of the bed. Driven by incentives of fantasy and expectations, she stood up, picked up her bag, and rushed through the door.

The building was quiet, as everyone had left by that hour. She observed with caution the long and empty corridor. Being alone had never bothered her before, but since the shooting was alert to any possible vulnerability or sign of danger. Max was sure that Yona would strike back. Unless the professionals caught up with him first. It was only a matter of days, weeks at most, before the professionals dealt with Yona. That's what Max said.

Brenda thought a lot about events of the last month. Before all this had started, she was prepared to risk her future, or even her life, to get what she wanted. It turned out to be much, much more than that. Now, she was the reason Max had nearly died. If the bullet had struck an inch lower, it would have hit his liver, and he would be dead. The only man she loved would be dead. Why? Just because he loved her? How could she use his love for her selfish plans? The thought of losing Max made her shiver. As for her own life, it was wonderful until she started her revenge scheme with Lucas. She had a job, love, and all pleasures of life. But then Lucas died. It was not eye for eye, as she had imagined. Lucas haunted her in her nightmares. And now, Max's wound. What other random horrors might be lurking around the next turn? Would Yona retaliate? If so, how? And if not, would she be scared as long as he lived?

Brenda walked out of the emergency exit at the back of the building to the parking lot. Usually packed with cars in work hours, it was now almost empty; only three cars remained. One stood just two spaces off to the right of her car, facing the exit to the street. Its windows were tinted, which made it impossible to see inside.

Something about it made Brenda falter in her step. There was something in the air, something wrong. It was impossible to explain, as it was beyond borders of logic, common sense, of whatever was there that the mind could deal with. But her intuition, heightened by exposure to constant danger and in expectation of it, said Be careful. In a fleeting moment the brain captures some details, which, put together, cry out in warning. Sometimes it's a false alarm, but never the other way around.

She made a quick scan of the place. Everything looked peaceful and ordinary, as usual. She considered walking away, calling a cab, but she just wanted to get home to Max, so she shook off her worries and pressed the button on her remote door locks. Her car responded with cheerful flashes and a squeak. When she was two feet from it, the door of the closest car flew open. A huge bald man in a dark sweatshirt bounded out of it; his face was ugly and menacing, with a scar on his cheek and angry eyes. He held a gun in his right hand. He pressed its muzzle to her cheek, and grasped her hair into the fist of his left hand. Gripped with horror, Brenda did not resist. He hit her head with the butt of his gun and she screamed in pain. He yanked her to his car, opened the rear door, and threw her onto the back seat. He tore the bag off her shoulder; with quick, well-coordinated moves he opened the front door, jumped into the driver's seat, and threw the bag onto the passenger seat. The motor started almost at the same moment and the man turned back to her.

"One wrong move, and you're dead," he said, pointing a revolver at her face. No doubt he meant it. "Understand?"

"Yes," Brenda said. She nodded, succumbing to the instinct of fear. The next moment, though, her mind cleared. Anger and vicious hatred took the place of fear.

Her abductor was watching her in the rearview window. "Sit quiet. Don't try anything stupid." He made the car surge forward like a mad horse. The engine growled.

The attacker was not nervous, that much was obvious. With confident moves, he steered the car out to the street, and then to the exit leading to the highway. Not slowing at all, he turned his head back, looked into Brenda's eyes, and barked: "One wrong move, fucking bitch, and you are dead. Understood?"

"Sure," she said, grinding her teeth. She thought, You'll see soon what a nice catch you've got.

He watched at her in the rearview mirror. Nothing irritates hoods more than the defiance of their victims. She knew that from her years of incarceration. His eyes told her everything. In them was his intention to torture and humiliate her to the limits of his sick mind. But the car was already on the highway, it was still the daylight, and he must have known that it was not a good moment to demonstrate his superior power.

Brenda could not bear being at the mercy of hoods; it was far worse than death. What made people get into such misery was their desperation to survive at all cost. But she had for so long been prepared to accept any outcome, no matter how terrifying, as long as she did not submit weakly. Death? So be it. Better yet, death for both.

A crazy plan was forming in her head. Not a moment must be wasted, she thought, as she didn't know when the thug would turn off the highway, and how close they were to whatever final destination he had in mind.

Now, she thought, buckling up her safety belt.

"What are you doing there?" he asked, looking at her in the rearview mirror. Their eyes met again. The hood, seeing a stare as hard as his, scowled. Brenda detected anxiety and suspicion in his voice.

"I buckled up. Anything wrong with that?"

"What for?" The man's attention wavered between the road and the rear-view. They were heading north on a straight stretch of the highway, and, according to the speedometer, going about a hundred kilometers per hour.

"For safety," she said. "You drive like a crazy man."

He chuckled. "Good fucking broad. Wanna live, eh?"

"Sure, why not. Don't you?"

"What?" he roared. "What did you say?"

"Are you gonna kill me?" she asked.

He laughed. "We'll see. I was told that you're a dangerous bitch. Ha. You're no different from all the other broads I deal with."

"Who told you that? Yona?"

He laughed. "Clever twat. Wanna speak with him? We take care of nice twats like you all the time. Sure, you're gonna talk to him tonight. Happy?" He turned his head to her, and grinned the revolting smile of a psycho.

"Who else did you take care of, your grandma?" she asked, slowly sliding her belt from her jeans. To make her plan work, he had to be irritated to insanity. It was not a difficult task; in danger, even well trained, cold people lose control of themselves. Once he could not control himself, he would make mistakes. That would cost him dearly.

"Shut the fuck up." He glanced at her again through the rear view mirror, but the traffic was getting dense, and he had to concentrate on the road.

"You'll regret grabbing me for the rest of your fucking life," she said, wrapping one end of her belt around each hand. "But don't worry, that may not be that long."

"What?" His scream, it seemed, could shatter windows. He was not used to victims who didn't cower in fear. "What did you say, cunt?"

Their eyes met again in the rearview mirror.

"You heard me." She kept looking at him, tensing like a spring. The car moved to the rightmost lane, which meant that her abductor was nearing his exit. Time to strike.

She paused a few seconds before dealing the heavy blow to his pride. After all, it might be the last thing she ever did. Then she spat at her abductor: "Cocksucker."

She knew that the blow was coming, but it came faster than she had expected. His fist, hard like wood, landed on her face, almost knocking her unconscious. Almost, but not quite. She managed to jerk her head aside just in time, lessening the impact of the punch. She calculated, with mechanical precision, that after taking the time to hit her, he would have to turn his attention back to the road. He had to; he was driving a car at high speed on a busy highway. The moment he grasped the steering wheel with both hands, Brenda leaned forward and, firmly holding the belt, threw it over his head. Using it as a garrotte, she yanked it hard against his neck, shoving her feet against the back of his seat as added leverage. She pulled as hard as she could on the ends of the belt, straining to her capacity the muscles of her hands, back, and legs. The thug wheezed and tried to move forward to free himself. Finally, he let go of the steering wheel and grasped the belt at his neck with both hands. He was strong as an elephant, but not prepared for such an attack. He finally wrenched the belt from her hands, but at the same time, by instinct, slammed on the brakes. The tires screamed in agony, the steering wheel danced chaotically, the car wiggled its tail in a fatal dance.

Time slowed to a dream pace. Brenda heard a deafening sound as a car behind them collided with them, sending the abductor's sedan into another spin. It struck a car in the left lane, and then another fishtailed into another vehicle, and finally ran up over another car and took flight. They seemed to hover against the bright blue sky forever. Then the car landed with cracking and crushing sounds on its side, rolled over onto its roof, and back onto its tires.

Brenda had not lost consciousness, but she was totally disoriented. There was a searing pain in her right hand. She was slick with blood all over her. The driver was leaning forward, the deflated airbag shrouding his face. He did not move. A dense white cloud streaming from under the hood, masked anything beyond the windshield. Out the side window, she saw people running to her rescue. After a few powerful tugs, both front and rear doors of the car flew open. Someone unbuckled her safety belt and pulled her out. She groaned, feeling a sharp pain in her left side. Strong and gentle hands placed her on the grass, not far from the road. All traffic heading north stopped.

Brenda heard the sound of an approaching siren. She struggled to sit up, overcoming the pain, and looked around, searching for her abductor. He lay on the ground just ten meters away, apparently unconscious.

"Your safety belt saved your life," she heard someone beside her say. "It's not often that people who sit at the back seat buckle up. It's lucky you did."

Two police cars, lights flashing, came to the abrupt stop. A policewoman rushed to Brenda, and dropped to her knees, bringing her face level with Brenda's.

"An ambulance is on its way. Can you tell me what happened?" she asked.

Brenda stretched her left arm in the direction of her abductor. "He kidnapped me. He has a gun. It's probably still in the car."

The woman jumped, as if bitten by a snake, and rushed to other cops, who gathered around the abductor. She told them something, and two of them raced to the car. One dived into it, and the next moment appeared with the handgun. The policewoman rushed back to Brenda.

"What's your next of kin?" she kept asking. "Who should we call?"

Her first impulse was to name Max, but she thought better of it. The police might find out, but why tell them that she was a former con, that her boyfriend was in a biker gang, and that the man who had snatched her was from yet another gang.

"There's no one," she said. "It's just me."

The policewoman was asking something else, but Brenda didn't listen. She heard more sirens, and soon two ambulances arrived. Paramedics rushed to her. They also asked her questions, which she neither understood nor remembered, and then they placed her on a stretcher and loaded it into an ambulance. Every movement brought caused sharp pain in the left side of her chest.

"It hurts," she moaned.

"Where?"

"Here. Terrible. And my right hand."

The paramedic gave her a shot. She couldn't keep her eyes open. She felt dead tired. Her only desire was to rest, to sleep, to not be disturbed.

She woke up in a hospital bed, in a dim room with curtains instead of the door. Her right hand was in a cast, and her chest was wrapped with something firm but elastic. Using the metal rails of the bed, Brenda sat up. She found the red knob for the emergency call and pressed it. Immediately, a nurse came. She pulled the curtain aside, letting in a wide stream of artificial light.

"How'd you feel, dear?" she asked, with eyes that shone in admiration, detectable even in the semidarkness.

"What time is it?" Brenda asked.

"Five in the morning. You're doing well, dear. You have a broken arm, two broken ribs on the left side, and a broken nose. The police told us your story. They still don't know what you did exactly in that car, but they are sure you put up some kind of fight. They'll be by later in the morning to talk to you."

"Please, can you unhook me from these tubes? I wanna go to the washroom." When the nurse hesitated, Brenda said, "I'm okay. Quite well, actually. Please."

She came out of the washroom feeling much better, returned to hospital bed, and gazed at the ceiling, her mind running through the events of the last day. It was like a movie in a slow motion. She was immensely proud of herself. The memory of the choking kidnapper, the spinning and jumping of the car, the crushing and crunching sounds of metal beating the ground elated her. She had done it, in spite of the odds! Of course, now all hell would break loose. Now things would…

There was a rustle of curtains beside her, and then a warm, familiar hand clasped hers, and a smiling face appeared above hers. She relaxed, smiling. The man she loved sat on the edge of the bed, gazing down at her with anxious eyes.

"Max, dear," she whispered. "How'd you found me?"

"How'd ya feel?" he asked, also in whisper, letting the question pass. "The doctor said that you have two broken ribs and a broken arm. I can see that."

182

"Right." She could not take her eyes off him. "How'd you find me?"

"When it got late and you didn't come home and didn't answer you phone, I made a few calls. Bogdan got back to me and told me you were in this hospital. I got here after midnight, but the nurse wouldn't let me in. What happened?"

"I was leaving the office, and some huge jerk with a gun threw me into his car. I was in the back seat. When we were on the highway, I choked him with my belt. From behind, you know? He grabbed the belt from me, he was strong as a bear, but he lost control and we ended up rolling over. The car was a wreck." She chuckled. "I wonder if he's alive. Do you know?"

"Yes, he is." Max bent over to her, still talking in a whisper. "He's in a different hospital. Cops thought that it would be safer that way. Any idea who this sod was? He didn't have any ID, and the car was stolen."

"He was from the Yona's gang."

"Are you sure?"

"Positive. He said he was taking me to see Yona. I called him a cocksucker and he went nuts.... So I made my move."

Max ran his hands over her hair, then brought his lips to her ear and whispered, "My Wolverine. I love you."

"I could be gentle," she whispered back.

"I know, I know," he said. "So that son of a bitch...we have to finish him, the sooner, the better. Nobody needs him—not Yona's gang and not us. If he talks, he'll open a real can of worms."

"Right." She paused, thinking. "How?"

"I don't know yet. For some reason, there are a lot of police all around. Some undercovers even outside. I have no idea what's special about that sucker."

"You're tired, Max. Go home. I'm okay. Take a rest, and then come back."

"I won't. I'm not going home until you do." He leaned to her ear and whispered, as if telling her a big secret. "Love you, Wolverine."

Chapter 24

When Melissa and Larry came out of the elevator, the eighth floor of the hospital was quiet, with no people in sight. When they approached the nurse's station, a man came out of one of the rooms and walked by them. His stare was sharp, suspicious, and hard. Melissa recognized him in an instant as Brenda's boyfriend Max, whom she had seen for a brief moment during her visit to the mobile home village. The biker had changed noticeably. He was thinner, his face skinnier, colourless—all signs of some serious illness. There was something weird in his gait. He recognized Melissa as well, but chose not to show it.

At the station they were greeted by a young, good-looking nurse with skin the color of polished rosewood. The smile on her face shifted into a mask of official detachment when Melissa produced her badge while introducing herself and Larry.

"She's in room 806, right there." The nurse pointed at the number on the wall, the same room Max had exited a minute earlier. "She had a visitor. Perhaps she's sleeping now."

"Is she okay?"

"Yes, yes." The nurse smiled again. "She's doing remarkably well. She has two broken ribs and broken right forearm, but other than that, no serious damage, just some cuts and bruises. She was lucky she had her seatbelt on. She needs rest after that stress. She'll be plenty sore for a day or two, though, bouncing around like that."

"Is it okay to talk to her?"

The nurse nodded twice, to emphasise her consent. "Sure. She's a strong, healthy woman. We all admire her here. I mean, how many women do you know who would take on a kidnapper like that? Such iron character. Not even many men like that, for that matter."

"True." Melissa nodded, and then turned to Larry. "Wait here, please. I'll talk to her alone."

"Okay," he said, and turned to the nurse. The pretty woman shot him a meaningful glance, her eyes sparkling.

The room Melissa entered had no windows to the outside. It was dimly lit with a single table lamp. Brenda seemed to be in a deep sleep, but when Melissa sat on the wobbling plastic chair by her bed, she opened her eyes. To Melissa's surprise, she smiled.

"I was kind of expecting you. Although the police already questioned me."

"I've read the report," Melissa said.

"I told them everything." Brenda's tone suggested that she could not tell more than that.

"Almost all. Your account of what happened is quite detailed. It tells me that you were in complete control of the situation, with no lapses of memory, and that you remember everything."

"That's true," Brenda said, suspicion flickering in her eyes.

"So I won't ask you the same questions over again. But first, I'd like to express my appreciation of your courage and strength. You are a remarkable woman, Brenda."

"Thank you." Brenda eyed Melissa, in full alert.

"When you were in the car, you talked to the man. Right?"

"Right. Police asked me that."

"I know. I know. Did you, or your abductor, mention Yona? Did his name come up at all?"

Brenda turned her face away and stared at the wall. As she did not respond to the question, Melissa went on.

"Is the man associated somehow with Yona's gang? Any clue or hint?"

"I don't understand why you're asking me that." Brenda used the bed's controls to help herself to a sitting position. "What would Yona possibly have to do with what happened?"

"Yona was shot in the leg. You know better than I. He wants to kill you, for sure, as that would solve a lot of problems for him. Look, Brenda, I'll know everything soon anyway. Your abductor is alive, and soon he'll be able to speak. And speak he will. He's a sex offender, very violent, but he's not a gangster, he has no gang support, and has no stamina to keep his mouth shut. He'll make a deal. It's better if you tell me everything first."

"How it would change anything for me to talk if you'll know everything anyway?"

"I want to prevent a gang war. Once they get started, they're hard to stop. There would be lots of casualties, with you among the first, before the police can end it. Quebec is a good example."

Brenda sat silent, avoiding Melissa's eyes. "You know enough," she said. "Whatever I say will go against me, truth or lie, doesn't matter. I'm very familiar with police kindness."

This was a critical moment for Melissa's plan. For it to work, she needed unconditional trust from Brenda. To get that from a former con, especially one whose mistrust in the police and justice system was understandable, made the mission seem almost impossible. Melissa couldn't tell her any details. No one, not even Larry, could ever guess what she was up to. But it had to be done. For Brenda's good, and for the good of others. Melissa leaned toward her like an accomplice with the common goal.

"I'm questioning you not as a suspected criminal, but as a witness. You see, I don't even have a writing pad with me to record our conversation. I won't ask you to sign anything. You will have to testify during the preliminaries at and at court, if it comes to that. If… But a lot is now in your hands. Trust me, and I'll handle things.

My way. If not... This case will be placed in the hands of another investigator. It's quite simple, actually. All the material evidence is there, including the victim, who is the witness."

"What do you want from me, then?" Brenda asked.

"As I said, I want to prevent a gang war. I also want to stop you from committing any more crimes. You may call it revenge, or justice, or whatever you want...and I might sympathize with your reasoning...but what you're doing is still a crime. Unfortunately, there is nobody, including you, who wants to reopen the earlier case and punish the men who raped you. You know why, and you know what I mean. You wouldn't like it opened up, either, as many things would come out in the open, including the obvious involvement of your boyfriend and his gang in your recent crimes. Too much, isn't it?"

Her arguments hit the target. Melissa read in Brenda's eyes suspicion, intense thinking, and fear. As many before her had, Brenda was trying to guess how much Melissa actually knew, and how much was just gamesmanship. With her experience, Brenda knows that time is against her, and that the justice system is too powerful a foe to toy with or ignore. Most likely she has at stake a lot in her new life, too—a business, a boyfriend, a good car, and many other attributes of good life. Time changes values, and heals wounds. It was very likely that Brenda was not the same as she was when she left the prison. Melissa decided to press on.

"How's your boyfriend is doing? Is he okay?"

Melissa knew right away that she had hit the target the second time. Even in the dim light of the room, Melissa saw Brenda's face became a shade darker.

Brenda cleared her throat. "Eh...he's okay. Why do you ask?"

"Because he's a part of your life. He's your partner in everything."

"Not in everything."

"You know what I mean. As you suggested, let's cut the crap. He doesn't look well. You have to take care of him. You need money as well. Right?"

Brenda cast her eyes down.

"You put in danger your life, and his life. It's not fair to him."

"What's your point?" Brenda asked.

"I need very little from you," Melissa said, lowering her voice and leaning forward. "Just promise me you will stop seeking revenge. If you do that, I'll take care of the rest. I'll take your word for it. I know you already. I trust you. And I actually have a great deal of respect for you, and great sympathy. I'll close the case. You know what I mean."

Melissa leaned back and paused, waiting for Brenda's response. They both sat quietly, deep in thought.

"It is hard for me to trust you," Brenda said at last. "I expect no good from you."

"Take the risk, Brenda. Trust me. I'm on your side. In a broad sense, justice is on your side as well."

"Sure," Brenda nodded. The corners of her mouth curled down in contempt. "Justice can be bought and sold, in my experience. Or sold out, I should say."

"Look, Brenda. What happened before was terrible. No human activity, without exception, is without mistakes. Justice system is certainly not perfect, but…"

"Thank you for your wisdom. You advise me, the daughter of a cleaning lady, to put up with this fucking system, and what it did to me? My life is ruined. Broken to pieces. That should now be clear to anyone, even to your imbecile investigators. If not for another crime, it wouldn't be evident who really should've been in prison."

"Yes, they should all have been sent to prison. But you didn't go to the police. Instead, you lashed out."

"True. I was too young, too stupid, and too ashamed. I needed help and guidance, but had none. But what I did was nothing compared with what they did. They

189

committed a serious crime. I didn't start it. Now, with all the evidence, you can launch it again against me. Tell the rapists' parents that their kids were raped and videotaped, and that if I am arrested it's all going up into the Internet. Tell the police investigators who put me in prison five years ago. Tell the lawyers who defended those brats. Ask them if they want it all opened up again. Ask the guys who raped me if they wanna start it all over. My advice to you? If justice is really your concern, dig deeper into my case. It wasn't just the rapists who fucked me. The system fucked me, too. Go after the lawyers…the judge…the rich brats' parents! Oh, to see them go down I wouldn't mind getting sent back to prison. Tell the journalists to—"

"Calm down, Brenda. Think about it. Do you really want all that? Sure, I can open the old case, and go after you in the new ones, but if I do, nobody wins, and everybody loses. Brenda, I know who raped Lucas. I can incarcerate Max for a few years. Do you want that?"

Brenda deflated like a poked balloon, and raised her eyes to the ceiling.

"Do you want that?" Melissa repeated, this time without friendly notes in her voice.

"No," Brenda whispered, avoiding Melissa's eyes.

"I understand you, Brenda. I can't promise that the system will treat you well, but I can promise that you can trust me, that I'm really just interested in closing this case."

"What's your incentive?" Genuine surprise flickered in Brenda's eyes.

"You can think about that later. Tell me, Brenda, would you be receptive to making a deal with the men who raped you?"

"What kind of deal?" Brenda was flabbergasted. She took a glass of water from the shelf and made a few gulps.

"I'm just asking hypothetically. If one of them calls you and offers you to meet and discuss a deal of some sort, would you be willing to listen?"

Not taking her eyes off Melissa, Brenda said in a low voice, "Yes. I would. What about Yona?"

"I'll take care of him. Trust me."

"I want to trust you. But if I'm wrong, you should know that I know how to defend myself."

Melissa stood up. "You are a remarkable woman, Brenda. You've done many wrong things, but you deserve respect, if not admiration. I wish you all the best in your life. I hope that this is our last meeting. Hopefully, I won't see you again. But if anything goes wrong in your life, call me. You know my number."

She left the room. Larry stood alone, leaning at the station desk. She nodded, and he joined her on the way to the elevators.

"Did she tell you anything interesting?" he asked.

"She's a good diplomat," Melissa said, avoiding the direct answer.

"If we play it rough, all of them will spill the beans," he said. "That would be lots of fun, wouldn't it?" They stepped inside the empty elevator, and the doors closed.

"Yes," Melissa agreed. "But a lot of headaches for us as well. I have enough headaches as it is, and I don't want more. And what would we achieve? Justice? Or just an excuse to punish whoever comes alone?"

"I agree. But…"

They went out, and strode along a lengthy, crowded corridor toward the exit. "I mean, it's our job, isn't it?"

"You know as well as I that we could send more people to prison than we actually do. The reason we don't is obvious. We know better than anyone that it doesn't stop the sickness. Humanity is a sick entity and always been. We can arrest all the prostitutes, but why? The next day the streets would be filled with new ones. We can arrest all drug dealers, right? We know many of their names—they're right there in our file—but we don't haul them all in because the next day there would be new dealers out, ones whose names we don't know, even in greater numbers. And all those arrests would overload the courts and flood the penitentiary system. And yet, we have to fight crime. Weird, isn't it? Balance is the key. There is no final solution."

"What shall we do now?" Larry asked.

"Arrest Yona. Make a convincing case."

"Will do. I see what you mean."

Chapter 25

This was one of the rare days when Melissa made it home before seven. Nick rushed down from the second floor, screaming in joy. She caught him on the run, lifted him in the air, and kissed his cheek. Nick got furious. "I told you never lift me up," he protested. "Don't treat me like a tot." However, his anger quickly dissolved into his usual modus operandi. "Dinner is ready. Daddy bought me a sword; look, it's like a real one." He showed her a plastic imitation of a sword, really impressive.

Evan appeared from the kitchen and gave her a kiss. "Yes, dinner is ready. Today, I'm in charge."

"I don't see an apron on you," she said, heading to the kitchen dining area.

"It's because I don't have one. The only apron in our household belongs to you. Besides, I'm not a cook. But I'm a good manager. This is a take-out, but you'll like it."

"Good enough." Melissa sat at the table and picked up a fork and knife. Turning to Nick, she said, "How are you, sweetie? How was school?"

"Good." Nick swung his sword in the air. "Did you have any murders today?"

"Nick, Nick," Melissa said, reprimanding him gently. "There was no murder. What do you have for your homework today?"

"Nothing." He raised his sword above his head. "When I grew up, I'll be a policeman, mom. I'll kill murderers."

"Policemen do not kill. Put the sword down. Have you eaten dinner, Nicky?"

Nick ignored the question. "Then I'll be an Indian." He uttered a warlike call and ran back to his room, killing with his sword everything right and left.

Melissa sighed. "Soon, soon, I will be his mom again. And your wife as well."

"Thank you for considering me in your plans. Here you are." Evan filled up her plate with rice and fish. "It's not the first time I've heard that. Perhaps something new has come up in the Brenda case? The whole ordeal is very intriguing."

"It's a weird case, indeed," Melissa agreed, finishing a mouthful. "It makes me rethink a lot of what I thought I knew about justice, and right and wrong. Each new piece of circumstantial evidence falls into its expected place in the mosaic of the picture, which I have created from the beginning. It confirms my understanding of motives, and the methods of Brenda's crimes. I know almost everything about what and how things happened. But I have no material evidence yet, and no witnesses."

"You'll have it soon. I know you. You'll have both."

"Not that simple, Evan. Nobody would be willing to testify and tell the truth—not the victims, not the perpetrators, and not the people in the justice system. Everyone's got guilty secrets that they don't want to get out. There's another factor, too. Brenda is supported by a biker gang. That would intimidate witness and victims."

"This isn't the first time you've dealt with such circumstances," Evan said. "You'll make them speak."

"Here's the problem," Melissa said, pushing away her plate. "I don't want to lay charges against Brenda. I don't want to incarcerate her. She is…nice. She has character. She has good reason to be mad at the justice system and with the bullies who raped her. It's easy to put myself in her shoes and understand her motives. Besides, her smarts and unusual strength inspire admiration. I think deep down she's a good person."

"Humanity should not be a factor in investigation, I guess," Evan said. "You can't do much, other than behave by the book."

194

"I shouldn't, but I can. Here's where philosophy can help."

"I'm all ears."

"Of the four guys involved in the rape, three went on to become law-abiding citizens. Well, two, now, as one of them is dead. So, one has a spouse, another has a girlfriend. What can the justice achieve with putting them in prison? Broken careers, broken family life, parental grief, and basically ruined lives for many years to come, if not for the rest of their lives. What's worse, Brenda would be back in prison. This is the sorest point. Raped, incarcerated, released, took justice into her own hands, and got sent back to prison. Is it what it's supposed to be from philosophical point of view, Evan?"

"This is a treat for journalists, for sure. Particularly if corruption of justice is involved." Evan frowned, thinking.

"That's another point. I can ruin the life of Pamela Salazar, but that hurts her whole family: her two adolescent kids, and her husband, who is in a wheelchair for the rest of his life. Gary and his wife, Lucas's parents, would probably not survive the publicity, and the charges. All in all, there is no victim in this case who wants justice to interfere! How'd you like that?"

"Suppose you had the power to magically do whatever you believe is a just solution. What would you do?" Evan asked. "You cannot just let it go. As you said, Brenda won't stop. That means that she would commit other crimes until she gets what she wants. And there's a gang war looming, as you said. Doing nothing would lead to an explosion, which is worse than your scenario when justice does interfere. The way to solve the puzzle is just a matter of putting on scales the weights of different outcomes. It's purely theoretical, though, right?"

"No. That kind of logic is good for those who are remote from reality. That's why poets, scientists, artists, writers, and musicians seldom, if ever, are good

195

diplomats, politicians, managers, or policemen. Philosophers are in the same category."

Evan laughed. "This is so true! When philosophers suggest solutions to real-life problems, they seem clever. In practice, however, they are stupid in a very destructive way. Paradox. That's what life is about. What are you going to do?"

"I want to do unthinkable. And then I want to quit my job. For good."

"What are you going to do after you quit?"

"I'll take care of my two kids: Nick and you. Perhaps I'll have the third one.

"But why quit?" Evan asked. "You are a naturally born detective. Even Sherlock Holmes would envy you, if he were a real person. Finish with this case, and move along. If you believe in a higher judge, who is above our justice system and our loyalty to our duty, then you have to be faithful to the talent with which he blessed on you. This is your most important duty before God. Are you going to trash it?"

"But I cannot be above people and their understanding of my duty. I'm tired of confrontation with my own self. I need a break."

Chapter 26

While Max drove Brenda from the hospital to his house in Toronto, he was in a rather talkative mood, although he avoided any mention of Brenda's ordeal or Yona.

"There's a takeout dinner for you, hon," he said, smiling. "I'm not much of a good cook, and today I'm in no mood to cook anything. "You mind?"

"Not at all. Just being here with you makes everything good. That's why—"

"Not now." Max cut her off. "Relax, and then we'll talk."

Max walked directly to the coach. His face distorted with a grimace of pain. Holding his stomach with both hands, trying to sound casual, he said, "Hon, can you grab me a glass of water and two of those pills over there, the bottle that says Tylenol 2."

Using just her left hand, Brenda managed to remove the lid and get two pills, which she handed them to Max. She filled a glass of water at the tap and carried it over to him. "Max, why don't you go to a doctor?" she asked. "You're really sick. Whatever it is, I swear it's hurting you more than that damn bullet did. Though it seems it's been much worse since you got shot. Please, see a doctor. A real one."

"I will, I will, Brenda." He swallowed the pills, put the cup on the side table, lay back, and closed his eyes. "Don't worry, it'll pass. It's just a little stomach cramp. I'll be okay in a few minutes, then we can talk."

Brenda sat on the couch beside him and put her hand on his chest. "You might feel better in a few minutes, but you won't be okay, Max. You know that. You have something serious. You have to be diagnosed, and then you can be treated."

Max opened his eyes and gave her a sidelong glance. "Not just yet. Let me finish a few deals. I have to make some money, you know. In my line of work, I don't have health insurance, other than OHIP." He chuckled, and then sat up. "See, I'm better already. Now, what's the story?"

"I'll take care of you, Max. I have a good business. I make good money. I'll work twice as much if I have to. I have lots of energy, and I do a good job."

"How long will that last?" Max asked. "Please, pass me a beer. Thanks."

"What do you mean, how long will it last?"

"You know what I mean. Until Yona kills you. Now, tell me the story. What did those cops want?"

"Only Melissa talked to me. She said that she wanted to prevent a gang war. She said that if I stop chasing those guys, she can settle everything."

"Bullshit."

"She was pretty convincing. I kind of like her."

"Never trust cops."

"What's your solution?"

"You know my solution. Kill the asshole. There's no other way. Now you know exactly what he's up to."

"No, no, and no." Brenda felt blood rushing to her face and temples. "I'd rather close this chapter and forget about everything."

"Forget?" Max looked at her with condescending smile. "Don't give me that crap. Nobody could. You won't. And, by the way, it's not only you now. Yona's bullet may not be in my chest anymore, but it's still there in my memory. It will be forever, even after he's in his grave."

"You're right. I won't forget what they did, but..." Brenda took the bottle of beer from his hand and took a swig. "I think I'd rather live with those memories than—"

"Hold on," Max interrupted her rather abruptly. "Tell me something. You don't have much hard feeling against Lucas, do you?"

"True. Especially now, after he did what he did…because of me."

"His choice. But my point is, even if he was alive, he would be out of your mind. You wouldn't hate him anymore. Same with Christian. You don't hate him anymore, right?"

Brenda sighed. "Right."

"Even if Christian doesn't come through with the money, you'd still feel great. You forgive him now, right?"

Brenda nodded. She understood where Max was coming to.

"But Yona is your deepest wound. You'll be living with it for the rest of your life, unless you heal it."

"No killing. No." Her voice regained strength. "Maybe there's another solution."

"There is no other solution. And time is important. Now, what else did that cop Melissa say? And what did you say, for that matter?"

"She asked me if I'd be willing to make a deal with them. Not with the police, but with those guys. Don't ask me what kind of deal she meant; she didn't say. All she said was that she wanted to stop the gang war, and she asked me, if I was even open to listening if she could set up some sort of reconciliation. I don't know how much she knows…"

Max stood up and paced the room, looking at the floor.

"What are you thinking about?" Brenda asked.

"It's an interesting idea," he said, not looking at her. "Sometimes cops do things you would never expect from them. Let's wait a few days. In the meantime, I'll take care of the bastard in the hospital. Peter said that he's still in coma, but has a good chance to survive."

199

"Are you going to him?"

"I have to. If he talks, we're fucked. He'll tell the cops that Yona hired him. Then it will all blow up— Yona, your rape, a full-blown investigation, news reporters, all that shit. No question I'd get hauled in and questioned, and who knows what else could happen?"

"You could get caught, and be in prison for murder until the end of your life," said Brenda.

"No. This will be done clean. He'll be dead tomorrow."

Chapter 27

As soon as a criminal appears on the police radar, an arrest is just a question of timing. Even if the police have no material evidence of a crime, they will, if it's at all possible to obtain. Undercover agents can often lead the investigators in the right directions, and they are particularly useful in narcotics operations. Everyone in the drug trade is vulnerable, from the big distributors and middlemen to the guy on the street dealing out of his coat pocket. It's an open field, accessible by anyone.

Of course, the police have limited resources. They can't arrest everyone. Besides, doing so is not expedient; if they arrest the traders today, by tomorrow the market will be filled with others, and the cycle will begin anew. But when an arrest is necessary, and promises to yield good results, that's another story. Melissa had such considerations.

"Larry," she said. "We have to arrest Yona as soon as possible. We have to isolate him. That will solve a number of problems. If he turns for us, gives up some names, we might even be able to arrest the whole gang, but I doubt it. However, he's the target. He has to be incarcerated."

Larry gave her a long look. "So, you decided to go that way," he said in a low voice. It wasn't clear if he approved or disapproved of her decision.

"If you'd like, I can explain my reasoning after everything is settled, after I've worked it out," she added. "But right now, there's no time."

"No need. I understand. One way or another, the bastard belongs to jail. But if you rush it now, we probably won't get sufficient evidence for a federal sentence. In a year or two, he'll be back out."

"I know. I know. But his kind never stops. He'll go back a second time, and soon."

"Okay. As a matter of fact, the undercovers are already at work in the Rooster and a few other places. They know a few dealers there. Yona might be one of them."

"Thoughtful of you," Melissa said. "By the way, how Brenda's abductor doing? Has he recovered enough from the crash for us to question him yet?"

Larry frowned. "He's dead."

"Dead? Yesterday I got a report that he seemed to be coming out of his coma."

"I know. The medical staff is puzzled, too," he said.

A few moments passed in silence. "Has an autopsy been done?" she asked.

"No. Not yet."

"Was there any police guard?"

Larry shook his head. "The thinking was that the son of a bitch was of no interest to anyone. Not worth pulling cops away from real work for a special detail."

"Damn. I should have seen it," Melissa said, looking out the window with half-closed eyes. The day was dull, cloudy, with all the indications of approaching rain. It was a good day for a generous cup of coffee.

"Seen—?" Larry asked, as if continuing their silent conversation aloud.

"Both Yona and Brenda had an interest in shutting the suspect up for good. And both Yona and Brenda are connected to gangs. His testimony would have opened the floodgates to a full-blown investigation. As usual, one thing would pull in another…you know the drill."

"I asked the staff if they had seen anything suspicious before he died. They said it was a busy afternoon, with lots of visitors, doctors, and nurses hustling about. One nurse said she thought she remembered seeing someone in a medical gown near his room. Soon after, all his monitors began beeping, but so were monitors in some of the other rooms. That happens a lot in intensive care. Nurses can't attend to all of them at once. When one of the nurses checked on him, she found him dead. No sign of violence."

"I see," Melissa said, and then sighed. "We'll deal with it. In the meantime, bring me Yona."

"Will do."

And he did. Just three days later, Larry appeared in Melissa's office with his customary toothy smile on his face.

"Yona is waiting for you," he said. "As usual, he'd love to talk to you."

"Where is he?"

"Here, in the jail."

"Tell me the story."

"There were three undercovers in the Rooster. Yona came in, limping, but still running his business as usual. One of our guys asked to buy some pot. They made a deal in the washroom. Two uniforms just 'happened' to walk in during the deal and arrested them both—you know, not to blow our guy's cover. They hauled 'em both in, though of course the undercover will be 'released' after they make sure Yona sees him going through booking. No sense blowing his cover just for this dickhead, right? By the way, the stuff on Yona considerably exceeds the limit. It's a no-brainer to lay formal charges against him."

"Good." Melissa nodded. "Let's talk to him together. Press him hard. I'll be a good cop. Okay?"

"Sure," Larry agreed, and left her office.

Yona was brought to the interrogation room without handcuffs. He was limping. His face was pale and covered with a few days' worth of stubble, his long hair in disarray. His expression, though, was defiant and arrogant. His stare was hard and unyielding.

Larry explained to him his rights not to answer questions, to have a lawyer, and other procedural details.

Yona nodded, visibly unimpressed. He avoided Melissa and Larry's eyes, and generally behaved as an experienced criminal—unusual for someone who had no record of ever having been interrogated before.

"Do you have a lawyer?" Larry asked.

"No. What for?"

"Just to help you."

"Don't need one," he said. "I'm not a criminal. Why would I need a lawyer?"

"You were arrested while selling illegal drugs, that's why."

Yona gave Melissa a grim, sidelong glance, and shrugged. "It was the first time in my life," he said, turning his face away. "Never done it before."

"Never?" There was metal in Larry's voice. "You were carrying quite a bit. Enough to incarcerate you for long."

"Not true. It wasn't much at all."

"Not much. Huh. Well, we'll see what the court says. Who's your supplier?"

"Supplier? I don't know what you mean."

"You know very well what I mean," Larry said. "Who's the wholesaler, the one who sells you the stuff?"

"There you go again," Yona said with a sneer. "I told you. This was my first time. Never bought it before, never sold it before."

"Right, your first time," Larry nodded. "So who is the person who sold it to you, this one time?"

"A guy I just met that day for the first time in my life. In another bar. He promised me good money if I helped him out. I decided to try. Sorry."

"Sorry for what?" Larry asked. "Sorry for telling me bullshit?"

Yona shrugged his shoulders. Larry paused, waiting for his words to sink in.

"Who was the guy who sold you this stuff the first time?" Larry asked.

"I don't know. He didn't show me any ID."

"Would you recognize him, if you meet him again?"

"For sure, yeah," Yona said. His enthusiasm was obviously meant to show the cops how stupid he considered them to be.

"We've videotaped your dealings with a hidden camera in the Rooster's washroom," Larry said. That was true. The police had done a good job with this. They'd recorded multiple transactions between Yona and his buyers.

"Bullshit," Yona murmured.

"No, not bullshit," Larry said. "I can show you these videos if you'd like. Would that help your memory any?"

Yona cast his eyes down, and said nothing. It was time for Melissa to step in.

"I talked to the man who abducted Brenda. Myles is his name. You know whom I'm talking about." She stopped, examining Yona's face. His eyes were wide open, exuding hatred and fear.

"Interested to know what he said?" Melissa continued.

"I don't know who you're talking about," he said. "Who's Myles?"

"You know. You do. You hired him."

Melissa had never had a chance to talk to Myles. Apparently Yona did not know that Myles was dead. Otherwise, he would have put on his usual arrogant expression.

"Don't try to hang your bullshit on me," he said, glaring at Melissa. In his eyes, Melissa read the hatred and menace of a mature gangster. Anyhow, he was already in the trap.

"There's a long list of charges we could lay against Myles, like would be with abduction, aggravated assault, using a firearm in commission of an offence, possession of a weapon for dangerous purposes, kidnapping, dangerous operation of a motor vehicle—"

"Yeah, yeah, so what?" said Yona.

"So you are the one who hired him, so you're culpable in every one of his actionable offences. He was supposed to take Brenda to you, but he had trouble handling her. She got the better of him, and he had no choice but to cut a deal with us. Of course, you can deny everything, and that's fine with me. It will be a long, long time before you're out of prison anyway. Especially since there are some other things that we can add to those charges. I think you know what I mean."

Melissa thought that a minute or so of silence would break Yona's resolve.

"Can I see a copy of his testimony?" Yona asked.

"Of course," Melissa bluffed on. "All supporting documents will be available for examination to you and to your lawyer. But mind you, we don't have much time, patience, or interest in dealing with people of your kind. Do you want to make a deal, or not?"

"What kind of deal are you offering?"

There was a brief moment when the hope of a big deal flickered in Melissa's mind.

"You tell us everything about your gang—your sources of supply, your permanent clients, all about your gang members. We offer you a witness protection plan, reduced or no sentence. All other conditions would be open for negotiations. Even money, for that matter."

Yona crossed his legs. He was all arrogance and defiance.

"Fuck you both," he said.

"Attempted murder charges, then, along with the rest of it," Larry said. "That's what your choice is."

"I don't care," came the reply. Yona turned his face to the wall, apparently accepting his fate.

Tough nut. "So, you refuse to cooperate with the investigation?" she asked. Yona kept looking aside, saying nothing. Further interrogation wouldn't bring much fruit, Melissa concluded. They had plenty of evidence of his illicit drug trade, sufficient to isolate Yona for a few years. For her purposes, that was good enough.

Chapter 28

It seemed sometimes to Brenda that the memories in her head lived a life of their own life. Scenes from the rape and the aftermath flashed through her mind unbidden, though she tried to erase them; there was nothing gained by dwelling on that polluted water under the bridge. Quite the opposite: it was a hindrance to clear thinking and a sound decision making. These flashes of reminiscences were rarely lately— the intensity of her new life did not afford the time for them—but when they did pop into her mind, the bitter taste of the past churned her stomach. After coming home from hospital, she had a few uncontrollable splashes of memory that disturbed her sleep for many nights.

"Please, Brenda," her lawyer begged her before the arraignment. "Admit your guilt. There is undeniable evidence of your crime. It would be much easier for me to defend you at the court hearing, and it would certainly affect the final verdict. If you won't do that, there's not much I could do. Please, Brenda."

That was the lawyer that Sury had hired to replace the legal aid lawyer. The new lawyer was also young, but with some experience, and eager to win.

"What about those jerks who raped me?" she asks, holding back her boiling rage. "Make them sit with me in the box. If they admit their guilt, I'll admit mine."

The lawyer kept explaining the complications, but Brenda wouldn't listen. She entered the courtroom feeling edgy, but tried her best not to show her fear. The guard led her to the thick glass enclosure designated for dangerous offenders. Her lower lip trembled when the judge entered the courtroom. After procedural formalities and a quick review of the available evidence, the judge, an imposing middle-aged man with a mane of gray hair and dark, frightening eyes, turned to her.

"Do you understand the charges against you?" he asks.

"Yes, I do."

"Do you plead guilty, or not guilty?"

"Guilty of what?" she asks. "I was raped. The so-called witnesses and victims should be—"

"Defendant!" the judge interrupted her in the burst of anger. "Answer the question."

"I'm guilty of committing a crime against criminals," she said. Her fear vanished. She felt a weird mixture of a cold, clear mind, an urge to fight, and a controlled fury. She was ready for the worst. She was determined to fight for the truth and justice at any cost.

After a short but meaningful pause, the judge resumed his grilling.

"When you were at the party, did you threaten to kill Lucas, Jonathan, Christian, or Bob?"

"After Sury rescued me? After those animals raped me? I did not mention each of them by name, or confront them individually, but I definitely wanted them punished—in prison or dead. They have to be in—"

The judge interrupted her again with the intensity of a righteous man. "Do you still contemplate inflicting physical harm to them?"

"If you are concerned about their safety, put them in prison for their crime."

"Defendant!" the judge roared. "Answer the question."

Brenda can still recall the intensity of the judge's anger. Why did he seem to take her accusations of rape so personally? What was the matter with him? After all, none of those jerks was related to him. He should have been professional, detached, and fair, and punished everyone in accordance with the crimes committed.

After that, everything went from bad to worse. The prosecutor, Pamela Salazar, the hateful bitch, spoke eloquently and convincingly...and untruthfully. The defendant, she said, is dangerous and revengeful. She admits her dangerous intentions, and will carry out her threats, as she proved with her vicious attack on Lucas. Pamela strongly objected Brenda's release on bail. But there was no one to put up a bond for Brenda anyway. The judge agreed without a moment of hesitation. He declared the court adjourned and appointed the court hearing.

* * *

Brenda pushed away the unpleasant memories and stared at Max's face. In sleep, it was relaxed, peaceful, but still bore traces of a tough man with a strong, dangerous will. She closed her eyes, but in spite of her determination to fall asleep, she found herself back to the past.

The courtroom was packed with curious gawkers who had nothing better to do than put their noses into other people's affairs. Brenda sat in the defendants' enclosure, clad in her jail outfit, watching Gary, Lucas, Yona, Christian, and Bob. The four rapists were being treated as victims and witnesses. All of them except Yona avoided her eyes.

Pamela Salazar, the prosecutor, asked Brenda in a very calm, friendly voice, "Did you have an intention to kill Lucas when you assaulted him with the knife?"

Brenda understood where Pamela was leading her. "I was mad at them," she started. "But I didn't—"

Pamela interrupted her, "Did you intend to kill Lucas? Please, answer the question. Yes or no?"

"I didn't know at that time what I wanted. I was mad at all of them," she pointed to where the witnesses sat. "They raped me, don't you understand that?"

In the middle of Brenda's speech, Pamela began shouting, while approaching the defendant's box. "Yes or no? It's a simple question. Answer the question: did you, or did you not, intend to kill Lucas? Yes or no?"

Brenda completely lost control of herself. "Have you ever been raped? Have you ever had four guys hold you down and force themselves on you?" she screamed. "If not, I hope you do!"

There was a commotion among the spectators. Sury was among them. In a split second, Brenda saw her pale face, usually emotional and animated, now still, like a stone.

Pamela's words are drowned by the uproar. The judge used his gavel, and shouted for order. Brenda's lawyer tried to show his character, and gave her a sign to calm down, but nothing helped. The inflamed spiritual wound of her soul burst open and bled openly for all to see.

"I hope your daughter gets raped, and you have to be her prosecutor!" Brenda cried out. All of a sudden, the noise level dropped to an unusual, unexpected silence. The judge held his gavel high, as if ready to hit someone on the head.

"If this happens again," the judge said, exuding anger, "I'll hold those responsible for the disturbances in contempt of the court. Please proceed. Defendant, you will please answer the questions asked, truthfully, and obey the order of the court. You, attorney, please remain in your place. There is no need for you to approach the defendant." The judge, it seemed, was at least friendlier to Brenda than the prosecutor. This gave her some sense of support, and calmed her nerves.

"Did you, or did you not..." The prosecutor began again.

"No, I did not. I did not wish death on anyone. Then or now."

"Why, then, did you take the knife?" The prosecutor requested permission to show the weapon. "Although it is a kitchen knife, you can see that it is large, sturdy, and quite deadly. You chose this before you sought out and assaulted the victim, didn't you?"

"He's not the victim here, I am!" Brenda blurted, tightening her fists. "He's the criminal…"

"Answer the question!" the judge warned again. "You'll be given an opportunity to express your opinions later."

"Thank you, Your Honour," Pamela said, and then turned to Brenda. "Did you, or did you not, assault Lucas with this weapon?"

"Yes, I did."

"Did you understand that you could have killed him, if the wound had been in his chest, not his arm?"

"Objection!" Brenda's lawyer shouted, but the judge dismissed it.

* * *

With some effort Brenda stopped her train of thought and left the bed. Max was still asleep, snoring lightly. Would she behave the same way if it happened now? No, she would have done many things differently. But it was easy to analyse things now, when a great distance of time and life experience separated her from the action, when emotions flew high and there was no time for thinking.

She heated a half glass of milk and drank it slowly, enjoying the warm, soothing liquid. Her mother used to give her milk and honey before bed if she was too excited to sleep. It was a tranquiliser, as good as a sleeping pill. Tomorrow is another day, she thought. There will be new worries, new problems, and new dangers. It's better to have a sound sleep and be refreshed for the new battles. With this thought, she returned to bed and lay back on the bed. But the moment she closed her eyes, her memories yanked her back to the court.

In the morning, the prosecutor began speaking. The public benches were packed. Some of Brenda's former classmates were there, and some older people, perhaps parents or relatives, or just bored retirees.

Pamela Salazar approached the podium with the proud posture of a veteran attorney. She gave Brenda a long, hard, disapproving glance. Brenda made an effort to respond with an iron, unyielding, even menacing stare and was pleased to see in Pamela's eyes a trace of imbalance, if not fear. However, the bitch regained her poise quickly, and looked at Brenda with double fury. Only much later did Brenda come to understand how much people in power hated to be intimidated, and hated those who make them feel that way. Indeed, how dare a helpless teenage girl show her iron will to a prosecutor, at whose mercy she was that day?

That was the first time Brenda learned that even clever people can make mistakes if they are in the grips of uncontrolled emotions.

"Your honour," Pamela began, this time addressing the judge. "With all my heart I am inclined to be compassionate toward a teenager. After all, we all make mistakes, and particularly so in younger age, when the human mind is not yet mature enough to make sound decisions in critical moments. Yet although I'd like to feel compassion for the defendant, my heart is not with her. During this hearing she has shown herself to be a hardened criminal, one completely unrepentant for her crime, and one who refuses to admit her guilt."

"Objection, Your Honour!" Brenda's lawyer rose to his feet. "My client did admit that she committed the crime."

"Sustained," the judge said, nodding.

"Exactly," Pamela continued. "She admitted that she committed the crime, but she did not admit her guilt. She does not feel guilty. She shows no remorse. As the evidence shows, she is a person of very low moral standards. After having a consensual sex with more than one of her schoolmates, she accused them in rape, just because someone noticed it."

"That is a lie!" Brenda said. She had not spoken loudly, but because of the courtroom's quiet, her words sounded crisp and clear.

"Quiet!" the judge shouted.

"There were photographs on the Internet," Brenda said.

"Next time you interrupt this hearing, and I'll order you removed from this courtroom." When order was restored, he nodded at Pamela. "Please proceed." He was red with anger. He could have removed Brenda right then, but for some reason he chose not to. Brenda noticed a journalist scribbling something on his writing pad.

Her lawyer motioned toward Brenda in an attempt to calm her down.

"There is undeniable evidence, Your Honour, that the defendant is very, very dangerous. During the party, she hit one of her classmates on the head with a frying pan."

There was a suppressed laughter from the visitors' benches, along with brief applause. The judge smashed his gavel down, shot an angry look at the gallery, and soon the quiet returned.

"This was a very heavy object. She could have killed the victim, or left him permanently disabled. As if that was not enough, next day she attacked another of her classmates, this time with even more dangerous weapon, a sharp knife, and in a public place in broad daylight! Luckily, she did not kill him, but she did inflict a serious wound. When that wasn't enough, she chased him, still brandishing the knife. Had it not been for the quick response of our faithful public servants, the young man, newly graduated and headed for university and a bright future, would have bled to death in the street. Well, even that would not prevent me from taking a softer stand toward her. But her aggressive behaviour and repeated threats and outbursts throughout these proceedings clearly demonstrate that she feels no guilt, only hostility and animosity. We all heard her open threats, addressed to the victims and witnesses. Her own lawyer must have made her aware of the importance of recognizing her mistakes and cooperating with authorities, important factors influencing the verdict, and yet still she has been disruptive, unapologetic, and verbally abusive.

Pamela paused before dealing her final blow. She turned to the judge.

"The accused is not forthcoming and cooperative," Pamela said. "There is a pattern of unprovoked physical violence toward her schoolmates. That very afternoon of the party, she let the middle of a volleyball game to strike one of the witnesses, in full view of dozens of onlookers, and returned to the game as though nothing had happened! Her indecent behaviour has been well documented. Given her family background and upbringing, perhaps we should not be surprised that there has been some suggestion that she drinks heavily and uses illegal substances, which would obviously feed her proclivity for violence. Her consistent threats to the victims and witnesses should be considered as criminal acts in accordance with Canadian laws. But more so, they are evidence of her disturbed, dangerous character. Coupled with her violent acts, there is no doubt in my mind that if she is not incarcerated, she will carry out her threats and cause grievous bodily harm to more than one of her classmates at her earliest opportunity."

Pamela turned her head and looked at Brenda, and then back at the judge.

"You will make your decision having plenty of facts, Your Honour. We have to defend our society, particularly the best and the brightest of our young people, from the most violent and dangerous criminals. The stereotype of a violent criminal as a male is now changing with alarming speed. More and more women are being charged for acts of violence, including murder. This defendant is dangerous, revengeful, and has to be isolated from society for the maximum term."

Damn it, Brenda cursed, opening her eyes in the darkness of her room. This was one of those times when her efforts to push her memories away and get a good sleep failed completely. Even if I had been mellow and sobbing, nothing would have changed, she thought. But she hadn't been. She'd been angry and aggressive, which was the wrong thing to be in court. Everyone has a right to be bitter, angry, and revengeful, but not the defendant. Judges can shout at anyone, openly showing their anger. Prosecutor can shout at defendants and their attorneys, risking only a reprimand from the judge. But defendants must be angels, humbly admitting their guilt, promising good behaviour in the future, and crying at all the right times. Everything in Brenda's nature had rebelled against it then, and did now. Even though she was the victim, painfully abused and disgraced publicly, she should admit her guilt and promise a good behaviour? Perhaps if she had done that, she might have gotten a lesser sentence, but those brats would still have remained free to enjoy life, without a single black mark against their records. It was obviously a rigged game. Certainly some money and influence were involved. They all knew the truth, but chose to ignore it.

Brenda went to the kitchen and heated up some more milk. This was the last try, she decided. If the milk didn't work, she would give up and forget about sleeping for the night. She turned on a small spotlight under the kitchen cabinet and looked at the clock. The time was two in the morning.

Max stopped snoring. A moment later he said, "Are you okay, hon?"

"Yes, dear. Just a little insomnia. Sorry for waking you up."

"No worries." He turned over in bed and soon his snoring resumed. Brenda finished her milk with a few gulps and returned to bed. It would have been nicer to punish those bastards at that time, not five years later. Now they were different people, and she was different too. And yet, they still deserved something. Not because it would change them, and not even because she wanted revenge. Max was right when he said that after each blow, her anger toward them had almost vanished, leaving space for peace of mind. And she wanted that peace of mind.

There was another consideration. As far as she remembered, she had always kept her word. If she promised something, either to herself or to someone else, she made all possible effort to deliver on that promise. And she had promised to pursue them all. She had promised them hell on earth. And she was almost, if not fully, there. She smiled in the darkness when her memory brought her again to the courtroom.

"Your honour," her lawyer said, "Please take into consideration the defendant's age and lack of life experience. She committed an impulsive crime, and she has admitted it. But I would like to emphasize that at that time she was in great distress, and had little understanding of what she was doing. Her reactions here in court could be forgiven in light of the fact that her mother, the only family she had in the world, died just days after—"

"Objection!" Pamela shouted.

"Sustained," the judge agreed. "Please stick to the facts pertinent to the crime."

"I have no doubt that Brenda was raped by these four hooligans." Her lawyer pointed at the bench.

"Objection! Your Honour! This is an outrageous breach of court ethics!"

There was an uproar from the benches. Brenda laughed aloud. She would have applauded, if not for handcuffs.

"Sustained," the judge said, with angry glances at Brenda and her attorney. "Please restrict yourself to appropriate language, counsellor. You are here in this court to defend your client, not to accuse anyone of a crime or to call malign witnesses with names that are utterly inappropriate. If this happens again, I will hold you in contempt to the court. Please proceed."

"Sorry, Your Honour. Let me say it this way: the defendant believes that she was raped by—"

"Objection!" Pamela screamed. Brenda smiled, and looked at the benches. Gary was not there. He had come to the hearing only once, and not returned since.

"Sustained."

Brenda's lawyer, young though he was, held his ground. "Your Honour, we do not minimize the significance of the events, not in any shape and form. But she is the person who has no proclivity for unprovoked violence. We heard here an argument that she needs anger management. No objection, Your Honour. But in order to diagnose the problem, we have to answer the question: why she is angry? Is she angry all the time, and reacting inadequately to any irritating factor, or there was only one issue, one terrible tragic event, that which triggered her violent reaction? If there is only one issue, then anger management won't do much good, and I believe that it is our task to solve the problem at its root."

"Stick to the point," the judge demanded.

"I am making my point, Your Honour. The medical examination concluded that the defendant is not psychotic, and that she has a completely normal response to any matter other than this particular case. There has to be a compelling reason to be that angry. Otherwise, she would have to be declared insane, and prone to killing anyone for any trifling irritant, but the psychiatric experts have sworn that this is not the case. The prosecution has implied that the use of illegal drugs led to this violence. Such drugs were used at the party, but not by Brenda. Some of the witnesses and so-called victims did use those drugs, and I have witnesses who can confirm that. Brenda was severely beaten up at the party by those same so-called victims, and again I have witnesses. This is a

218

crime, Your Honour, let's make no mistake on it. They deserve to stand trial for it at the court of law."

"Objection," Pamela cut in.

"What's your point?" the judge asks. "You are free to initiate the case, but this court considers another crime."

"My point is simple, Your Honour. I shudder at the thought that four strong men physically abused a woman. Isn't that enough to make young girl angry as hell? This is a crime, which tells us about morality of these men, and confirms their proclivity for violence, including rape."

"Objection, Your Honour," Pamela shouted, jumping up from her seat. She was at the peak of her outrage."

"Sustained," the judge agrees.

Brenda opened her eyes again. The light was seeping through the blinds.

It would have been such a pleasure to hit Pamela on the head with the above-mentioned heavy object. The bitch knew the truth, but she didn't care. Although…Pamela had been right that Brenda was dangerous to the so-called victims. She was probably gloating about that now. Yes, you were right, madam prosecutor, but there's nothing you can do. You're afraid for your own sorry ass.

The judge, after announcing his verdict, made an angry speech about the unyielding, strong, and dangerous character of the accused. When he said something about her morality, Brenda erupted with anger.

"You will all pay the price," she said. The judge raised his gavel, but Brenda shouted through the noise, addressing the victims. "I will be after you for the rest of your lives. You won't find rest, not on earth, and not in hell!"

"Quiet!" the judge screamed. "Quiet!"

When courtroom return to order, and was quiet again, Brenda repeated in a calm voice, "Until the end of my life…or yours. Whichever comes first."

Sury told her later that when she had spoken to Brenda's lawyer, he said that he had heard Pamela saying to a colleague, "I admit that I have never come across a woman of such strength and determination. She behaves like a hard terrorist. I can only imagine what a danger she would be when she leaves the prison. I only hope that she commits another crime there so she won't be out of the prison gate soon."

You hoped, madam, Brenda said to herself, and fell asleep.

Chapter 29

Only proud people keep their word. It takes integrity, strength of character, and courage to accept, without any reservation, full responsibility for actions and consequences. Melissa had no doubt that she was one of those proud people. And yet, it wasn't easy for her to pick up the phone and start—as she thought of it—the grand finale. But she did. A familiar voice at the other end of the line said, with the calm confidence of a seasoned executive, "Gary Kroner."

"Good day, Gary. Detective Bonar. How are you?"

"Good day, detective. What can I do for you?" His voice remained calm, but just a bit solemn.

"I wanted to speak with you. It won't take long. It's not a strictly official conversation. Do you mind?"

"Not at all. When do you wish to meet? And where?"

"I can be in your office at two o'clock. Is that a good place for you?"

"That's fine. What's this about?"

"We'll have plenty of time to discuss it."

She hung up and sat quietly for a few minutes. It was true that her visit was not meant to be official. In fact, it was a breach of protocol, in a sense. Under the circumstances, though, it was of no significance that she would be meeting him alone. The mission that she had taken upon herself would be no easier than her first conversation with him had been.

The corridors of the office building were bustling with people engaged in loud conversations in the thresholds of open doors, and echoing with the musical rings of cell phones.

Gary answered the door.

"Please, come in," he said, and gestured at an armchair that sat by his huge desk.

"Thanks." Melissa took it, and swept her eyes around. It was a nice place, with expensive, tastefully selected furniture, a bronze statue on the table, and a gold fountain pen casually thrown on a writing pad. A large picture in the style of surrealism hung on the wall. A wall-to-ceiling window let in the flood of light from the bright, sunny day. "Nice office," she commented.

"Thanks. Anything new?" asked Gary.

"In a sense. There is a circumstantial evidence that Brenda was involved in the circumstances related to your son's suicide. There was no intent to kill Lucas, or do any harm beyond what he did to Brenda. That's how I understand it."

Gary shifted in his chair. He grew pale, and his lips began twitching. He moved a few papers from one place on his desk to another, apparently with no particular purpose. "What do you mean?" he finally asked, and cleared his throat.

"I think you understand what I mean." This time, Melissa had no need to be tactful and diplomatic. "My understanding is that Brenda wanted to rape the rapists, and upload the obscene pictures on the Internet. Nothing fancy, and nothing more than what they did to her. Again, as I said, I have no material evidence to lay formal charges against her." After a moment of silence, she said, "It'd be to your advantage to be frank with me, Gary. I intend to be frank with you."

"I still don't—"

"Well, if you still don't, then I'll have to be even less diplomatic. It changes things from a friendly discussion with an honest exchange of perspectives, but it will be the shortest way to conclusion. So, what I mean is that Brenda arranged for Lucas to be raped. She took pictures, just as they did, and planned to post them online, just as they did. You want to say something, Gary? Are you thinking of denying it?"

Gary covered his face with both hands, but just for a few seconds. When he showed his face again, it was a mask of a much older man.

"There was no evidence," he said in a raspy voice.

"There was. And still is. You can't play the same game with me, Gary. No chance."

"What game?" Gary asked. His eyes were pale, wide open, filled with the horror of a trapped, doomed man.

"You know very well what game. That you are innocent. What you did is called bribery. You bought off the prosecutor and the judge to get Brenda out of the way and make the accusations of rape go away. Now, I intend to make all of you who were involved confess to obstruction of justice, and other crimes. I have evidence that you knew about the rape, and I have the paper trail that links you to Salazar and Price. You could try to fight it, but it would be very messy and public if it comes to the point where I have to lay formal charges against you and the others. Not one of you would be able to save his or her ass, if you'll pardon my language."

"If it comes to that point?" Gary repeated, with a glimmer of hope.

"I am sorry to have to tell you things that disgust me as much as they do you, but if I am forced to arrest Brenda, then the video showing your son being raped will end up all over the Internet. We can't stop it. She's backed by an outlaw biker gang. We can try to do something after it's posted, but I think you know how impossible it would be to find every copy once it's out there. We don't know where the video is, but we know that it does exist. That's why she arranged the rape: to make this video. To humiliate Lucas and ruin his life as he did hers."

Gary nodded. He was in trance, at the bottom of his despair.

"If I am forced to arrest Brenda, the original rape case will have to be brought up. Your son's role will be exposed. You know that the justice system has no feelings, no compassion. It's a system, a set of procedures, a machine that operates on the gears and pulleys of cold logic and evidence. I have proof that you bribed Pamela Salazar, and she will testify to that fact, too. Now, your money will work against you. Unless..."

Blood rushed back to Gary's cheeks. He straightened up in his chair, looking at Melissa with renewed hope.

"Anything." It was almost a groan.

Melissa paused. The turning point of her career, and perhaps many people's futures, had arrived. It was not easy, although she had rehearsed the scene many times in her head. "I have spoken with Brenda," Melissa said. "She has agreed, in principle, to make a deal. No, not with the justice system, and not with me. There will be no bribing the law to look away this time. She agreed to make a deal with you."

"What kind of deal?" he asked.

"I don't know. And I don't need to know. The only thing I need to know is, after you speak, whether or not you and she have come to terms. If yes, I can close the case. Both cases."

"We will," he said, voice trembling. "Thank you. Can I do something for you? Please."

"No. I don't want any favours from you. Call Brenda. This is her phone number. Good luck."

Chapter 30

It took a week after the car crash for Brenda to feel sufficiently recovered. Her ribs were still sore, but healing nicely, although walking or any strain on her chest still caused some pain. She wrapped her chest with a towel, and it eased the pressure, and gave her some support. Her right arm was in cast, but she could move it, and use her fingers to peck on her computer keyboard. Idleness was against her nature. There was a backlog in her work, and she attacked it with vigour and renewed energy.

Max had left in early morning hours; much to Brenda's relief, he had an appointment with a surgeon. At last she had won the battle and convinced him to take care of his health. After his appointment, he was going to inspect a few sites to choose one for his car repair shop. He would likely be gone all day, as they were in different locations.

After three hours of intense concentration, Brenda leaned back in her chair. She was not tired; in better times, she would work even longer hours without taking a break. She liked her job. For many, accounting and bookkeeping meant dealing with dry numbers, a bore, and it was definitely not for everyone. For her, numbers were honest. They lived their own life. They told her a lot about her clients, too: their habits, spending patterns, business and personal decisions, and much more. It was fun to eventually reconcile these numbers, and make sense of them, and prepare final reports that could pass any scrutiny or audit.

But now, after the abduction, car crash, the hospital, and her talk with Melissa, she found that she had to make a huge effort to concentrate on the work. Her mind kept going over everything that had happened, replaying the previous week, with all its emotional and physical upheavals. Life had become much more dangerous and confusing than she could have ever imagined. Even her office had not been safe, so she had closed it and was working from home for now. Would that help? For how long?

Yona had turned out to be a much tougher bastard than she had expected. If he was determined to kill her, or Max, then the gang war was unavoidable. Killing him would probably be the solution, but the very thought of it terrified her.

She stood up and walked to the window overlooking the backyard. Last mowed a month ago, it had been taken over by weeds of different kinds, giving the house the look of an abandoned place. Max had not felt at all well lately, and had no enthusiasm for almost anything, and Brenda was too busy—and too sore—to deal with a lawnmower right now.

Her train of thought was broken by the sound of the garage door opening. Max must have decided to tell me about the doctor visit before scouting shop locations. She went to the kitchen to make coffee. She knew Max would want it. They would chat a bit, as was their habit, over a cup of coffee, in the seclusion and quiet of his home. Actually, their home, as Max said it lately.

Max came into the kitchen and ran his hand over her back and bottom. "Nice. Coffee," he said, and squeezed her butt.

"I heard you coming," she said, turning around. "What's new? What did the doctor say?"

"When I have coffee first, I'll tell you everything."

He retreated to the family room, where he sat on the sofa and stretched his legs. As there was no separating wall, she could watch Max from the kitchen. His customary countenance of confidence and iron will has softened. He seemed unbalanced, if not insecure. Brenda brought him coffee and sat across from him, cradling her cup.

"It's not good, I can see that. What did the doctor say?" She took a sip, as Max did not rush with his answer.

"You know—there's good news, and bad news. Which one do you want to hear first?"

"I prefer bad news. It prompts me into action. The good news doesn't mean as much."

"Wrong," Max said, with his usual confidence. "Have it your way, though. The doctor said that I need an operation. I had kidney stones before. They've grown bigger, and the bullet did not improve things."

"Is it serious?"

"Not life threatening, but I will have to spend some time in the hospital, and then at home."

Brenda tried to detect a sign of worry on his face. There was none.

"When?"

"He said about three weeks, though he would try to do it sooner." The corners of his mouth dropped. "I thought that I could open my business next month. Bad luck."

Brenda narrowed her eyes and regarded him in silence. "Max, everything will be okay. You have me. I'll stand by you, take care of you, you know that. You'll do it after your recovery. It's only a few weeks or a couple of months more to wait, right. It's not a big deal."

Max nodded a few times, but it was not a sign of agreement. "Yeah. But my money is drying out. I'll have to go back to my other car business."

"No way!" Brenda said. "I'll work twice as much. Forget about money for now, Max. We'll survive, trust me."

Max laughed.

"Okay," said Brenda. "Now, tell me the good news."

"This is really fun." He brought the cup to his lips, and gave Brenda a sly look. He took a sip and placed the cup back on the table, all to enhance the dramatic effect of the news. "Bogdan called. Yona's been arrested. He's in jail, and Bogdan says that he won't be getting out any time soon."

Brenda had to put her cup on the table. Her hand began trembling.

"Really," she murmured. Melissa's face flashed through her mind. "That's awesome. It solves everything."

"Not everything." Max took another sip of his coffee. "There's still Christian. He owes us money."

"Max, Max," Brenda pleaded. "Drop it. It's over. I don't want his money."

"You don't, but I do. You have a partner, don't you? It's my business as much as it is yours. You think that fifty grand is nothing? It'll be over when it's over."

Brenda stood up and went to the window. Her cell phone rang, but she didn't pick it up. In a minute, it rang again. Neither of them spoke. Her phone rang the third time.

"Someone wants to speak with you badly," Max commented. He rose to his feet and went to the kitchen. Brenda took the call.

"Hello," she said, irritated by the interruption.

"Is this Brenda?" a calm, confident voice asked. A new client?

"Yes."

"My name is Gary. I'm the Lucas's father."

Brenda felt an incapacitating weakness in her legs. She sat down in her chair and said, "Good day."

"Would you...would you mind meeting with me?" he asked. "It's not for long. Fifteen minutes, or so."

A host of thoughts swirled in her mind. She totally lost her balance.

"I...I...well, I suppose. Why not? What's this about?"

"Just something recommended by...a mutual friend. I'll tell you all about it when we meet. Please, Brenda."

His voice suggested that he meant no harm. If anything, it sounded contrite. It was rather convincing.

The lesson of letting down her guard, of feeling safe at her officer one moment and being shoved into a car then next, was not lost on her. "Someplace where there are people, right? Where and when do you want to meet?" she asked. At that moment, Max came back from the kitchen and sat on the sofa.

"Who's that?" he asked. Brenda made an impatient gesture for him to be quiet.

"I'm in Toronto right now on business matters," the calm voice continued. "We can meet anytime, anywhere you wish."

"Timothy's. The one on the corner of Bloor and Sherbourne."

"When?"

"I can be there in two hours, if that's okay with you."

"Yes." His voice sounded friendly and solemn. "See you there." He hung up.

Brenda sat in silence, feeling Max's questioning stare.

"Now, it's your turn to tell me the news," he said.

"You won't believe it." She downed the remaining coffee, which was already lukewarm. "That was Gary Kroner. Lucas's father."

A trace of surprise showed in Max's eyes, but otherwise he remained unperturbed. "What did he want?"

"A meeting."

"Really?" He frowned. "What for?"

"He said that it's better to discuss it face-to-face. He sounded friendly, though."

"Interesting," Max said, and joined left and right hand fingertips together, as if holding an invisible ball.

"Melissa's behind it. That's what it is. I'm sure. But I'm scared."

"Don't worry. I'll go with you."

229

"Not that kind of scared, Max. I'm not worried about my life," said Brenda. "I'm scared that won't be able to look into his eyes. My hatred is gone forever. And now he's gone through such a tragedy."

"Bullshit," Max grumbled. "Just recall what you've gone through."

"I know, Max, I know. But I didn't become tougher. I wish I had, in some ways, but it's beyond me. Maybe something is broken inside. I guess it's wrong, but I can't—"

"You didn't want it. I didn't want it. It's not our fault that things went that way."

"It's not about fault. I knew there would be things we couldn't control, but I never wanted anyone to die."

"Dress up," Max said, in a commanding, angry voice. He rose to his feet. "I'll help you. Which dress do you wish to put on?"

"Jeans, and the gray sweater. It's fairly loose, so it'll cover the cast. It's on a chilly side today."

With her left hand, she helped Max pull up her jeans.

"You are too nervous, hon," he said, noticing her trembling hands.

"I'm okay."

The right sleeve of her sweater stretched to its limit over her cast. A wrinkle in her looks, she thought, but there was nothing she could do about that.

They arrived at Timothy's fifteen minutes early. Max wanted it that way. Brenda took a seat by a huge window that was more like a glass wall. From there she could see busy city people going about their lives, and the fading leaves of the trees across the street. Nature, it seemed, had grown tired of its vigorous summer life; the leaves had lost most of their lustre, and some of them began changing their colour. It was not Indian summer yet, but close to it.

Max settled at the bar, taking a seat where he could see both streets and the entrance, and remain inconspicuous. Brenda had seen Gary in court, but that had been five years ago, seemingly in another life. Had he changed much? I hope I recognize him, or he recognizes me. She was looking at the entrance when Gary came in, holding a wrinkled grocery plastic bag. It seemed out of place with his appearance, a well-to-do gentleman dressed sharply but not conspicuously. His suit was dark brown, his shirt a shade lighter, and his tie a sedate pattern combining the two. She recognized him the instant he walked in. His hair had turned completely gray, but otherwise he looked the same as he had when she saw him in court. A little more tired, perhaps. Older. Sadder. With a nod to ask her permission, he pulled out the chair across from and put the plastic bag on the table.

"Good day, Brenda," he said. It was a formality of politeness, without a smile or any expression of warmth.

"Good day, Gary," she said in the same manner. She looked at the plastic bag. Why he brought his groceries? Weird. She forced herself to meet his eyes. They were blank, but somewhere deep inside them Brenda caught a glimpse of grief and distress.

"What happened to your arm?" he asked.

"Broken. A car accident. It's okay now."

"Sorry."

"It's okay. Nothing serious. It will heal." She paused, waiting. After all, he had invited her, so it was his duty to support the conversation. And he did. He cleared his throat. It was obvious that it was not easy for him to start.

"I know that what happened was a tragedy for you. I mean, that you were raped. Believe me, it was a tragedy for all my family." The words stuck somewhere deep in his chest. "Lucas was horrified by what he did. He was under influence of drugs at the time. He bore his guilt until his death."

231

Now it was Brenda's turn. She swallowed a large, stubborn slump. Her heart began pounding, like a frightened bird trying to escape its cage.

"Perhaps it would've been better if he, and others, had been punished at the time," she said.

"Maybe." After a short pause, he shook his head. "Frankly, I don't know. He had a weak and unstable psyche. I was horrified to think of what would have happened to him in a prison with violent criminals. You know what I mean."

Brenda nodded. A prison with violent criminals. She knew exactly what he meant. She looked out of the window. In spite of approaching fall, the day was bright and beautiful. The thought occurred to her that Gary thought she had murdered his son.

"That's why you arranged things? Why you saved him?" she asked, turning back to Gary. He didn't respond. She felt an urge to tell him her feelings.

"I never wanted Lucas to die. Never. I just wanted him, and others, to go through what I went through. Not all of it—not through prison, parole, a broken life—just the shame, the disgrace, and the nightmare. When they raped me, the ruined my faith and trust in others. But when they placed those photos on the Internet, they ruined my life, my future."

"It wasn't Lucas who did that," Gary said. "As I said, he was in a deep depression after that."

"I didn't expect this outcome. If I had known that this would cause him to take his life, I would never have done this. Trust me. I often think about that, and it hurts like hell."

For the first time in many years, she could not hold back her tears. She picked up a coffee napkin and wiped them. However, she quickly regained her composure. She had to remain tough.

"Lucas was very weak," Gary said. The rims of his eyes were also brimming with tears. "Well, we can't replay the past in a different way, can we?"

Brenda shook her head sadly.

"I think that our best choice is to close this chapter. This book. There have been enough casualties, don't you think?" He looked out the window for a moment, and then turned back to Brenda. "We can repair nothing. But we are still alive, and can do something about our present and future."

"Maybe you're right," she said. His eyes had become too sad for her to look into them. He said, "In this bag is one hundred thousand dollars. Would that do to finish it all? I mean, everything, for everyone. You know what I mean."

Her first impulse was to tell him to go to hell. Then she looked into his eyes. They were too sad for harsh words. Then she looked at Max. He sat, his back to her, leaning against the bar. He had a wound in his chest because of her. He had risked his life for her, and all he wanted was an auto shop of his own. Who knew what might happen to him after the operation? Melissa's face flashed in her mind in a split second. Then she looked around. No one was paying any attention to them. Her anger was gone. Yet the world was still spinning on its axis. The sun was still shining.

"I'm not for sale, but I do know what you mean," she said, hardly hearing her own words. "It's time to end it. I'm ready to move on, and rebuild my future. And yes, this will help. I'll close this chapter. You can trust me."

"I know. I know," Gary said. "Good-bye."

He stood up and left. As soon as he was out the door, Max took his place.

"What's the scoop?" he asked, with a sidelong look at the plastic bag. "He brought you a loaf of bread? What's inside that shitty bag?"

"Money," she said flatly. "One hundred grand."

"Kidding," he grumbled, regarding her with suspicion.

"Check it out."

Max opened the bag and looked inside. "This is clothes," he said, putting his hand inside. He removed the clothes and said, "Fuck," as if he had been struck by lightning. He quickly dropped the clothes back, a wild fire glowing in his eyes. "Fuck," he repeated. He took Brenda's cup for a greedy gulp of coffee. "Fuck. That much money, eh? I can't believe it." He reached into the bag again to feel the clothes, and what was wrapped inside them. Then he looked around with suspicion in his eyes. "Let's get the fuck out of here. Christ! Wolverine!"

Brenda had never before seen Max so agitated. He picked up the bag and rose to his feet. Brenda did the same and followed him for the exit. Max, it seemed, was in a hurry. He crossed the road on a red light, disregarding the protesting honks from the cars and the screech of tires. When they sat in their car, Max laughed aloud.

"Wow," he roared, and gave her a bear hug. "Paula was right. You can tear a man's balls off with one pull. Real wolverine. That's something. Huh? Now, when we collect Christian's money…"

"We aren't going to collect Christian's money," she said firmly. She had a mixed feeling about Gary's bag. On the one hand, she was happy with it. Now she could take a good care of Max's health. Even more important, it means that all this was over. It was a great relief. But getting money was a sort of admitting that it was adequate compensation, as if Gary had bought her forgiveness. To hell with it. The deal was done. The condition was accepted. She had given her word to two people: Melissa and Gary. It was over.

"What do you mean, we aren't going to collect Christian's money?" Max repeated. "Fifty grand! Are you crazy?"

"I'm not crazy. I gave my word that it's all over, and I'll stick to it. Don't argue with me, Max. It's over."

"I agree that it's over," he said with a frown. "But we don't have to do anything. He'll bring this money himself, without a reminder."

"I said no!" Brenda raised her voice in anger. "You know full well that if I give my word, I keep it. You like it when I give my word to you. So you have to put up with the fact that I keep my word to others."

"Fifty grand," Max grumbled. "Are you stupid, or what, Wolverine?"

"Stop it, Max." She returned to her confident, but somewhat abrupt voice. "It's done. And that's the last time you will ever again call me by that nickname. Wolverine." She leaned to him and put her head on his shoulder. "I'm not an animal. I'm a woman, Max. I don't want to be anything else." She sighed, straightened up, picked up her cell phone and dialled. When Christian said "Hello," she recognized his voice right away.

"Good day, Christian. This is Brenda."

"Oh." Christian stumbled for a second. "Hi, Brenda. Look, can you wait a bit longer? I can't sell my..."

"Stop it. Just stop, Christian. Don't sell your house. Don't do anything. I don't want your money. It's all over. Forget everything. Life goes back to normal now, finally."

The silence lasted a long time.

"Are you there?" she asked.

"Yes, I am."

"Do you understand what I'm saying?"

"Yes. Thank you, Brenda. Please forgive me, if you can."

"Good-bye, Christian." She hung up and lowered down the back support of her seat.

"It's all over, Max. It's all over," she whispered. Max met her eyes, then turned his attention to the road. He said nothing.

Chapter 31

On Melissa's last day at work, Larry was silent, the frown never leaving his face.

"What happened to you?" Melissa asked. "Unrequited love?"

"Sort of," he grumbled. "With you."

"I guess you won't cry when we split up for good?" she joked. But Larry was in a different mood.

"What are you going to do, Melissa?" he asked. "I know you well enough. I can't imagine you in the role of a housewife. You have the strength and brains of a great man."

"Really? Maybe I should give them back...he might miss them," she joked. She winked. "Anyway, why didn't you say that I have the strength and brains of a great woman?"

"I wanted to give you a compliment. I didn't mean to offend you." He winked back.

Melissa laughed. "Rascal. Male chauvinist. I should have fired you from my team a long time ago."

"You missed your chance," Larry said, pointing out the obvious. "You did not answer my question, though. What are you going to do?"

"What I'm going to do? I will learn."

"Learn?" Larry exclaimed. "What, for Christ sake, will you learn? Are you pulling my leg?"

"I'm serious. I'll learn how to be a woman."

"Are you a male chauvinist too?" Larry spread his arms, as if for a bear hug. Melissa stepped back.

"I know, I know. You're a woman. A pretty one, too," he said with a grin. "If I didn't tell you that before, you shouldn't take it to heart. It's no reason to retire."

"Insolent rascal," she said, without any hint of anger.

"Seriously, what are you gonna do? I'm sure you'll be back."

"Don't be so sure. There are plenty of things that I can do."

She reached out her hand for a last handshake. "I'll miss you, Larry. Your ugly looks are not a factor. Wish you luck."

"I'll miss you badly," he said, this time in all seriousness. "I learned a lot from you. We'll all miss you, Melissa."

When she returned home, it was late afternoon, when the sun was only an hour or so from completing its descent from on high. Evan and Nick were lounging around, waiting for her. She headed straight to the veranda, where the table was set for an early evening meal. Nick began telling her the latest news. His teacher had reprimanded him for punching a girl in the arm, but of course it was the girl's fault; she was a bully, and she started it.

"That makes me very sad, Nick. I never thought you would do such thing. You're a big boy now, and you need to treat others with respect. Use your wits, not your fists. Nothing good comes of bullying bullies. You have to be the stronger person."

"I love you, mom, but you talk like you were never, ever a kid," Nick said.

Evan laughed. "Now your son can teach you something, madam investigator," he said.

"I'm not an investigator anymore," she said, watching Nick with a smile. He ran away, and disappeared into the house. She looked around the backyard and veranda.

The trees in their neighbourhood had already begun changing colours, unlike in those in most other parts of the city. The air was crisp, still warm, but spicy scent of approaching fall filled her nostrils. The scenery was beautiful, but there was something sad and hopeless in the beauty. Nature seemed to be saying farewell to the creating color and life, the joys of blooming. We could all be happier, Melissa thought, if not for the ills and stupidity on the part of humanity. The devil of disaster always seemed to be waiting around the corner, and no one was safe from its assault. Cruelty and injustice hovered in the sky, invisible but real. There were principles of justice as created by people, and then there were over which people held no dominion, those whose true meaning was known only to God.

"You are deep in thought, darling," Evan said. "You want to say something, don't you?

"Yes. Sorry. I lost my balance for a moment. Such a happy and sad day. Weird, isn't it? I closed the case—Brenda's case. There was no single material evidence of the crime. There was no one to accuse." She chuckled. "It was my most successful case ever. I know everything, but presented nothing. And now I have retired, Evan. It's over. Now I am ready to learn from my son."

"Welcome back." Evan gave her a meaningful look. "For how long, though? I can't see you doing nothing."

"I'll do something. But other than welcoming me back, what do you think? I mean, when I started my career, I thought that I could change the world. If not the whole world, then at least my small part of it. I thought I'd make a contribution. But it seems that the devil's ability to recreate himself is endless."

"True, but society can keep him in check, as long as there are people like you who wish to make your small contributions. You contribute to your small world, but the universe consists of myriad such small worlds. Mind you, bad things happen not only from ill intentions. As you know, a lot happens just because of stupidity, and even the caprice of providence. I bet the majority of the inmates in prisons are just plain stupid. But there are many clever people who have, on occasion, done stupid things, including committing crimes. But once a crime is committed, really smart people come on the scene: attorneys, defence lawyers, judges, journalists, you name it. And, as in this case, people with money and connections join the crowd as well. Nothing new. Why has this case shattered you so much?"

Melissa spread her arms in a gesture of surrender.

"Because of its contradictions. It tested my sense of duty and justice, and of right and wrong. I have a lot of respect and sympathy for Brenda. But by the letter of law, she should have been put in jail. Could she have achieved her idea of justice without the help of her biker gang friends? Not a chance. And yet they were more loyal to her and each other than her own classmates had been. There were no good guys or bad guys in this case. Everyone involved in this case was a criminal, if judged by the strict formulation of law. My solution was a breach of my duty, although no one but me knows that. Well, and you. But I believe that there is a higher judge, above the laws written by man, and there is a divine justice, which should come from the heart. Anyway, for now at least, I'm all yours, and Nick's. Let's crack a bottle of wine to celebrate my success."

END

CPSIA information can be obtained
at www.ICGtesting.com
Printed in the USA
LVHW081024120323
741287LV00012B/251

9 781926 720548